RELATIVE HARM

CAROLINE FARDIG

SEVERN RIVER
PUBLISHING

Severn River Publishing
www.SevernRiverBooks.com

ISBN: 978-1-64875-472-2 (Paperback)

ALSO BY CAROLINE FARDIG

Ellie Matthews Novels

Bitter Past

An Eye for an Eye

Dead Sprint

Parted by Death

Relative Harm

Sins of the Father

To find out more about Caroline Fardig and her books, visit

severnriverbooks.com/authors/caroline-fardig

To my family

PROLOGUE

The only light in the old barn came from one of the hanging light fixtures overhead. The back half of the barn was swathed in ominous shadows. But nothing was scarier than the butt of the axe handle that came straight at her, punching her in the sternum and knocking the wind out of her. She stumbled backward and lost her balance. The dirt floor of the barn didn't make for as soft a surface as she'd hoped as she fell hard on her ass.

"You don't . . . have to do this," she croaked, her breath coming and going in spasms.

Her attacker circled her. The business end of the axe glinted when it caught the light. "Get up."

Fighting through the searing pain in her lungs and the violent ache in her chest, she cried, "Don't do this. *I'm* the . . . bad person here. Don't ruin your life . . . over me. I'm . . . not worth it."

"I said, get up."

Hauling herself up to her knees, she pleaded, "Please. Don't."

"Don't what? Do the world a favor? You're a disease. Now *stand up*."

She did as she was told, dragging herself to her feet. "I know . . . I'm . . . a disease. I know everyone in this end of the state thinks so." She wheezed out a breath. "But I don't want to die."

"Too bad."

Before she could react, the axe came at her like a baseball bat. And then everything was dark.

1

Earlier that evening

"Wait. Say that again."

Detective Nick Baxter glanced over at me worriedly. "That's the third time you've asked me to repeat that part. Let's take a break."

I shook my head and fought back a wince. My head was pounding and I was having trouble focusing, but I didn't want to stop working. I had promised Baxter I'd type out his case report from our last investigation as he drove and dictated it to me, and I wanted to deliver.

I said, "Why don't we stop and get me another awful gas station coffee? That should keep me sharp."

He frowned. "You've already had two. What I think you need is some rest, Ellie. Take a nap. I got this from here. We may have a long night ahead of us."

I glanced at his troubled profile in the darkened vehicle. We were headed to his hometown in southern Indiana to track down his younger brother. During the past week, Baxter had been juggling some serious family issues while trying to investigate a high-profile homicide. Our case wrapped up only a few hours ago, and I convinced him to drive down and take care of things in person, promising we'd get our reports done and filed electronically. Unfortunately, the two minor head injuries I'd received while trying to free myself from our suspect weren't allowing me to hold up my end of the bargain. Baxter seemed much more worried about my well-being than getting any of the reports done, not that I would have expected anything different.

Shifting in my seat so I could face him and rest my head on the head-rest, I said, "True, but a nap would mean giving up alone time with you. I'm not wasting a precious commodity like that on something as useless as sleep."

He grinned at me. "I'm flattered, but—" His phone rang through my car's audio system. He'd been receiving calls all night from his older brother, Tom, keeping him in the loop of his family's search for his nine-teen-year-old brother, Shawn. Answering the call, he said, "Hey, what's up?"

Tom Baxter's tired and somewhat irritated voice said, "We found Shawn at a friend's place. He's not talking to me or Dad right now because we had to physically remove him. He's in his room crying to Mom."

I saw Baxter visibly relax. "Thanks for tracking him down. I'll handle the rest. We're about thirty minutes out."

"Cool. See you soon."

After he ended the call, I said, "That saves us a ton of time, which means I don't need to waste a half hour of my life on a stupid nap."

Baxter reached over and took my hand. "Okay, you win. Oh . . . I should probably mention that my family might not give you the warmest welcome when I introduce you . . ." He trailed off uncertainly.

"Because?"

"Because the last they knew, you'd chosen Manetti over me and I was angry about it."

I gaped at him. "What? That was like four months ago. You've talked to them since."

"You were still with him two months ago, and then we were together for a whopping five minutes, and then we weren't . . . so I didn't ever bother to update them."

A lot had happened in two months. Vic Manetti, an FBI agent we'd both butted heads with and I'd dated for a while, was now one of my best friends. "Well, you can update them tonight."

He frowned as he exited I-69 for a smaller highway. "It's probably for the best that we don't. The fewer people who know we're together, the better."

Baxter and I had a rough start getting together. It never seemed to be the right time for us to be able to add a romantic relationship on top of our working partnership. And it still wasn't the right time—in fact, now was the worst possible time. Two months ago we worked an investigation that ended with me getting kicked off the task force *and* becoming a victim while Baxter ended up solving the whole case. With us being on opposite sides of the investigation, it was a bad look and a gray area for us to be romantically linked until the trial was over. We'd tried to stay apart, and we'd succeeded for two months. But being thrown back into another investigation together reminded us how miserable we were without each other. Rules be damned, we decided to allow ourselves to be together, but we had to keep it quiet.

It was for the best, but I hated that the first time I met his family it would be under these conditions. "Then how are you going to explain me tagging along on an overnight road trip with you?"

He shrugged. "We could say you owe me one for saving your life a couple of times."

I smiled. "That's true. We could say that."

"Or we could say we had work left to do to wrap up our case and we figured we could do it just as easily on the road as at the station. That's at least part of the truth."

"It would probably be good to stick to as much of the truth as possible."

Squeezing my hand, he said, "I wish we could tell them everything, but right now, I'm just happy you're with me."

I'd forgotten how much he made my heart flutter. "Me, too."

∼

THE BAXTER FAMILY lived just outside the city limits of Boonville, a small Indiana town not far from the Ohio River.

"I had no idea you grew up on a farm," I said as Baxter pulled up to his parents' home. I was struck by the beauty and serenity of the rolling fields and rustic barn in the distance, lit brightly by the full moon in a cloudless sky.

He parked the car and shrugged. "It's not a real farm compared to most of the ones around here. All we ever had was a few cows and some sheep and chickens. Now they're down to only two cows."

"Considering I never had so much as a goldfish growing up, to me, that's a whole ass farm."

"If you're so interested, I'm sure Dad would let you help him feed the cows tomorrow morning."

I wrinkled my nose. "Oh, I don't want to touch one or anything. I just think the idea of someone else having a farm is cool."

"Ah." He leaned across the console to give me a soft kiss. "Ready to pretend we don't like each other again?"

"As long as I know you're pretending this time, I think I can manage."

He cradled the side of my face that didn't hurt. "You don't know what it means to me that you came down here with me. I can guarantee tonight is going to be awful, and I apologize in advance."

"We're in this together. We can handle awful."

He kissed me again, this time like he really meant it. "Let's get this over with."

Baxter led me to the house's back door, which opened straight into a homey kitchen that smelled of the freshly baked cookies his mom was taking out of the oven. "Hey, Mom," he said, enveloping her in a hug.

"Oh, Nicholas. I'm so glad you're here," she said, her voice thick with emotion as she clung to him. She broke their embrace and turned to me with a frown. "You must be Ellie."

I smiled, thankful he'd given me a heads-up about the icy welcome. "Yes. Nice to meet you, Mrs. Baxter. You have a lovely home."

Her gaze narrowed on the left side of my face. "Where'd you get that black eye? Does your FBI boyfriend slap you around?" Not what I expected out of such a sweet-looking woman, although I detected a slight slur to her voice. I imagined the slur had been brought on by the half-empty bottle of gin sitting open on the kitchen table. I hoped the pithy remark had as well.

While Baxter stared at his mother in horror, I managed to keep my composure and reply, "No . . . never . . . and I'm not seeing him anymore. This is from an altercation I had with a suspect earlier this afternoon."

"Hmm," was her only response as she turned her attention back to her cookies.

Baxter quickly ushered me into the living room. Two men sat staring at a basketball game on TV. The vibe in the air was tense, not that it was a surprise. This family had had a difficult day, and this evening wasn't going to get any better.

"Hey, we're here," Baxter announced.

Both men hopped up from the couch and came over to give him a hug.

Baxter said, "Dad, Tom, this is Ellie Matthews. Ellie, my brother, Tom, and my dad, Jim."

I smiled at them, hoping this introduction would go better than the last. "Hi. Nice to meet you both." Both men shook my hand.

Tom Baxter, basically a dark-haired version of his brother, said, "Thanks for keeping my brother company on the trip down. I'm sure you had better things to do."

I felt like that was kind of a leading comment, so I made sure to convey our cover story. "Not really. We had reports to do, so we knocked most of them out during the drive."

Mr. Baxter nodded, his eyes kind like his son's always were. "Well, we appreciate your time."

"Is Shawn in his room?" Baxter asked, glancing toward a nearby hallway.

Tom shook his head. "He's in the barn blowing off some steam. Good luck."

Rather than going back through the kitchen and past his mom, Baxter took us out the front door and down a long rock driveway toward the barn. I didn't know what we were walking into out there, but I was sure it would be an even more tense atmosphere than the one inside the house.

The youngest Baxter brother, Shawn, was a troubled teen, always needing to be bailed out of some kind of mischief. He'd been a kidnap victim when he was four years old, taken from his family and held for seven months by Marie Collins, a friend of his mother's. His captor had been released earlier in the day from serving her stint in prison. Even after fifteen years, the Baxter family wasn't emotionally ready for the monster who'd ripped apart their family to rejoin society, Shawn especially. He had been nowhere to be found most of the day, notably around noon, when Marie Collins's sister's home—where she planned to live after her release— was vandalized. Not surprisingly, the police suspected Shawn of the vandalism. That was why we were here—to get Shawn to agree to turn himself in and avoid a more severe punishment for evading the cops. The other members of the Baxter family hadn't had any luck so far with convincing him, but out of all of them, Nick had the best relationship with him.

As we approached the barn door, I caught Baxter's arm and said, "Do you want me to wait outside? This is going to be a touchy subject for your brother, and I don't imagine he'd want a stranger butting in."

"We may need a neutral third party. Or possibly a referee. Besides, you can talk to kids his age like it's your job."

I smiled. It *was* my job, as a professor of criminalistics at Ashmore College, to talk to kids his age. Plus, I had a twenty-one-year-old sister who lived with me, along with her three-year-old son. I prided myself on being able to communicate with new adults better than most people.

Baxter entered the open barn door ahead of me and called, "Hey, Shawn."

As I set foot inside the barn, something whizzed past my head and slammed into the door. I whirled to find an axe buried in the wood of the door not ten feet from my head. I let out a little yelp as a chill swept through me, and I had to will myself not to stand there and shake like a leaf. After spending my afternoon being held at gunpoint, getting smacked around, and then being bound at the wrists and ankles and thrown in a walk-in freezer, I had very little emotional control left.

"What the hell are you doing?" Baxter bellowed, stalking toward his brother. "You clearly saw us and still launched that thing."

"Sorry, bro," Shawn replied, his tone anything but contrite as he took a drag from a vape pen. I'd heard how much of a hot mess he was, but once I laid my eyes on the kid it was hard to hold anything against him. He was the spitting image of Baxter, only twelve years younger—the same boyish face minus the beard, with the same piercing blue eyes. He nodded in my direction, his expression wary. "Who's she?"

Working to calm back down, Baxter replied, "This is Ellie Matthews, my partner—"

"That bitch you wouldn't shut up about at Christmas?"

I couldn't help but laugh. "That would be me."

Baxter cuffed his brother on the back of the head. "Watch your mouth." As Shawn rubbed his head and pouted, Nick continued more gently, "Look, Shawn, I know it hasn't been a good day. And you may not have any good days for a while until you can find a way to work through what you're feeling. But you're going to have to sack up and be an adult first. Did you vandalize Margo Watson's house?"

"What if I didn't do it?" Shawn fired back, his tone undeniably defensive.

"Then I'll help you stand up to the police and get your name cleared."

I saw a flicker of a smirk cross Shawn's face. He said, "So you can negotiate some kind of cop favor or something?"

Baxter must not have noticed what I had. He said sincerely, "No, not exactly, but I'd be in a better position than most people to help find you some reasonable doubt and be able to have a frank discussion with them. Ellie can help with that, too."

"Or you could just bone your old cop girlfriend again and get her to pull some strings. Mom said she asked about you last week."

While I worked to keep a straight face, Baxter's cheeks reddened and he snapped, "That's not how the justice system works."

Shawn shrugged and inhaled deeply from the vape pen. "Whatever. It's not as big a deal as you all are making it. The cops'll move on in a day or two, and I'll be off the hook anyway."

"That's also not how the justice system works."

"It's how my buddy Chase got out of a possession charge. He laid low until the cops got tired of looking for him."

I seriously doubted that. Shawn was clouding the issue with extraneous information.

Shawn went on, "What I really need is to get the hell out of this town. Make a fresh start."

Baxter scoffed. "With what money? You can't hold down a job."

"I can find a place to crash." I studied Shawn as his demeanor shifted.

He kicked at the straw on the ground with the toe of his boot and said quietly, "Maybe with you? You're the only one who gets me."

Oh, he was good. And Baxter fell for it. "Well . . . yeah, I'd let you live with me for a while, if you think it would help."

Shawn smiled. "That'd be sick, bro. I'm ready. I can go pack up right now."

I couldn't hold my tongue any longer. "Cut the shit, Shawn. You vandalized that house. Own it."

Shawn's bright blue eyes snapped up to meet mine. "You don't know me."

"I work with and live with people your age. Your manipulation style is excellent, but I've seen it before."

Baxter frowned at his brother. "You said you didn't do it."

I chimed in apologetically, "Actually he said, '*What if* I didn't do it.' You heard what you wanted to."

Shawn's expression had turned stony. He spat at me, "This is between me and my brother."

"No, it's between you and the cops. You're an adult, and they're going to treat you like one. They'll track you down sooner or later, move or not. Your only hope is to quit blowing smoke up your brother's ass and hope he'll still help you try to clean up your mess. You go it alone with your shitty attitude, and you could be looking at six months in jail for this."

Shawn snorted. "Yeah. That's why I'm not going to the cops."

Grabbing him by the collar, Baxter growled, "You evade the police, and you can tack on a whole lot more, plus a bunch of fines the rest of us are going to have to pay. Either go turn yourself in, or I call the cops and tell them where you are."

"I'll run."

"I'll find you. It's what I do."

Baxter was steaming mad, and I could tell he was going to get nowhere with his brother if they kept fighting this way. We needed a different tactic. I had an idea, but it would involve some serious soul-bearing on my part. Baxter and his family were worth it to me, though.

I let out a shaky breath. "I generally don't talk about this, but . . ." I raised the hem of my sweater and pointed to a quarter-inch circular scar on my stomach. "See this? If anyone happens to notice it, I tell them it's a bad chickenpox scar. It's actually a cigarette burn. I got it when I was eleven from one of my stepfathers. He was mad because one day I came home from school and interrupted his afternoon delight with my mother."

"What does that have to do with me?" Shawn snapped.

"If someone ever were to put out a cigarette on your bare skin, what do you think any member of your family would do?"

For a moment, he seemed taken aback, but he quickly slipped back into his disinterested teenage persona and bought himself some time by taking another drag from his vape. "I don't know . . . go ape shit and probably try to kill them with their bare hands."

I nodded. "Exactly. You want to know what my mother did? She called me a dumb bitch, told me I had it coming, and made it a rule that I had to knock before entering my own home. What I'm trying to make you understand is that you have an amazing support system who'll stand beside you even when you're being a piece of shit."

While I was speaking, Shawn's bravado had wavered again, but he managed to sound unmoved as he replied, "Okay, so I'm lucky. How is that going to keep me out of jail?"

"Is that all you care about?"

"At the moment, yeah."

Baxter, who'd been listening to my story quietly appalled, shook his head and backed away from his brother. "You know what, Shawn? I've had enough. I'm out. You want to push your family away with both hands? Do it. You've clearly got everything figured out. You don't need us." To me, he said, "Ellie, let's go."

As I started to follow Baxter toward the door, I watched Shawn's reaction. His façade was beginning to crack.

Eyes wide, Shawn's voice faltered as he said, "You're leaving right now?"

Baxter stopped and turned to face him. "We ditched work during a case to come down here to help you, but you obviously don't want it. Dad, Tom, and I, and especially Mom, have coddled you all your life. Maybe it's our fault you turned out the way you did. But you're an adult now, and it's time we let you be your own man. Run if you want. Or don't. Sooner or later you're going to do something really stupid and pay the price for it. And I'm not going to lift a finger to help. I hope you enjoy prison, because that's where you're ultimately headed." He took my elbow and started steering me with him toward the door.

Shawn said quietly, "Please don't give up on me, Nick."

Baxter's grip on my arm tightened for a moment and then released. He turned to his brother. "What are you saying?"

Shawn hung his head. "I don't want to run. But . . . I'm terrified of going to jail." He raised his eyes, now glazed with tears, to meet ours. Finally, the real Shawn. "I need you. Please don't go."

2

Baxter sighed. "Okay, I won't. But no more bullshit."

Shawn nodded.

"And you'll let us take you to the station to 'fess up?"

Closing his eyes, Shawn nodded again.

"Go on and tell Mom and Dad and Tom what's going on. We'll wait for you in the car."

Shawn shuffled out the door.

As soon as we were alone in the barn, Baxter put his arms around my waist and pulled me close. "Thanks for the help."

I shrugged. "It takes a teenage delinquent to know one."

His face clouded over. "You've never told me that story."

"I've never told anyone that story. Rachel was only two when it happened, so she doesn't remember." I sighed. "There's no point in telling her. She doesn't need another reason to hate that man. Or our mother."

His grip on me tightened. "You've carried this around for nearly twenty years without talking about it?"

"It's embarrassing."

"Only for the people who abused you."

I shook my head. "I wish. Marcus Copland loved that he gave me something to remember him by for the rest of my life."

His jaw dropped. "Wait. Rachel's father did that to you?"

"I told you he was a sadistic bastard."

"I'm so sorry, Ellie. Did he—"

Knowing where this conversation was going, I cut him off. "I appreciate your sympathy, but we don't have the time—and I don't have the energy—to unpack this tonight."

He pulled me into a tight hug. "You're right." When he released me, he added, "You don't have to go the station with us if you'd rather get some rest."

I smiled. "You're not getting rid of me that easily."

~

As BAXTER, Shawn, and I rode to the police station in silence, I was able to take in a little of the area. What I saw of the Boonville town square reminded me of the town square of my home in Noblesville, a century-old (or more) courthouse in the center with well-kept, ornate old buildings around it housing locally owned shops and restaurants. The police station building was equally old and beautiful, the words PUBLIC LIBRARY carved into the stone above the front doors.

Baxter spoke to the front desk officer, and we only had to wait a few moments before another officer came to get us. He took us downstairs to their interrogation rooms, but stopped Baxter and me when we tried to follow Shawn inside.

"The sergeant wants to speak to you all separately," he told us.

Shawn's eyes grew wide. "They don't get to come in here with me?"

Baxter eyed the officer and said to Shawn, "It'll be okay. Be polite."

The officer closed the door on a terrified-looking Shawn and escorted us to the room next door, which had a two-way mirror for other law enforcement officials to watch and listen to the interview. "Sergeant Woods will be with you in just a moment."

After the door was closed and Baxter and I were alone, I said, "I don't think I like this. I thought we'd be able to be in there as Shawn's legal backup."

Baxter said nothing, his attention on Shawn through the two-way mirror. The poor kid was beside himself. He reminded me of myself the time I'd gotten caught shoplifting as a teen and hauled to jail.

I put my hand on Baxter's shoulder. "But I'm sure it'll be okay."

The door opened, and I dropped my hand. An older sergeant came into the room and smiled when he laid eyes on Baxter, hand outstretched. They shook hands.

"Good to see you, Nick."

"You, too, Sergeant Woods." Baxter nodded to me. "This is my partner, Ellie Matthews. She's a criminalist for Hamilton County."

Sergeant Woods shook my hand and smiled. "No introduction needed. You two are legends around here."

"Oh," I breathed, hoping that wasn't true.

The media had tried repeatedly to give me my fifteen minutes of fame over the explosive cases we'd investigated over the past several months, but I'd done my best to stay out of the spotlight. That didn't keep them from talking about me and plastering my photo everywhere. It was good for my professorship at Ashmore College—everyone suddenly wanted to take my criminalistics classes—but not so much for my privacy otherwise.

His gaze on Shawn, Sergeant Woods said to us, "Thank you for convincing your brother to come in. I'll admit we don't have anything on him but suspicion. But given the fact that he doesn't exactly run with the best crowd around here, I'd love to scare him straight before anything actually bad happens."

Baxter visibly relaxed and nodded. "We're hoping the same thing, Sergeant."

"I'm going to get tough with him, but I'm hoping I can convince Margo Watson not to press charges. That way we can have Shawn clean up his mess and be done with this business, no harm, no foul. And hopefully learn a valuable lesson."

A wave of relief washed over me. Sergeant Woods was doing for Shawn what Jayne Walsh, Hamilton County's sheriff (and Baxter's and my boss), had done for me during my wild youth. She'd taken me to the station over some petty shoplifting and thrown me in a holding cell with a bunch of crazies. That one act put me on the right path, and I hoped this one would do the same for Shawn.

"Thank you, Sergeant," Baxter said, looking as relieved as I felt.

The sergeant left us and appeared in the room next door. As jovial as he'd been during our conversation, he'd managed to turn that all around and command a frightening presence. "Shawn Baxter?" he barked.

Shawn shrunk back in his seat. "Yes?"

"I'm Sergeant Woods." He sat down across from Shawn and sat still for a moment, I assumed to intimidate him with a stare-down, since I could only see him from the back. "You've been hiding from us today."

Shawn's face turned even paler, if that was possible. "No, I—"

"Don't lie to me, son," the sergeant bellowed.

A tear escaped from one of Shawn's eyes. As bad as I felt for the kid to have to go through this situation, especially on today of all days, there was no question in my mind how much good it would do him.

Shawn cast his gaze down. "I was . . . hiding out. I don't want to go to jail." His last word hitched on a stifled sob.

"You weren't thinking about that when you were destroying Margo Watson's flower beds and porch furniture, were you?"

Shawn shook his head.

"You want to tell me why you felt the need to trash this woman's home?"

Shawn hesitated, tears starting to fall down his cheeks. He said so quietly I could barely hear him, "It's not fair. What she did to me . . . I can't get past it. She doesn't deserve to be walking around free. She took me away. She . . . told me my family was dead. I can't—" He put his head in his hands, sobbing.

Blown away by his words, I murmured to Baxter, "She seriously told a four-year-old kid his whole family had died?"

Baxter wiped a tear from his own eyes. "Yeah. That's how she got him to accept her as his caregiver and kept him from wanting to escape. She told him a bad man came and killed us all, and that he couldn't tell anyone who he really was because the bad man was looking for him, too. That our mom had charged her with keeping him safe and being his new mother." He let out a sad huff. "He'd started calling her Mom and everything."

I put my hand on his shoulder. Now I understood the depth of hurt this family had endured because of Marie Collins. I mostly only knew the facts I could glean from newspaper articles and the bare minimum Baxter had told me. I hadn't known about the psychological abuse and manipulation. No wonder Shawn had never moved on—and no wonder his family had gone so easy on him all these years.

The sergeant dropped his bad cop act. "Look, Shawn, I'm sure you'd never vandalize this woman's house for the hell of it. It's obvious to us that you were lashing out over Marie Collins's release. The only outlet you had that would inflict even a little damage on her was to the place that she was going to be staying when she got out of prison. It's perfectly natural to have those feelings. It's unfortunate you destroyed someone else's property while dealing with them, but you did. No one likes it, but your actions, to me, are understandable. We appreciate the fact that you've owned your mistake, and we're not going to hold you for this."

Shawn lifted his head. "Does that mean no jail time?"

He nodded. "*If* Ms. Watson decides not to press charges. I'll go contact her now."

The sergeant left the room, and Shawn collapsed onto the table, looking thoroughly spent.

I said, "Wow. Sergeant Woods wasn't dicking around."

Baxter shook his head. "I hope this sticks with my brother."

Now that there was considerably less tension in the air, I changed the subject and joked, "So, did you see your old cop girlfriend here tonight?"

He kept his eyes on Shawn. "No, she's with the sheriff's department. She's a detective."

"Oh, so she's you."

He shrugged.

Evidently there was some tension left. I knew better than to push him. "Sorry. Trying to lighten the mood."

"You're welcome to bring it up again after we get this shit show taken care of. Maybe it'll be funnier then." He seemed to be trying to keep it light with a little sarcasm, but there was a definite edge to his voice.

We waited in an uncomfortable silence until Sergeant Woods returned to the interrogation room.

The sergeant said to Shawn, "You're one lucky young man. When I told Margo Watson it was you who'd done the damage, she said she'd never press charges against you of all people. She felt she owed you something for what her sister did to you."

Shawn nearly fell out of his chair with relief.

Sergeant Woods's voice took on a more serious tone. "You've been given a gift, Shawn. And now it's time you made a change. The degenerates you've been running around with lately are only going to get you into more trouble. Don't think we haven't noticed that you've been in the vicinity a lot of the time when we've been called out to various noise and loitering complaints."

Shawn seemed taken aback. "You mean I have to find all new friends?"

"That, or convince those fools they need to start behaving better. Come on, Shawn. You know you guys are getting out of control. It's only a matter of time before one of those boneheads does something that'll get you all in trouble. And I'll tell you right now—we won't go easy on you again."

Shawn hung his head. "I understand."

"Good." Sergeant Woods stood. "I'll coordinate a time when Marie Collins will be away from Margo Watson's home so that you can go over there and clean up the damage you caused. You'll hear from me tomorrow."

"Okay . . . thank you, Sergeant," Shawn said.

～

SHAWN'S HOMECOMING was joyful and tearful and honestly more than I could handle after the day I'd had. I slipped out of the house and sat in my car until Baxter finally came out and opened the door to ask me, "You planning on sleeping out here tonight?"

I smiled. "I felt like I was intruding."

Grabbing our bags, he threw them over one shoulder and took my hand as we walked toward the house. "After what you did for my brother tonight, encouraging him to have a change of heart, you'll always be welcome here." When we got to the front door, he dropped my hand.

His mother met us in the living room. To me, she said with a little less chill in her tone than before, "You can sleep in the boys' room." To Baxter, she said, "I'm afraid that means you'll have to take the couch, dear."

Fighting a grin, Baxter said, "No problem. I'll get Ellie settled."

Still trying to win her over even though it felt like a lost cause, I smiled at Mrs. Baxter and said, "Thank you. Goodnight."

Baxter led me down the hall to a no-frills bedroom with two twin beds. "Tom's and my old room."

"Aww. Which one was your bed?"

"The one on the left," he replied as he set our bags on the other bed.

I plopped down on his old bed with a devilish grin. "I'm going to need the full rundown of all the action that was had here. Please, leave nothing out."

"I'm afraid you're going to be sorely disappointed." He gestured toward the open door. "Open-door policy when there's a female guest in the Baxter house. No action was had in this room."

"Ever?"

"Ever." He jerked his thumb toward Tom's bed. "Two beds here, and we're both grown-ass adults, yet my mother made it a point to let me know I'm sleeping on the couch."

"She's not wrong. It would be odd for two work colleagues of the opposite sex to share a room." When he frowned, I whispered, "Or did you forget our cover story already?"

"Okay, smartass." He took some pajamas and a toiletry bag out of his duffel and backed away out the door. "Sleep tight."

∾

I COULD HEAR MUFFLED voices coming from down the hall, but that wasn't what was keeping me from falling asleep. My head would not stop pounding. I'd taken more than the advised dosage of Advil, and it hadn't eased the pain even a little. I hadn't treated my face or head with ice since I'd been at Vic's house, so the swelling had returned around my eye socket. It made my eye feel tight and squishy, which served to generally irritate the hell out of me and make me borderline nauseous.

More than all that, there was the highlight reel that wouldn't quit playing in my head when I closed my eyes—being bound by the wrists and ankles with zip ties, having a gun thrust in my face and poked in my ribs, plus of course the backhand across the face and the slam of my head into a wall causing said injuries. Although the person responsible for my duress was currently sitting in a cell three hours away, the fear I'd been able to tamp down earlier to focus on getting out of my situation was starting to bubble to the surface.

I had a shaky feeling inside my chest I couldn't stifle, no matter what sleeping position I tried. Before I knew it, tears were running down my face uncontrollably and my breath was hitching.

There was a knock at the door, and Baxter leaned his head in to say, "Ellie, are you okay? I thought I heard—" When his eyes landed on me, he quickly shut the door behind him and rushed to my side. "What's wrong?"

I was full-on sobbing, unable to control my emotions anymore. I choked out, "Today."

Kneeling beside my bed, he gathered me into his arms and held me. "I wondered when it would hit you. It's okay. Let it all out."

I cried against his shoulder for only a short time, the safety of his embrace dissipating my fear. I was never afraid of anything when I was with him.

Once I'd calmed down, I groaned, "Damn it. I freaking hate crying. It did nothing for me but make my head hurt worse."

He leaned back and grinned at me. "There's the Ellie I know. Can I do anything for you? Drugs? Ice pack?"

I talked tough, but the thought of him leaving made me want to cry again. "You could stay here with me. That would help more than anything."

With only a flicker of hesitation, he replied, "Of course." He stood and moved to get into Tom's bed.

"I meant a little closer than that."

He turned to face me. "I was hoping that's what you meant, but I didn't want to assume."

I smiled. "Make no mistake, you have zero chance of getting lucky with me. When I say, 'Not tonight, I have a headache,' you know it's legit."

He chuckled as he slid in next to me under the covers. "I know."

As he pulled me close, I said, "Thanks for staying. I don't want to get you in trouble with your mom."

He gave me a soft kiss. "For you, I'll risk it."

3

I slept surprisingly well but still awoke with a splitting headache. That said, waking up in Baxter's arms made me so happy I nearly forgot about the pain.

"Hey."

I smiled and shifted to face him. "Hey."

"How's your head?"

"About the same." I wrapped my arm around his waist and burrowed tighter toward him. "Everything else is pretty awesome, though. You think we could stay here forever?"

Grinning, he said, "You mean quit our jobs and live with my parents? I don't think you want that."

"I do if it means we could do this all the time."

He kissed my forehead. "We will, soon."

"Not soon enough."

"No, not soon enough. But eventually."

Last night the house had smelled of cookies, but this morning another heavenly aroma filled the place. "Do I smell bacon?"

He grunted. "Is that one of your rude cop jokes?"

"Ha, ha. I'm asking if my overnight stay comes with breakfast."

"Oh, yeah. My mom makes a mean Sunday morning breakfast."

I sighed. "Then I'm going to ask again—you think we could stay here forever?"

"Considering my mom has probably figured out by now that you seduced me away from my spot on the couch, I'm betting it's going to be a hard no from her."

I made a face. "Moms never like me."

"Two alpha females in one house never works out."

"No joke. Jayne invited me to stay with her over one Christmas break when I was in college. She never made that mistake again."

He laughed. "You and the sheriff can stand your ground better than most people. It's scary for the rest of us when you two aren't on the same page."

I frowned. "Speaking of which, we'd better be heading back soon. I know I was the one who pushed you to make the trip down here, but the more I think about it, the more I think it wasn't my brightest idea."

He tightened his arms around me. "I thought you wanted to stay here forever."

"In theory, I do. In reality, I'd prefer Jayne didn't fire us for skipping town when we're supposed to be wrapping up a case. I figure if we roll in around noon she might buy that we worked late and slept in."

"I doubt she'll jump straight to firing, but there's plenty of disciplinary action she could take," he said uneasily. "I'd do it again in a heartbeat, but I still get the feeling this decision is going to come back and bite me in the ass."

I smiled. "Then let's haul that sweet ass of yours back home ASAP."

$\sim$

WE ATE breakfast with Mr. and Mrs. Baxter, which was pretty stilted and painful, unable to be lightened by the bad jokes being lobbed back and forth between Baxter and his dad. Now at least I knew where he got his flair for terrible jokes. We then quickly got ready to leave and went to say our goodbyes to his family. As we were heading toward the door, Baxter's mother pulled him aside and launched into an in-depth conversation with him, which made me again feel like I was intruding. I went ahead outside and put our bags in my trunk. I went to get into my vehicle to sit and wait for him, but I figured some fresh air would do me more good. I set off on as brisk a walk as my still-sore head would allow.

Their property was even more lovely in the daylight, the rolling hills starting to green up and the woods in the distance filling in with spring foliage. I walked the perimeter and began heading back. The barn had fascinated me last night, and since I didn't see much of it in the dark, I figured now was a great time to poke around. I walked around the outside of it. The exterior boards were a weathered gray, giving it the quintessential old Midwestern barn look.

When I neared the open door, I heard some rustling in the brush just around the corner. Figuring it was Baxter coming out to get me, I headed that way. But when I rounded the corner, I found a different Baxter than I'd hoped. Mrs. Baxter was leaning tiredly against the barn wall, a flask-sized bottle of gin in hand, drinking deeply with her eyes tightly shut. I stopped dead in my tracks and shrank back around the corner, out of her sight.

This was certainly a conundrum. There was now no doubt in my mind Mrs. Baxter was an alcoholic, and now that I thought about it, I was betting she was the alcoholic Baxter had told me he'd accompanied to AA meetings in the past. Did I, as a fellow sufferer, butt into her personal business and offer support? Or did I, as possibly her least favorite person on the planet, keep my damn mouth shut, pretend I didn't see her, and go the hell home? I didn't know the right answer. Since I wanted to spend the foreseeable future with her son, I needed to be able to get along with her. And if that meant not rocking the boat less than twenty-four hours after I'd met the woman, maybe it was best I let this go. I remembered how angry I'd been at Baxter when he'd pointed out my problem to me, and I cared about him and respected his opinion. I couldn't imagine her response to someone she could barely stand the sight of.

I decided to let Baxter know what I'd witnessed, and he could do whatever he thought best with the information. Before I could make myself scarce, I heard her footsteps in the brush sounding like they were coming my way. Mrs. Baxter finding me spying on her private binge would be worse than any intervention I might perform. I panicked and rushed into the open barn door to find a place to hide.

It smelled terrible in here, worse than it had last night when it had only stunk of manure and wet straw. It reminded me of a crime scene, sort of—various stenches rolled into a sickly, putrid odor. I assumed an animal had crawled in here to die. I dove quickly toward the nearest corner, behind a large tractor attachment. I heard some shuffling and slurred muttering outside, something about Shawn forgetting to do something again. There was a loud squeak, and it suddenly got dark in the barn. Then there was a clank. She'd closed the door. I breathed a sigh of relief, but instantly regretted it. The smell in here was not getting better, but I had no choice but to stay put until I knew Mrs. Baxter was back at the house.

I waited several minutes before I left my hiding spot. I crept back to the door in the darkened barn and put my ear against it to listen. I heard nothing, so I decided to go for it. I pushed against the door, but nothing happened. I pushed again, hoping it was heavier than I'd assumed and I hadn't pushed hard enough. No luck. It was then that it dawned on me that the clank I heard had been the metal latch falling into place. I was locked in.

Damn it. I texted Baxter, *Locked in barn.*

I waited for a response from him, but nothing was popping up. I assumed he might have been talking with his little brother since Shawn had just rolled out of bed as we were saying our goodbyes. I imagined his last conversation with Shawn before leaving would be a heartfelt one, so I didn't blame him for ignoring me. To pass the time, I decided to peruse the barn. Breathing through my mouth, I turned on my phone's flashlight and walked farther into the darkened barn. There had been a couple of lights on in here last night, but I didn't know how to turn them on, so the meager light from my phone would have to suffice. The crime scene aroma was getting stronger as I went. I shined the light to my left, toward the animal stalls lining one wall.

I gasped and fumbled my phone. Lying on the ground was a woman, an axe driven through the side of her head.

Snatching my phone up from the ground, I scrambled away from the carnage and walked several paces away to try to get myself under control. It wasn't that I was afraid of a dead body—far from it—but seeing someone's head split open so far the brains were seeping out was a hard thing to digest when you weren't prepared for it.

No more texts. I called Baxter.

He answered with, "Got yourself locked in the barn, did you?"

I replied shakily, "Uh . . . that's actually the least of my worries. Can you come here, alone? Don't tell anyone where you're going, and *do not* bring any of your family members with you."

He chuckled, evidently oblivious to my trembling tone. "Is this a booty call? Are you interested in a literal roll in the hay?"

I couldn't bring myself to verbalize what I'd seen—and was locked in with. He also didn't need to hear this grisly news over the phone. "Can you just get here fast?"

He finally figured out this was no joke. "What's wrong? Are you okay?"

"I'm okay. I. . . . You need to see this." I ended the call without letting him get in another word.

My stomach lurched as this situation began to sink in. Why was there a dead woman in the Baxter family's barn? And more disconcertingly, who was out here killing her while the rest of us were sleeping a couple hundred yards away?

The sudden thought popped into my mind that the killer could still be in here, and I got a chill. That was always a concern, especially for criminalists—that the killer would return to the scene of his crime and sneak up on us while we were concentrating on gathering evidence. The department always provided exceptional security for us, so I was never terribly worried for my personal safety, even though we'd all heard the horror stories that had happened in other places. Here, I didn't have any backup besides Baxter, and as I'd realized during our last case, the fact that I now cared so much about him had made me protective of him.

I grabbed the nearest weapon—a pitchfork leaning against the wall— and hurried around the perimeter of the barn, looking for hiding places and poking every human-sized lump of hay. I made sure to stay far, far away from the primary crime scene, which seemed at first glance to be confined to a small area around the body.

The barn door lurched open, and Baxter appeared in the doorway. "Ellie? What's going on?"

I hurried toward him, pitchfork still in hand.

Before I could say anything, he asked, "What the hell are you doing?"

I threw the pitchfork on the ground and grabbed his hands. "Okay, don't freak out, but . . . there's a dead body in here. A woman."

I felt his grip tense, then he pulled away. "What? In here?" he breathed, his eyes darting around as his face clouded over.

I shined my phone's light toward the body. "Over there. It's pretty brutal. Be prepared."

He pushed past me and got out his own phone, shining the flashlight as he slowly approached the body. I followed him, my focus now on him and what this situation had to be doing to his already fully frayed nerves. Not only that, Baxter had a strange initial reaction to crime scenes. He vomited. Every time. After he got it out, he was completely fine to get up close and personal with the grossest of corpses. I assumed it was going to hit him at any moment.

I said, a little more motherly-sounding than I intended, "If you're going to puke, do it outside. This isn't our scene, so—"

"I know," he snapped. It was a fairly sore subject, especially since his partner, Jason Sterling, took every opportunity to rib him about it.

"Sorry," I murmured, keeping an eye on him nevertheless.

He continued to circle the body, giving it a wide berth, until he got around to the other side, where he could see the woman's face. His expression registered shock, but then suddenly turned to what I thought seemed indifferent and almost relieved.

"Do you know who it is?" I asked.

He raised his eyes to meet mine. He didn't look upset in the least. Barking out a mirthless laugh, he replied, "Marie Collins."

4

My jaw hit the ground. I stared down at the body at a total loss for words. I walked over to stand next to Baxter so I could get a good look at the woman's face, which I hadn't bothered to do before. It wasn't likely I would have recognized her anyway, only having seen a few photos of her online. Baxter and I stood there for a while, taking everything in.

I couldn't tell what was going on inside his head, but a really bad batch of ideas was beginning to form in mine. Marie Collins brutally murdered inside the Baxter family's barn was a bad look any way you considered it.

Marie Collins had ruined the Baxter family. Shawn was a teenage degenerate. Mrs. Baxter was a depressed alcoholic. Mr. Baxter looked older than his years, I imagined because he'd been the one holding the family together all this time. I didn't know much about Tom, but he'd dropped whatever he had with his own family to spend most of the previous day looking for Shawn. And then there was Nick, who'd become a detective and made it his mission to get justice for victims and their families, no matter how hard he had to work or what it cost him. Marie Collins had in one way or another shaped the trajectory of each of their lives. In my mind, any of them had a number of perfectly acceptable reasons to end her. And that was a real problem.

Baxter wiped a hand down his face and muttered, "I'll be back."

Based on the green tint to his face, I was sure he was heading out to heave up his breakfast. But I wasn't positive he wouldn't bolt and run back to the house to announce the good news to his family, so I followed him. I kept an eye on him as he retched into the brush on the back side of the barn. Based on the glare he cut me as he returned to where I stood at the barn door, my moral support, or babysitting, was not appreciated.

I caught his arm before he reentered the barn. "Where's your head right now?"

"Thinking about how much I want to high-five whoever did that," he replied stonily, jerking his thumb toward the scene.

This wasn't him. His heart bled for the victims of the crimes we investigated. But I understood how much relief he must have felt for what this meant for his family. They were finally rid of the person who'd been a specter haunting their lives for the last fifteen years. But I worried that the ramifications of Marie Collins meeting a violent end on their property—and who'd done it—would only end up being a fresh hell for them to endure.

I said gently, "Do you, uh . . . have an idea of who might be on the receiving end of your high five?"

He frowned at me. "You seem to."

I rolled my eyes. "You can cut out your grumpy-ass bullshit with me right now, Baxter. I've endured it for two weeks, and I'm done. I am *always* on your side, in case you've forgotten. You know damn well I'd help you bury that body if it were you who did it, so don't give me any attitude."

His eyebrows shot up, then he cast his gaze down and took my hand. "I'm sorry. This is all a little much."

I squeezed his hand. "I know. We need a plan."

He dropped my hand and took out his phone. "The plan isn't the question here. We have to call this in."

I put my hand over his before he could start dialing. "I think we need to think about it first."

He frowned. "You of all people should understand the protocol here, not to mention our duty to follow it."

"True, but it's not like there's a time element to the protocol."

"There most certainly is."

I held out both hands. "Go with me here—the moment you make that call, all of us are suspects. You, me, your mom and dad, Shawn, and maybe even Tom depending on TOD."

"And we all have a right to protect ourselves from trespassers on our property under self-defense laws."

"You really think any of us can cry self-defense on *that* level of malice?" I cried, gesturing toward the open barn. "We all have excellent motives for ending that bitch in there—maybe me not quite so much, but I had means and opportunity, and two out of three ain't bad. That said, the police are going to be so busy figuring out which one of us to pin it on they'll never bother to entertain any other suspects. One of the Baxters is going down for this, guilty or not, and we will have no way of defending ourselves . . . unless . . ." My eyes trailed toward the open door.

Baxter's face had gotten paler and increasingly drawn as I was speaking. "Ellie, no. It's not right."

"No, it's not right. But it's necessary."

He shook his head. "We can't."

"We've already looked at it. I just want to look at it more closely and for longer." When his only reply was a frown, I added, "Don't you believe I can get in and out of a crime scene without a trace? No one will know."

"I'll know."

I took his hand again. "I love that you're such a good man, but I won't sit by and watch one of your family members fry for something Marie Collins had coming."

He pulled me toward him and wrapped his arms around me, burying his head on my shoulder. His voice was shaky as he said, "What if one of them did it?"

I held him tightly. "You can't think that. I don't know them well, but I can't imagine any of them are capable of this."

"You'd be surprised," he muttered into my hair.

My heart broke for him. I couldn't imagine even entertaining the thought that my sister Rachel would be capable of murdering someone. My mother, maybe, but she'd been a horrible woman. I couldn't imagine Shawn, after his genuine breakthrough last night, would have done this. He'd already taken his aggression out and was spent from the aftermath.

Not unlike a worn-out toddler, he'd nearly fallen asleep in the car on the way home. And even though Mrs. Baxter hadn't been nice to me, I didn't believe her to be a bad person. She seemed like a mama bear who'd do anything to protect her children. Then again, I supposed if push came to shove, that could include murder. I still wasn't seeing it, even in a drunken rage, out of the woman who bore and raised my sweet Nick Baxter.

"Look, everyone is innocent until proven guilty, so we don't need to jump to any conclusions. Give me thirty minutes and then you can call whoever you want."

He pulled back from me. "You don't have your gear or anything to collect any kind of samples. And if you were to collect a fingerprint, you're essentially destroying evidence because it won't be admissible. It could actually hurt us."

I smiled. "I know how evidence works. I'm just saying if we can glean anything from the scene, we should. If we're all suspects, the detectives aren't going to give us even a smidge of information about this case. We have to know what we're up against."

"I'm not going to talk you out of this, am I?"

"Nope," I replied, backing away from him. "I've got some gloves in my car. I'll be back."

"I thought we decided we weren't touching anything," he called after me, his tone stern.

"It's only a precaution."

Seeing as how he'd only begrudgingly given me thirty minutes to work a whole murder scene, I sprinted to my car. I grabbed a few pairs of gloves out of the box I kept in the trunk. My nephew Nate was a puker, and car sickness would strike the poor kid at random. With gloves, I could clean up the mess fast and not have it all over me when I was finished. I never imagined I'd need them for a clandestine field investigation. I rifled through my cosmetic bag and found a hair tie, tweezers, some cotton swabs, and a cleanish Ziploc bag. I also snatched up my stash of plastic grocery bags and disposable masks from my vomit-cleaning arsenal and then raced back to the barn.

Baxter continued his crisis of ethics as I stopped outside the barn to tie two of the grocery bags over my shoes as makeshift booties. "Seriously,

Ellie, if you leave any trace of yourself behind, *you're* going to be the one going down for this."

As I ran my fingers through my hair to rid it of loose strands and pulled it into a messy ponytail, I replied, "I am the queen of crime scenes. I don't leave traces of myself at the ones we process, so why would I do it now when it matters? This one is no different. Give me your hat."

He took the baseball cap off his head and put it on mine. "It's different in that you have literally zero authority to be in there."

"I found the body. I can't unsee it, so there's no harm in looking at it more."

"Is this how you justified your teenage delinquency? Splitting hairs like this?"

"Yes. Isn't that how everyone does it?" I donned a pair of gloves and a mask, feeling sufficiently suited up to enter the scene. "You're welcome to leave me to it if you'd like some plausible deniability."

Frowning, he said, "Not a chance. If I can't stop you, at least I can help you."

I smiled and handed him a pair of gloves, a mask, and two grocery bags, excitement running through me at the thought of working a scene with him, even under these conditions. "I was hoping you'd say that."

Grumbling under his breath, he put on his own protective gear and followed me into the barn.

"Can you turn on some lights without smudging any possible prints that might be on the switches?" I asked.

He went over to one wall and flipped some switches. The barn filled with a decent amount of light from the four fluorescent fixtures high above. It wasn't great lighting, but it was better than nothing. We approached the body again, making sure to stay away from the blood pooled around her head, lest we made footprints.

I said, "Obviously you and I can't pinpoint TOD without a coroner's assessment, but we know it had to be after eleven, right? That's when we left here to take Shawn to the station."

"Right," he replied. "The blood looks sticky but not necessarily dry, so I imagine it's been several hours since . . . the incident."

"Agreed." I got out my phone and started taking photos, just as I would at any other crime scene—wide-angle first, then moving to midrange.

Baxter stepped in front of me. "I don't think you should have evidence of this on your phone. If the police take a look through it, which is a real possibility, you're looking at obstruction charges at best."

"That's why I'm going to upload them to a burner Google Drive and delete them from my phone and the cloud as soon as we're done."

"I don't like this."

"Really? I hadn't noticed." When he glared at me, I added, "Now get out of my shot."

Baxter moved, and I continued to take photos, stepping in for some close-up shots of the murder weapon. As I worked, Baxter griped about how I was getting way too close for his comfort, not that I expected anything less. I'd gotten my hopes up that the killer had left behind some patent fingerprints in blood on the axe. I zoomed in on the axe handle as far as my camera would go and used a magnifier app to look closer, but there was nothing. With only one swing of the axe, there was no blood castoff and probably not a lot of back spatter. Damn. That was unfortunate, because I could have at least determined the killer's fingerprint pattern and been able to exonerate some of the Baxters.

Whoever had driven this axe through Marie Collins's skull had done it with malice. And they had decent aim—her head was split in two like a watermelon, dead center through her right ear. For reasons I didn't under-stand, the thing I found most disconcerting about her wound wasn't the brain matter bulging out of her cracked skull. It was that her ear was now in two blood-drenched pieces dangling inches away from each other.

"The murderer is a lefty," I said, turning toward Baxter and away from the carnage. "That should narrow it down to a tenth of the population. Know any lefties with a grudge?"

He furrowed his brow, murmuring, "Swung that thing like a baseball bat."

"Yep." I didn't want to ask the next question, but it bore asking. "Um . . . is this by chance the axe—"

Before I could get my whole question out, he said, "No. Shawn was throwing a hatchet last night. Shorter handle. They call the sport 'axe throwing,' but you generally don't throw this type of long-handled axe like you'd use to cut down a tree."

"Oh. Well, good. At least his prints won't be on it." I hesitated, not wanting to ask this question either. "Unless . . . was this axe here already? Does it belong to your dad?"

He paused before answering, "Maybe. Probably."

My heart sank. "So this is going to be another instance where the killer used the tools at hand to kill his or her victim, and the unfortunate property owner is going to automatically look guilty? I wish people would come prepared once in a while when they set out to kill someone."

He huffed out a chuckle. "Yeah. Unprepared killers are the worst."

I gave him a sympathetic smile behind my mask. He was trying to inject some of his classic gallows humor into this situation, but his heart wasn't in it. I couldn't imagine how scared he was right now. We had to figure this out.

I pulled myself together and took out a cotton swab. I stuck it into the rift in the victim's skull and got a good sample of blood that was still liquid.

"Gross," Baxter said. "Do we really need a sample from her? That blood's clearly hers."

"It's one sample I can take without getting caught. It won't hurt to know her blood type."

He stared at me. "You have a blood typing kit with you?"

"No, but I can get one easily enough." I had a thought. "Speaking of her info . . ." I pulled my mask down, took my phone out, and called my friend and fellow criminalist, Amanda Carmack.

She answered with, "Hey, how are you feeling today?"

"My head is killing me." When Baxter gave me a pained look, I added, "No pun intended. But I'm . . . recuperating. How's Sterling?"

Baxter's partner, Detective Jason Sterling, had been with me during our big showdown with our suspect. He, too, had received a nasty head injury as a result of the altercation and had ended up with a full-blown concussion.

I could hear the smile in Amanda's voice. The two of them had recently reconciled their on-again, off-again relationship. "Crabby as hell that he can't be here today for the wrap-up. Speaking of which, Nick isn't here either."

I flicked my eyes his way. "He's got a family thing to take care of. I heard him mention being back later today, maybe."

Baxter shrugged and shook his head sadly. With this new issue at hand, I imagined we wouldn't be going home anytime soon. And that could spell trouble for both of us at work.

Amanda said, "Cool. It's been pretty chill around here. We had a short meeting first thing, but now it's down to paperwork."

"That's good." Jayne had given me a pass to take it easy today because of my injuries, although she did expect me to come in at some point. But maybe if Baxter and I could get all of his reports finished, he wouldn't be in too much hot water for missing the meeting. I got down to what I called for. "Hey, totally off subject . . . could you look in AFIS for me and see if someone's in there?"

"Sure. What's the name?"

"Marie . . ." I mouthed to Baxter, "Middle name?"

He pulled down his mask and whispered, "Ann."

"Marie Ann Collins." Since she'd been in prison, I assumed her fingerprints would have been input in the Automated Fingerprint Identification System either when she was arrested or when she entered prison. But if not, I didn't want to let my chance go by to collect her prints in person.

After a moment, Amanda said, "I found a Marie Ann Collins from Indiana, charged with kidnapping. She did a fifteen-year stint in Rockville . . . just got out yesterday. Is that her?"

"That's her. What's her pattern?"

"Central pocket whorl," she replied.

"Perfect. Thanks."

"Is she a new person connected to the case?"

"No . . . I was just being nosy."

"Oh. Okay." Thankfully, she changed the subject. "You want to grab lunch sometime this week?"

"Absolutely. See you soon." I hung up with Amanda to face a frowning Baxter.

He said, "If she hadn't been in AFIS, you were considering collecting prints from her cold, dead fingers, weren't you?"

I shrugged. "Coroners do it all the time. And you know I touch way grosser stuff than corpse fingers."

"And again, you probably don't need her vital info, considering she didn't swing that axe herself."

Instead of getting into an argument with him, I put his detective brain to work. "Point noted. I need you to start spitballing how Marie Collins got into your barn in the first place. Clearly this is the primary, because you can tell she hasn't been moved since the blood started flowing. Why in the hell was she here? And how did she get here, considering I haven't seen any other vehicles on your property besides mine and your family's? Oh, and could you poke around and look for anything she might have left behind—purse, jacket, phone? You know the drill."

While he mulled over my questions and searched the barn, I kneeled down next to the body and studied her clothing, looking for traces of anything that might have come from the killer. I was finding a whole lot of nothing, aside from the fact that this woman was dressed to party.

Between the grays that had been missed by her bad hair dye job, the aging skin on the backs of her hands, and the wrinkles on her face and neck, I'd guessed she was fiftyish. However, her impressively toned prison body and the tight tank top, miniskirt, and gaudy heels she was wearing made her appear much younger. The last time she'd been out and about in the world, she was in her late thirties, in the prime of her life. It stood to reason that she might have been trying to fit back into society exactly where she'd left off. It was kind of sad when you thought about it—her life screeched to a halt fifteen years ago and the world went on without her. Not that I felt sorry for her after what she'd done. But she was human, and I was sure she'd had a rough time of it.

I forced my train of thought back to my task. As far as I could tell, there were no signs of struggle aside from the large axe lodged in her head. No dirt or straw looked roughed up anywhere, her hair wasn't mussed (aside from the blood that had seeped into it), and her clothing was clean and even looked new. I was itching to get my hands on that murder weapon to process it, but I knew I couldn't lay a finger on it. Not only that, I wasn't convinced I could pry it out of her skull without help.

As I kept looking for something—anything—to help identify who might have killed this woman, Baxter said, "I suppose she could have come out here looking for Shawn, to apologize. She'd written him a bunch of letters from prison, but my parents kept them from him."

"Even after he turned eighteen?" I asked as I studied the victim's face, arms, and hands.

She didn't seem to have been punched in the face and knocked out. Her wrists were smooth and unblemished, so she hadn't been tied up and brought out here forcibly. I saw no other wounds besides the painfully obvious one, unless there were some under her clothing. And speaking of corpse fingers, I got close enough to note there was no blood or dirt or other refuse under her fingernails, which would have been present if she'd scratched at an attacker or tried to claw her way away from one. If she'd been brought out here against her will, she'd had to have been drugged. Or I suppose she could have been blackout drunk.

He replied, "I know it maybe wasn't the right thing to do . . . but they did what they thought was best. They knew he wouldn't want to dredge all that back up, and no one in this family has ever been interested in her pathetic attempts at making amends."

"That part I understand." No way would I have entertained an apology from my sister's abductor, and now that I thought about it, I probably would have tried to protect her from all communication from him as well. Good thing that asshole was dead so I never had to worry about it.

He went on, "So say she comes out here to apologize, and it doesn't go well . . ." He trailed off, ripping his mask off as his face went ashen.

I got up and went over to stand in front of him. "Nope. You shut that shit down right now. None of the Baxters did this." At least I hoped not. If one of them had, it would crush him so badly I didn't think he'd ever recover. "Someone had to have followed her."

"How did she get here and not leave a vehicle behind? I doubt she walked here from town. It's too far."

"She's been in prison for fifteen years, so she probably didn't have a vehicle anymore. For a person without transportation, a couple miles isn't far. Trust me, I've been there. Maybe she walked out here, someone followed her and killed her, then they drove away. That would explain why no vehicles got left here."

Baxter said uneasily, "That's a lot of moving parts."

I frowned, thinking about Marie Collins's shoe choice. "You're right. And considering she hadn't had her feet in a pair of high heels for fifteen years, there's no way in hell she'd try to walk all the way out here. I'm going to amend my theory—maybe someone gave her a ride out here, noticed the barn, and saw an opportunity for a secluded murder spot."

"You mean someone was out cruising Boonville for single females needing a ride? I feel like anyone with that much of a serial killer vibe would choose a more populated area."

"Maybe, but it's much more likely she knew the person."

He shook his head. "Now that we're delving into it, I'm realizing the timing is crazy. Why would she come out here after eleven p.m. to try to talk to any of us? She had to know there was a good chance no one would be awake."

"Maybe she couldn't sleep until she said what she felt she needed to say." I frowned. "Or, if her alleged amends-making was as shady as you all seemed to think, maybe she came out here intending to do some damage to your place in retaliation for what Shawn did." I looked around. "Anything seem damaged to you?"

"Not really," he murmured, pulling up his mask and taking another walk around the barn.

I went back to examining the area around the body. I wanted so badly to be able to move her to look underneath her, but I couldn't risk it. I hadn't seen a purse anywhere, so unless the killer took it, whatever she'd brought with her would have been on her person. I would have loved to dig through her pockets, but I didn't dare, especially with how much Baxter already disapproved of my plan.

He came back to stand next to me and mused, "What if she was forced to come out here?"

I held out my wrists, the ligature marks less red than yesterday but looking more bruised. "Like bound at the wrists and ankles and put somewhere she didn't want to be? I checked, and no, it doesn't look like our dearly departed kidnapper here suffered the same fate I did."

He winced. "Was it too soon to bring up that type of scenario?"

I chuckled. "No, it's fine. I know I was a mess last night, but my rational brain knows my situation yesterday is over and no harm was done."

His worried gaze landing on my black eye, he replied, "I wouldn't say *no* harm was done."

"I meant no real emotional harm. I've been in much scarier situations."

He took my hand. "I know, and I hate it. I've come close to several heart attacks because of the 'situations' you keep getting yourself into."

"And I hate that. I promise to try to be more careful, although I take no blame for this last one. Sterling and I were following a lead Jayne gave us. I wasn't going rogue or anything. It just . . . happened. Bad luck."

He shook his head. "Bad partner. Once his concussion heals, I'm kicking Sterling's ass for not looking out for you better."

Smiling up at him, I said, "You know I'd never stand in the way of anyone kicking Sterling's ass for any reason, but it honestly wasn't his fault, either." I crouched down next to the victim again. "Now back to work, Detective. My arbitrary thirty-minute time limit is ticking away."

He chuckled and began studying the path between the door and the body.

Moments later, we both jumped as we heard a voice say, "What are you doing in here?"

5

Mrs. Baxter approached her son. "I thought you were leaving, dear."

Ripping off his mask and gloves and shoving them in his pocket, Baxter headed her way. "Mom . . . I have something I need to tell you, but let's talk outside."

Her eyes locked on mine, then slid down to the body I was kneeling beside. She jumped back, a strangled cry escaping her lips. "Is that . . . a . . . a person?"

Baxter put his arm around his mom and steered her so she faced away from the carnage. "Um . . . yes. Someone was killed out here."

"*What?* Who?" she cried, darting a look over her shoulder, then covering her eyes and shuddering.

"It's . . . Marie Collins."

His mother snapped her head up and whirled around. Wrenching herself out of his grasp, she began striding toward me and the body, her face a combination of fury, shock, and elation. Baxter made a move to stop her, but she was a woman on a mission. After a terse, "Nicholas," he took a wary step back from her. She pursed her lips, and I had a feeling what was coming next. I scrambled up and put my hands out in time to stop the mouthful of spit Mrs. Baxter had intended to land on her archenemy.

When her projectile hit my gloved hands rather than her intended target, she turned her wrath onto me. "Out of the way."

By that time, Baxter had gotten his act together and positioned himself in between his mother and me. Finally asserting himself to her, he said, "Mom, you cannot under any circumstances spit on that corpse . . . or kick it, or anything. None of us can, no matter how much we might want to. If your DNA gets anywhere near that body, you could easily be charged for the murder. Do you understand?"

Panting from sheer fury, she choked out, "I haven't laid eyes on that bitch in fifteen years. Do you know how much I wanted to give her a piece of my mind?"

Removing my soiled gloves, I gestured toward the body and said, "Hey, if you look closely, you can literally see a piece of *her* mind."

Mrs. Baxter flicked her eyes toward the victim's cracked-open skull, horror evident on her face. Baxter frowned at me.

I scoffed. "Oh, come on. You were thinking it."

He finally relented and let out a single snicker. "Okay, fine. I was thinking it."

Mrs. Baxter's expression had relaxed, and now it seemed as if she was fighting a grin. "I can see—a little—why you were drawn to her, Nicholas. You do share the same terrible sense of humor, like your father." She let out a giggle. "A piece of her mind. I certainly can see a *piece* of her mind." The giggling turned into full-on belly laughter.

I hoped it was solely my wit rather than the booze from earlier combined with the shock and relief at seeing the bane of her existence dead that had made her laugh. Maybe after she found out the truth she'd actually even like me.

Baxter watched his mother worriedly. "We need to get you out of here, Mom." He put his arm around her and began walking her toward the door. Over his shoulder, he said to me, "Once I get her settled, I'm calling this in."

Shit. My opportunity alone with this scene was about to end. I redoubled my efforts, quickly taking more photos and scouring the place desperately to find any telltale evidence, keeping my ungloved hands to myself. Aside from possible latent fingerprints I couldn't hope to see without my gear and wasn't allowed to dust for, the killer had left nothing behind. Not even a footprint, that I could tell. Damn.

I decided to calm down and completely start over. I hurried to the entrance of the barn and looked inside as if I were entering for the first time. It had been nighttime when the incident occurred, so for Marie Collins to have made it that far into the barn, she would've had to have some light to see. She could have used her phone, or . . . I hurried over to the wall where I'd seen Baxter go when he flipped on the lights. It was a fuse panel with four smooth, wide switches—ones that could hold a whole fingerprint. I longed to dust them for prints, especially since Baxter had gloved up before he'd touched them. It was dark in here when I'd gotten locked in, so it stood to reason that the killer had turned off the lights before they had left—and that meant the last prints on there had to belong to them.

Alas, they were not mine to collect. But they soon might be if the local criminalists were of the same caliber as my nemesis, Beck Durant, the lead criminalist for Hamilton County. He had the job because of his mother's influence, not because of his skill. Anything he processed, Amanda and I had to come by and recheck. Thanks to Beck's incompetence, searching for evidence someone else had missed was a talent of mine. That was why after the locals released this scene, my plan was to process the hell out of it.

Baxter entered the barn again, his shoulders slumped and face drawn. "That was a difficult conversation."

Removing my mask, I walked over to give him a hug. "I imagine it was. But I don't suppose too many tears were shed."

"No, but I had to threaten my dad and little brother with bodily harm if they came out here."

"Ooh. Sorry. Did you also make the call?"

"I did."

I huffed out a sigh. "Boo. That means my clandestine scene processing op is over."

He eyed me. "You were having fun, weren't you?"

"I was. You know I love what I do."

Grinning, he said, "Nerd." His face fell as he took my hand in his. "Life is about to get real shitty . . . again."

I squeezed his hand. "Then lean on me. I got you."

He ran a finger over the bruising around my wrists. "Lean on the woman with two head injuries and some nasty ligature marks?"

I chuckled. "Maybe don't physically lean on me."

He began walking out of the barn and pulled me with him. "Come on. We'd better at least pretend we weren't in here for the last half hour."

Once we got outside, I removed my bag booties and wrapped my soiled gloves and my mask in them. "Where did you put your stuff?"

Baxter replied, "I threw it away in the kitchen."

"That won't do. What if they go through your trash?"

"They shouldn't, because the house has nothing to do with the crime scene. And it's not like they have to search for the murder weapon."

"True . . ." I thought about the bloody swab in my pocket. "I should probably hide my blood sample, though."

He shook his head tiredly.

Before he could admonish me again, I said, "I know, I know. Spare me the lecture."

◆

BY THE TIME I uploaded my photos to my new Google Drive, deleted them from my phone and from the cloud, and hid the blood sample and the used gloves and bags, a sheriff's department cruiser was pulling up to the house. I joined a very nervous clan of Baxters in their living room as Mr. Baxter opened the door for the deputy.

The deputy nodded. "Good morning, Mr. Baxter. I'm responding to a call about a deceased person found on your property."

Mr. Baxter replied, "Good morning, Jared. It's . . . uh . . . she's . . . out in our barn."

The deputy glanced at Baxter. "Nice to see you, Nick."

Baxter nodded. "You, too, Jared."

Getting down to business, the deputy said, "I ask that you all sit tight here while I secure the scene. Our detectives will be along shortly to speak to you. I'll warn you that it's going to be a madhouse around here for a while." He gave a rueful half-smile to Baxter. "But I guess I don't need to tell you that."

Once he'd left and the door was shut, Mr. Baxter turned to the rest of us, his shoulders slumped and expression full of worry. "What do we do now?"

Baxter said, "We tell the truth."

Mrs. Baxter flicked her gaze toward me. I gave her a slight nod, hoping she understood it to mean the version of the truth with the wishy-washy time line that didn't advertise the fact that I'd nosed around the scene for a good while. And the version of the truth that didn't involve me barely stopping her from spitting on the corpse of her mortal enemy.

Shawn had been leaning against the wall, a shell of the cocky degenerate he'd pretended to be last night. His eyes welling with tears, he said, "So what is the truth? Why is . . . *she* . . . dead in our barn? Did one of you guys . . . did one of you—" He broke into a sob, unable to finish a question no child should have to ask of his family.

Mrs. Baxter rushed to her youngest son and swept him into her arms. "Of course we didn't hurt her, sweetheart. None of us did. Someone else must have come onto our property last night."

Mr. Baxter asked quietly, "Has anyone spoken to Tom yet this morning?"

I felt Baxter stiffen next to me. "I'll call him," he said. He covered giving my hand a squeeze by brushing past me as he retreated to his room.

That left me with the rest of the family, again feeling like I was trespassing. Thankfully, Mrs. Baxter steered Shawn to his room. Then it was just Mr. Baxter and me, but I wasn't convinced it was any better.

After a few moments of uncomfortable silence, he rubbed the back of his neck and ventured, "I . . . uh . . . don't reckon you envisioned your weekend ending up like this, did you?"

I tried to smile, but couldn't hold it. "I didn't, but had I known, it wouldn't have stopped me from making the trip. Honestly, I'm glad I was the one who found . . . it."

He sighed heavily. "Honestly . . . me, too. I don't know that any of my family could have handled it like you seem to be. I'm sure you have no qualms about dealing with death, but having it sprung on you out of the blue like this can't be easy."

"Strangely enough, it's not the first time I've discovered a victim. That's actually how Nick and I met. He had to question me about a young woman I found deceased."

"Oh. He never mentioned that."

"I hadn't been on that side of an investigation before, but he instantly put me at ease. He has a way of making difficult subjects easy to talk about. His empathy for people is unmatched. It's what makes him such an amazing law enforcement official, head and shoulders above the rest. You should know how well-respected and liked he is in our department and in our community."

Mr. Baxter's gaze was focused on something over my shoulder. "Have you ever told him that?"

"Yes, I have. Many times. Your son is the best man I know."

He shook his head, a frown furrowing his brow. "If you truly believe that, then I don't understand why you—"

Baxter's voice boomed from behind me, "I just talked to Tom. He's coming over."

I turned to him and murmured, "Is that advisable, considering?"

Baxter gave me a pointed look. "They'll want to question him once we tell them he was here last night." Flicking a glance behind me at his dad, he added, "Ellie, can I speak to you for a moment?"

I followed him to his room, and he shut the door behind us. "What happened to the Baxter house's open-door policy for girls?" I joked.

He didn't laugh. "We need to have a private conversation." His voice low, he demanded, "Why were you saying all that stuff about me to my dad?"

"What do you mean? He and I were having a nice conversation about how good you are at what you do."

"You were getting a little too familiar about me for being a work colleague."

I took a step toward him and slid my hands up his chest to clasp them behind his neck. "Did I fangirl too much over the sweeter half of the Dream Team?" An FBI agent had called Baxter and me that a while back, and the name had stuck as a joke around our department.

Baxter reached up and gently removed my hands. "Yes. You can't do that."

I looked up at him and wrinkled my nose. "So do you want me to treat you like I treat Sterling, or what?"

"Maybe somewhere in between."

I overexaggerated a sigh. "Fine. But you're going to have to quit being so wonderful and handsome and stuff."

That got a smile out of him. "I'm not sure I can—"

A knock at the front door interrupted us.

His face fell. He said in a rush, "Ellie, I'm so sorry you got pulled into all this. Please promise me you won't try to protect us and get yourself in trouble in the process. If you were to get slapped with obstruction charges because you were trying to help me, I'd never—"

I stopped his anxious speech by pulling him toward me and pressing my lips against his. He wrapped his arms around me and deepened our kiss, his lips needy and almost desperate. I never wanted him to be in turmoil, but I had to admit the kisses we shared in the midst of emotionally charged situations were unparalleled in passion.

When we broke apart, he caught me in a crushing hug. It was a good thing, because I was dizzy as hell, and not from my head injuries. I said, "I won't do anything stupid. The last thing I want to do is put more pressure on you. I came down here to support you, not cause you more stress."

He pulled back a little so he could look at me. "There's no one I'd rather have in my corner than you."

I smiled. "Same."

His expression turned serious. "Game face."

The last-minute pep talk phrase he often used with me before we dived into tense situations was more of a comfort than he could ever know. To me, it meant all I had to do was pretend to be confident and he'd have my back through whatever came next. This time, though, he needed me. This time, it was up to me to have his back, and I could not have been more honored to be the person he was counting on.

Nodding, I echoed, "Game face."

6

When Baxter and I entered the living room, we found a striking woman speaking to his dad. She was tall and beautiful, a dark brunette whose mere presence commanded the attention of everyone in the room. Her painted-on skinny jeans, knee boots, and stylish leather jacket put the whole package together.

The woman landed her laser gaze on Baxter, and she cut her quiet conversation short to say to him in a smooth tone, "Hello, Nick. I'm sorry we have to meet again under these circumstances."

Baxter nodded. "Hey, Corinne. You're assigned to the case?"

She smiled slightly, her perfect cheekbones taking on a lovely rosiness. "I am, along with my partner. You remember Patrick Martin."

"Yeah."

As they spoke, I'd wondered what was with all this familiarity, but then it hit me. This woman was Baxter's ex, the detective who'd been asking about him, according to Shawn. My confidence took a serious hit knowing she'd be the one I'd have to go up against to keep the Baxters from going down for this crime. She was one of those larger-than-life people who instantly and inexplicably dominated any situation. I never had been able to get the upper hand around people like that, always feeling inadequate. And if I didn't already feel like enough of a loser, Mrs. Baxter's half-empty bottle of gin started calling my name from the kitchen, and I despised the flavor of gin.

I struggled to get hold of myself, clenching my fists until my fingernails dug into my palms. This was not the time for a meltdown. I thought about why I came here and how deeply I cared about Baxter—and how that was the only thing in the world that mattered. Making it about him centered me and gave me a decent idea. Why couldn't I be the formidable one this time?

Drawing on my recent undercover experience of pretending to be a rich, above-it-all socialite, I gathered my courage and straightened my posture. Not waiting for Baxter to introduce me, I approached the detective with my hand outstretched and took control of the conversation. "Hi there, I'm Ellie Matthews. I found Ms. Collins in the barn. I suppose you'd like to speak to me first."

She seemed a bit taken aback, but only for a moment. She shook my hand and smiled at me warmly. "You're Nick's partner."

"I am."

"Detective Corinne Barnes." She shot a glance at Baxter. "Nick and I are old friends."

I nodded knowingly. "You used to date. I heard. And yet you've still been assigned to this case?"

"It was ages ago. We were kids." She changed the subject. "I've read a lot about the two of you. You've had an eventful year."

Baxter let out an uncomfortable laugh. " 'Eventful.' That's one word for it."

Taking back over, I said, "Not to be rude, but Baxter and I need to get back to work soon. Can we get started?"

Detective Barnes smiled again, but this time it didn't reach her eyes. "Follow me."

She led the way out the door. Rather than stopping to have a conversation with me in a neutral area, she began heading straight toward the barn. Evidently we were going to talk at the crime scene. A pretty ballsy move for an investigator, but I imagined she was going to try to use the scene to rattle me. That wasn't going to happen, at least not if I could keep up my bravado. I fell into step next to her. Her legs were much longer than mine, so it was a bit of a stretch for me to match her strides. Luckily I was used to it, thanks to all the running I'd done with my long-legged friend Vic during the last few months.

She said, "So this is the second time you've found a homicide victim?"

"Yes. I didn't realize you were so serious when you said you'd read a lot about Baxter and me."

"I like to follow my fellow law enforcement officials' careers, especially when they're old friends. Why do you call Nick by his last name?"

I shrugged. "I call most of my male colleagues by their last names. It puts a little distance between us and makes me feel more like one of the guys."

"Makes sense." I felt a shift in her demeanor. "Ms. Matthews, can you tell me what time you discovered Marie Collins's body?"

Baxter and I were the only ones who knew how long we'd sat on the scene before calling it in, so we had to stick to our vague time line. "I didn't pay attention to the exact time. It was right before Baxter called it in, whatever time that was."

"You were in the barn alone?" she asked.

"Yes."

"Why?"

"The family was having a private conversation, so I wandered around the farm for a while to give them some space."

She narrowed her eyes. "But why go in the barn?"

"Why not? It's part of the farm, and it's got a cool rustic vibe." We had just reached the barn door, which was standing open, so I could see the lump on the floor that was Marie Collins's body. Frowning, I added, "At least . . . the vibe was pretty cool until it became a crime scene."

"Was this morning when you found the body the first time you'd gone into the barn?"

I smiled at her. "That's a slick way of asking me if I went in there another time while I was killing Marie Collins. Nice. I'll have to remember that. Oh, and of course interviewing me with a clear line of sight to the corpse is pretty hardcore, too. Sorry, it's not doing anything for me." I took a deep breath through my nose and had to work to keep my face passive as I said, "I don't even mind the smell of crime scenes. This one's a walk in the park without any overwhelming decomp. With the body being in there only several hours and it being fairly chilly last night, it stayed fairly fresh."

"You don't need to criminalist-splain how decomp works to me, Ms. Matthews."

Ooh. I held in a snicker. "Sorry. A hazard of my professor job—sometimes I overexplain. So how many homicides have you investigated?" Might as well go ahead and measure dicks and get that out of the way.

"Enough." I highly doubted that. She repeated her last question, "Was this morning when you found the body the first time you'd gone into the barn?"

"No, I'd been in there last night. Baxter and I talked to Shawn for a while before we went with him to the station to turn himself in for the vandalism he'd done at Margo Watson's home."

"Was Marie Collins in here at that time?"

Her line of questioning was cunning, but thanks to working so much with Baxter, I'd been in enough interrogations to know the tactics. I couldn't resist coming back at her with, "You mean alive or dead?"

The corner of her mouth tugged upward. "Either. Both."

"Neither. I'd never seen her in person until I found her cold, dead corpse."

She eyed me. "Then how did you know it was Marie Collins?"

"I didn't. I called Baxter, and he came out here and identified her."

"What was his reaction when he realized who was dead on his family's property?"

I shrugged. "A normal one. He was suitably appalled at the manner of death and understandably not very torn up about the victim's identity. When he told me who she was, I felt a decided decrease in sympathy for her as well. We're all human. I'm sure you're not going to lose any sleep tonight knowing a convicted kidnapper fresh out of prison isn't going to be around to create any new crime in your county. In fact, I'd be willing to bet most of the county's residents will feel the same way."

"Are you saying you believe this homicide is justified, Ms. Matthews?"

"Absolutely not. I'm saying considering how many people know and love the Baxters around here, I can't imagine too many of those people shedding a tear over the woman who brought so much grief to them and to this whole town. That said, depending on how strongly the community feels about your victim's recent release back into society, you may have more possible suspects than you know what to do with."

Raising an eyebrow, she said, "Thank you for providing me with your take on the case, but I think I can handle it."

Damn, she was one condescending bitch. I liked her. Unable to keep the smile from my face, I replied in an equally sarcastic tone, "You're welcome, Detective. I have no doubt you can."

"Did you see anyone else near the barn at any time since you got here?"

Ooh. Mrs. Baxter had been out here drinking this morning, but based on the stickiness of the blood, Marie Collins was long dead before the light of day. In my mind, Mrs. Baxter's presence at that time didn't need to be mentioned. "No, not before I found the body. After Baxter met me out here, his mother came out, too, wondering why we were out here and not on our way home."

She nodded. "Speaking of the rest of the family, how has their demeanor been since you arrived here last night?"

"It's been tense, obviously. It was Marie Collins's release day. Shawn had lashed out and was hiding from the cops. Mr. Baxter and Tom had to get tough with him to get him to come home. Baxter had to get tough with him to get him to turn himself in. Mrs. Baxter had to deal with the drama of all that plus impromptu company at her home. I'd been held captive for a while yesterday and was injured. Baxter and I are going to have to answer for leaving town when we should be wrapping up a case. And of course now this. It's been a stressful twenty-four hours for everyone involved. We've all been on edge."

"On edge enough to snap and kill someone?"

Having to refrain from rolling my eyes, I replied, "There's no proper answer to that question and no reason for me to speculate."

"There's also no way you of all people don't have an opinion. You saw the crime scene. You spent the night in the family's home. Which one of them did it?"

I frowned. "None of them."

"Let me reframe that. Let's say Marie Collins came out here uninvited. Any of the Baxters have the right to defend themselves from a trespasser on their property. Now let me ask the question again: which one of them did it?"

"And I'll answer the question again: none of them. And don't try to blow smoke up my ass about this homicide being self-defense to try to trip me up."

She evidently didn't feel the need to keep from rolling her eyes. "It's going to be like this, then?"

Seriously? She was giving me shit for not playing along with her stupid speculation game? My temper rising, I snapped, "Like what? My purpose in life is literally to find and examine hard, tangible evidence to help identify suspects. I don't go around accusing random people I think are emotionally unstable. That's not how investigating works. If you don't know that, then maybe you're not up for this job."

That condescending edge came back to her voice in full force. "Are you worried you'll get another black eye if you don't defend the family? Blink once for yes."

"Holy hell, woman. None of the Baxters did this, and you of all people should realize that."

"Oh, so you have evidence that none of them committed this homicide? I'm all ears."

Shit. I had no answer for her. She'd rattled me, and I hadn't seen it coming.

A slow smile spread across her face. "Is that a no? It seems to me that exonerating people based on how much you like their son isn't how investigating works, either."

I gritted my teeth. "I think we're done here."

"Are we? Because I feel like I want to get to know you better. How about you meet me at the station later?"

Son of a bitch.

7

Vic had sent me a couple of texts during all the mayhem, asking if we'd been successful in finding Shawn and talking him into coming clean. I hadn't had time to answer him. But now all I had was time until the detectives finished interrogating Baxter's family and were ready to move the party to the station. I needed to hear a friendly voice. I called him as I trudged from the barn to the house.

Vic answered with, "Hey, how's it going?"

I replied, "The whole Shawn thing went well. Baxter's dad and brother had already found him by the time we got here, and it was easier than I imagined to get him to go turn himself in. The woman didn't want to press charges, so all he has to do is clean it up and he's good."

"That's great news."

"Well, that's where the great news stops."

His voice turned concerned. "What happened?"

I cleared my throat. "I found a dead body this morning."

There was such a long pause I thought the call might have dropped. Finally he said, "What? You . . . *you* found a body? Where? Who?"

I launched into the whole sad story, finishing with the excruciating interrogation by Detective Barnes.

Vic whistled. "Damn, Ellie. Do you need help? You want me to drive down?"

I smiled. "That's a nice offer, but I should be okay. I mean, I didn't do it, so surely they can't charge me."

Letting out a huff, he said, "Sounds like they could charge you with obstruction. Not your smartest idea."

"You're seriously taking Baxter's side on this?"

"Yes, because he's right and you're wrong."

I scoffed. "Some friend you are."

"Come on, Ellie. You get away with a lot of bullshit up here because of your relationship with the sheriff and because you get results despite your balls-to-the-wall approach to some things. Don't confuse that with being bulletproof."

"I hate being in the dark."

His tone softened. "I know you do. And I also know you're not going to be happy with the outcome of this case if any one of Detective Baxter's family ends up charged. Which means you're going to investigate it yourself . . . which means you'll need some objective help."

Sure, I'd done a half-assed examination of the crime scene, more for my own morbid curiosity and admittedly to see for myself that one of the Baxters hadn't in fact committed the crime. Had one of them done it, it would have been easier for me to believe (and stomach) if I'd determined that they were at fault rather than having to rely on someone else's findings.

But to actually investigate this homicide? What in the hell could I do with no evidence, no lab, no access to background records or financials, and zero jurisdiction?

I shook my head, not that Vic could see me. "No, I'm not going to try to investigate this. Right now, all I want to do is go home. Besides, my gut says none of the Baxters did it. I don't think it's going to be a problem."

"Whatever you say."

❧

WHEN I WENT to reenter the Baxter home, I was stopped at the door by Deputy Jared Neal. He informed me of the rules for the next few hours. I'd have to sit in the living room with him and the rest of the Baxters until the detectives had interviewed everyone. We were allowed to speak, but not a word about the case. Oh, and we couldn't use our phones, either, lest we try to communicate with each other on the sly.

Mr. and Mrs. Baxter were conspicuously absent from the room. Tom and a woman I assumed was his wife had shown up. Tom gave me a tired wave, but the woman didn't look up from the magazine she seemed to be nervously perusing. They were sitting on the couch with Shawn, who was staring off into space, still seeming shell-shocked by the whole ordeal. I steeled myself for an excruciating block of hours that was going to be awkward as hell.

However, nothing could have prepared me for the feeling I got when my gaze landed on Baxter, who was holding the most adorable baby girl I'd ever seen. She was by my guess about six months old, completely enthralled with him as he grinned at her and let her pinch his cheeks and grab his beard hair with her tiny fingers. Fair-haired and blue-eyed, she could have easily passed for his child. My heart felt like it was going to burst out of my chest.

When Baxter turned and saw me, his smile faltered. He flicked a glance at the deputy and slid his grin back into place. "You okay?" he asked, his tone light, but his eyes boring into me, an unspoken message that he was much more concerned about me than he sounded.

I didn't want to give him any more to worry about. I smiled. "Yeah. Fine."

He nodded toward the couch. "Ellie, this is Janelle, Tom's wife. Janelle, Ellie Matthews."

Janelle's head popped up. Seeming to snap out of her funk, she gave me a big smile and stood, holding out her hand. "Oh, sorry, I was off in my own little world and didn't notice you come in. Nice to meet you, Ellie."

I shook her hand. "You, too, Janelle." My focus returned to Baxter and the baby. "And who's this?"

He tickled the little girl's belly, making her giggle. My gut twisted again. "This is my niece, Olivia."

I said to Janelle, "She's beautiful. Those blue eyes."

She laughed, beaming at her daughter. "She definitely favors her father's side of the family, that's for sure. I would offer to let you hold her, but good luck getting her away from her Uncle Nick."

Thank goodness for the sudden unholy clanging of pots and pans from the kitchen that drowned out the deafening ticking of my biological clock. Never once had I had this feeling before, and I didn't like it.

Evidently Mrs. Baxter had been given clearance to putter around the kitchen. Based on her mutterings and the violence with which she was abusing her cookware, she was pissed about the family having to miss Sunday morning mass so they could instead be prisoners in their own home. At least this time her wrath had nothing to do with me.

After the clanging subsided, the room descended back into oppressive silence. The only noise punctuating the gloom was Olivia's intermittent cooing; she seemed only too happy in the arms of Uncle Nick. I took a seat on a wooden chair in the corner of the room that was more decorative than comfortable, where the two of them were out of my line of sight if I stared straight ahead.

After what seemed like an eternity, Mr. Baxter returned and Tom was called away for questioning. I noticed a look of panic cross Janelle's face as her husband left her side, but Mr. Baxter took the spot next to her and patted her shoulder. She seemed to relax, but I could tell she still held apprehension. I didn't blame her—she looked exactly how I'd felt since I stumbled onto the body.

The day was every bit as excruciating as I'd imagined. We sat somberly around the dining room table and picked at the lunch Mrs. Baxter prepared. None of us had much of an appetite except for Deputy Neal, who ate his weight in lasagna. The Baxters continued to be summoned and questioned, one by one, until Janelle, who'd been left for last. She returned to the house and collapsed into Tom's arms in tears. I imagined Detective Barnes played the alpha female card on sweet Janelle and won. I assumed she'd also badgered her with the awful question of which of the Baxters she thought had killed Marie Collins. It was a shitty question any way you looked at it, especially since Barnes couldn't make Janelle testify against her own husband.

A few minutes after Janelle returned, a plainclothes detective came in and addressed us. Handsome and confident, he was the male version of

Barnes. "For those of you who don't know me—" he nodded at me specifically, "I'm Detective Patrick Martin. I wanted to let you know you're free to leave and go about your day." He hesitated. "That said, considering you're all persons of interest in this investigation, I'm going to have to ask you not to leave town."

Tom's expression turned stony. He took a breath to, I assumed, challenge the detective, but Mr. Baxter laid a fatherly hand on his shoulder. Tom held his tongue.

Flicking his eyes at Tom, Detective Martin went on, "I can't stop you from speaking with each other about your interviews, but I can give you a friendly piece of advice. In situations like this, it's best to keep your mind from being clouded by other people's experiences and opinions. At some point you all will have to retell your story to a law enforcement official, possibly multiple times, and you'll want it to remain clear in your head. Especially with traumatic situations like these, our minds can take extraneous facts and try to fit them into our memories without us even realizing it. Please understand I'm not trying to muzzle anyone—I'm trying to help you keep your version of events as sharp as possible."

Detective Martin seemed to be much more of a straight shooter than his partner. He came across as kind, even in a room full of people his partner believed could have been harboring a killer. Honestly, his demeanor reminded me a little of Baxter's in a situation like this. I wished Detective Martin had been the one to interview me instead.

The moment the detective and the deputy shut the door behind them, the Baxters let out a collective sigh and all started talking at once.

Baxter snagged me by the arm and dragged me to his bedroom.

The only thing I had left in me was a bad joke. "I knew deep down that murder turned you on, but your whole family's right outside the door."

He snorted. "Your gallows humor still needs work." His gaze zeroed in on my black eye. "Seriously, though, are you okay? You've looked like a deer in headlights for hours. Is your head bothering you? Are you in any pain? Do we need to get you checked again?"

I dropped down onto the bed. "No, except for a dull ache where the bruising is, my head isn't what's bothering me. My pain is emotional."

He sat next to me and took my hand. "I'm so sorry you had to stumble across . . . that . . . this morning."

"I was talking about the awkward as hell house arrest."

"Ah. Well, if it's any comfort, I'm sure we were all on the same page about that. The good news is, our awkward as hell house arrest gave me plenty of time to think about this case. I have an idea of who might have wanted the world to think one of us killed Marie Collins."

I frowned. "Oh. Do you guys have enemies around here?"

He chuckled. "No, but there are a few people I could see justifying it as killing two birds with one stone."

"Wow. That's morbid."

"Morbid is what we do."

"Don't I know it."

"And speaking of what we do—"

I put my head in my hands. "We can't leave here today and get back to doing what we do. Probably for days . . . or more. We're going to have to beg Jayne for mercy. And for our jobs."

Nodding, he agreed, "Pretty much. But first, I want to get outside and check on what parts of the scene they've processed. I want to make sure they didn't miss any key areas."

I raised my head to stare at him. "Hello, pot. I'm kettle."

He smiled. "Ha, ha. I'm not going to barge in and contaminate the crime scene—I'm going to offer my expertise from a respectable distance. Loudly, if it comes to it."

"This, I want to see."

~

WE BYPASSED the cacophony that was still going strong in the living room and headed outside. There were fewer law enforcement vehicles than before. The only ones left were, I assumed, Deputy Neal's cruiser, the detectives' sedan, and the crime scene unit's van, all parked along the driveway near the house. There were no people milling about, either. Everyone must have been inside the barn.

As we walked toward the barn, Baxter griped, "See that? The only crime scene tape they've set is across the barn doors." He clenched his jaw.

I finished his thought. "So they're not even going to entertain the idea that someone else drove onto the property to kill Marie Collins."

"Oh, they're going to entertain it, all right."

"If nothing else, they need to at least look for some kind of evidence to show how she got out here in the first place. Barnes didn't ask me about that during my interview. Did Detective Martin mention how they think she got here?"

He shook his head. "Not exactly. He asked me if any of us contacted her yesterday."

"That should be easy enough to check through phone records. But she just got out of the joint—did she even have a phone yet?"

"I don't know."

I frowned as we neared the area of the driveway where someone would have parked to enter the barn. "From an investigative standpoint, I'm glad this isn't our case. Without a vehicle and probably no phone, bank account, or credit cards to speak of, Marie Collins has no footprint. There's no way to track her movements yesterday besides eyewitness accounts."

Baxter nodded thoughtfully. "Right, unless she took an Uber or something, which she would have needed access to a phone or computer to get."

"Or she had someone get one for her . . . which would mean there could be people out there who know she was here and maybe even why."

We stopped in the grass at the edge of the driveway and surveyed the area for anything that would point to the fact that a vehicle had been parked here last night. The crushed Indiana limestone gravel covering the driveway was fairly even, with few areas of bare dirt that would harbor tire marks. I didn't see any tire impressions anywhere. Damn. I'd been hoping for a big smoking gun clearly pointing away from the Baxters, but it didn't look like we were going to get it.

Baxter's expression was troubled. "I don't see anything, do you?"

"No," I said quietly.

"I still think it's their responsibility to process this area. Otherwise it looks like a witch hunt against my family."

I thought for a moment. "Would them overlooking this area actually help if a case was brought against you? If the detectives left out a key area of the scene, especially because they'd already made up their minds about the suspect pool too soon, a good defense lawyer could cast doubt on the whole investigation and—"

"Maybe we shouldn't let it get to that point," he said, his tone terse.

"Sorry. Just thinking outside the box, here. Our expertise has to help us figure out a way around this."

He frowned. "The way around this is to show none of us is at fault."

I turned to him. "How? I mean, sure, there's no hard evidence—unless there are fingerprints on the murder weapon—that one of us *did* do it. But means, motive, and opportunity? We all have it. Our team has held people on far less than that." The more I thought about it, the more convinced I was that someone in this family was going to jail today. I sighed. "Nick, I'm worried."

His eyes still roving the scene, he said absently, "I wouldn't be, if I were you. You don't have a motive."

"It's not me I'm worried about."

8

Baxter had evidently had enough of this discussion, because he strode purposely to the open barn door, stopping at the crime scene tape barring the entry. "Hey, detectives. I think there's a big part of the scene you've missed."

I followed him and stood next to him in a united front. Barnes and Martin, who were standing over the spot where Marie Collins's body had once been, both snapped their heads in our direction.

Martin frowned, but Barnes broke into a smile. I also noticed her shift her body to improve her posture. I wasn't sure if it was for my benefit or for Baxter's.

Strutting toward us as if she were a model on a catwalk, she said, "What's that? We missed something? Where?" Her tone was borderline patronizing, but not quite.

I couldn't really blame her too much, or Martin, either, who looked like he was trying to hold in an eyeroll. Had it been Baxter and me in their shoes and a couple of potential suspects barged in and tried to tell us how to do our jobs, we wouldn't have been at all receptive.

As he swept a hand toward the driveway, Baxter replied, "The area behind us is where Marie Collins—and the killer—would have parked last night. We think it bears processing rather than being dismissed because you already have a full suspect pool."

"Nick, of course that's not the case." Now her tone was fully patronizing. "We'll get someone out there shortly to have a look around. We're not leaving any stone unturned, and please don't assume we have our minds made up already. As you well know, it's much too early for that."

I noticed relief on Baxter's face. He said to her, "Thank you, Corinne. I appreciate your open-mindedness to outside ideas."

Barnes's smile widened. "Who could say no to a little insight from some celebrity investigators?"

Behind her, Martin turned his back on us, but not before I saw him cover a snort of laughter.

Baxter caught on to Barnes's game. He growled, "We'll be out here so you don't 'forget' to process the area."

Barnes feigned being taken aback. "Are you okay, Nick? Did I say something—"

I rolled my eyes, unable to hold my tongue any longer. "Cut the shit, Barnes. Nobody's buying it."

She let out a soft laugh, unwilling to give up her schtick. "Ellie, I'm not—"

I cut her off again. "We'll let you get back to work."

Before she could say anything else, I turned on my heel and walked away, hoping Baxter would follow my lead. He did, falling into step with me as I took off through the grass, giving the driveway a wide berth. I could tell by the set of his jaw that he wasn't any happier than I was.

"Was she that much of a bitch when you guys dated?" I blurted out. Thinking better of it, I added, "Don't answer that. I withdraw the question." I could be just as big an asshole as Barnes. She and I were alike in more ways than I wanted to admit, even to myself.

He griped, "Well, one thing that hasn't changed is that she'll do and say anything to control everyone around her."

Ouch. Now I knew why they broke up.

I changed the subject. "Hey, I know we've got a lot going on here, but I think we should be working on our reports while we wait. I wouldn't put it past Barnes to ice us for a while before she sends her tech out to process the driveway."

He nodded tiredly. "You're not wrong. I'll go grab our laptops."

"In the meantime, I'll call Jayne."

Sighing, he muttered, "There's no getting around 'fessing up to our crimes now."

Jayne knew how I felt about Baxter, and seasoned investigator that she was, she'd figured out how he felt about me as well. Only days ago, she had, as my boss, told me to stay away from him. And I'd agreed, which made me not only insubordinate, but also a liar. I hated this feeling, but it paled in comparison to the devastation I'd felt the last couple of months trying to squelch my feelings. As for us leaving town, especially together, there was no use trying to make excuses—Baxter and I had broken the rules, and now we had to come clean.

"Let me talk to her first," I said. "Maybe it'll make your conversation with her easier."

Shaking his head, he said, "You don't need to protect me, Ellie."

"I know. But given my relationship with her, I need to be the one to break the news."

As he walked away, I steeled myself for what was to come. I called Jayne's number, hoping she wouldn't pick up and I could put this off.

No such luck. As her greeting, she said, "I was wondering when I'd hear from you. How's your head?"

"It's been better."

Her tone became dark. "How's Detective Baxter holding up?"

Shit. I should have known she'd put two and two together. I sighed. "Jayne, I'm sorry—"

"You're not sorry. I appreciate that you go the extra mile to help out the people you love, but now—again—it's come and bit you in the ass."

"Wait—what do you know?"

"Everything."

"How?" I asked. Vic wouldn't have tattled on me to her.

She explained impatiently, "I pinged your cells when Detective Baxter missed the meeting this morning. I knew if you'd gone with him for moral support, trouble was brewing. One Google search for 'Boonville' nearly blew up my web browser. How you're such a magnet for trouble is beyond me, but I told you this would happen."

"I know."

She raised her voice. "Do you? Do you realize how disastrous this situation could become?"

I felt ill. "Yeah, I'm fully aware."

"I don't think you are. This could very well be a career killer for both you and Detective Baxter."

I started to choke out, "I—"

She cut me off. "You've been lucky thus far, Ellie, with your unorthodox methods, but I'm afraid your luck has run out. Ashmore College isn't going to stand for another of its professors being at the center of a homicide investigation. Especially after everything that's happened since last fall." She huffed out a breath. "And I can't afford to employ someone in that situation, either. I have to terminate your contract effective immediately."

I stood there, shell-shocked, my knees threatening to give way. "Jayne, I'm not a suspect. For that matter, neither is Baxter—"

"I've spoken to the sheriff there in Warrick County. He did me the professional courtesy of not sugarcoating your situation. It's not good, Ellie. You and Detective Baxter are up to your necks, and I can't let you drag the department down with you. We're already preparing for the worst. Every criminal either of you has had a hand in putting away will be poised to come after us if there's even a hint of real suspicion surrounding the two of you. You have to understand I have no other recourse."

My voice shaky, I replied, "I understand."

"Good." After a pause, she said in a much kinder tone, "Can I quit being your boss and be your friend for a moment?"

"Yes," I replied, my voice breaking as I choked back a sob.

"How are you coping after finding the body? I can't imagine you were in a good headspace this morning after . . . yesterday."

Tears leaked out my eyes, but I managed to keep my voice steady. "It's been rough. Really, the idea of the detectives believing someone in Baxter's family did the deed has been much harder to stomach than the initial shock of walking in on a crime scene."

"I'm sure that's true. How are they doing?"

"Not great. I won't lie; no one's exactly upset about the victim's passing, but . . ." I lowered my voice, although no one was in earshot. "The upsetting part is the fact that someone snuck out here last night and committed a murder while we were all sleeping."

She hesitated for a moment. I knew what she was thinking—the simplest explanation was often the correct one.

Before she could say anything, I added even more quietly, "I know the logical assumption is that one of the Baxters did it. But after watching these people all day, I can't imagine one of them doing it and neither Baxter or me picking up on any suspicious behavior. Even in the case of self-defense, I don't think one of them could have killed a person and not copped to it once they came to their senses."

"That's a fair assessment. So if none of them did it, who bothered to go out to their property—which I assume is in a rural area if there's a barn—in the middle of the night to kill someone who didn't live there? Do you believe the killer brought or lured the victim out to the Baxters' property?"

"They either brought her, lured her, or followed her out here. No vehicles of any kind were left on the property, and I'm pretty sure there are no tracks to be found, either. That's why we all look so damn guilty."

She let out a sigh. "I don't envy the position you're in, Ellie. If there's anything I can do for you, don't hesitate to ask."

"Thanks, Jayne." A sudden lump formed in my throat. "Um . . . if you wouldn't mind, could you look in on Rachel and Nate? She's got finals coming up, so my situation couldn't be worse timing for her."

"Consider it done. You keep your head up, okay?"

"Okay."

When I hung up with her, the tears that had welled up when I was talking about Rachel and Nate splashed down my cheeks. I was in the process of trying to wipe them off and compose myself when I heard footsteps behind me. I didn't know if it was Baxter or one of the detectives, but I didn't want any of them seeing me cry.

Baxter's voice said, "Did you talk to the sheriff?"

That lump came back with a vengeance. I didn't want to have to be the one to break the news to him that he was getting fired, but I also wouldn't allow myself to tell him less than the whole truth. After what we'd been through the past couple of months, we'd promised never to hide what we were feeling from each other.

I turned around to face him and cleared my throat. "I did."

One look at me, and his expression became worried. "What happened?"

Working to keep my tone even and light, I replied, "She spoke to the local sheriff here, so she knows everything."

"And?"

"And since I'm a person of interest in this case . . ." I paused to gather my composure. "She had to let me go." I felt a tear getting ready to escape, so I covered brushing it away by tucking a lock of hair behind my ear. My sadness wasn't as much for me as it was for him. I had another job, at least for now. He didn't.

Nothing got past him. He reached for me, but I said quickly, "You can't." When he dropped his hand and a look of hurt crossed his face, I added, "Not that I don't want you to, but I'm fine. It's fine. We'll fix this. But you should call her."

He clenched his jaw. "Losing my job is the least of my worries at the moment."

"You're right. Same for me. This isn't even the first time Jayne has fired me this year."

He didn't laugh at my feeble joke. Getting out his phone, he muttered, "Might as well get it over with," and walked out into the nearby field to have his own soul-crushing conversation with Jayne.

I took the opportunity to run over to my car and get out my cosmetic bag, hoping I could fix my face well enough that the detectives didn't have more ammunition for their war against me. Foundation and concealer covered my splotchy skin, but nothing could mask my red eyes.

Baxter met me at my vehicle, his expression the neutral one he'd sported for the past couple of weeks that I really hated. He'd never used his cop face around me before, but with everything going on with his family— and having to basically ignore me as we were working together—he'd had to wear it most of the time.

He set the laptop bag he'd brought on top of my trunk. "I'm on an indefinite leave of absence without pay, so I'm basically fired, too. Regardless, we still have to finish our reports."

～

BAXTER and I sat in my car in a depressive silence typing out the last of our reports from this past week's investigation. Deep in concentration to try to distract myself from the matter at hand, I nearly jumped out of my skin when a sharp rap on my window shattered the quiet.

Barnes's irritatingly happy face filled my driver's side window. "You want to point out where you think we should concentrate our search?"

Seriously? This was a total farce, but we clearly had to play along if we wanted any satisfaction.

Baxter and I got out of my vehicle and followed Barnes to the area in front of the barn.

As we walked, he said, "I think you should at least take a look at the length of the driveway, but I'd like to see a concentrated effort on the area in front of the barn."

Barnes nodded and went on ahead of us. "We'll get right on that."

My ass.

The narrow rock driveway started at the road, went past the house, and ended in front of the barn. Like Baxter suggested, I would have studied the entire driveway, concentrating on the area nearest the barn doors where someone would have been the most likely to park. But the detectives were only going to give us the bare minimum of their time and energy. As Barnes sauntered around in a wide circle and pretended to be deep in thought, Martin strode around with flags, hastily setting the smallest possible perimeter for their scene tech to examine. I could feel the frustration rolling off Baxter as we stood in the grass and watched.

Feeling helpless, I busied myself with trying to recreate last night's events in my head. As I conjured up an image of a vehicle pulling to a stop and the driver getting out, it dawned on me that Baxter and I were standing in an area where the killer might have taken a few steps as he exited his or her vehicle. Damn. I wish I'd thought about that before we'd trampled a little of the grass. It was too dry to bother to look for footprints. I kept my feet stationary, so as not to do any more damage, and looked down, hoping something might have fallen out of the vehicle or the killer's pockets or something. Behind me, in a clump of weeds, I noticed a piece of plastic. Feeling a rush of excitement, I opened my mouth to speak, but my words died on my lips. I took a casual step back and set my other foot lightly over my find, my pulse pounding.

9

Baxter griped, "They're not taking this seriously."

I cleared my throat, hoping my voice would sound calmer than I felt. Matching his disgruntled tone, I said, "Not even a little."

The detectives had finished marking off the area by the barn and were now moseying down the side of the driveway like they were out for a stroll in the afternoon sun. When the duo reached the end of the driveway and had their backs to us while they stopped to confer, I gestured their way and asked Baxter, "Do you think they coordinated their outfits? Fancy leather jackets and tight jeans might be standard issue for TV detectives, but not so much in real life."

He turned his attention their way and let out a chuckle. "It's a big day for them. They probably wanted to look as badass as they're pretending to be. Plus, they've got to look good for their close-ups." He pointed down the road at a couple of news vans sitting on the other side of a police barricade. At the moment, no one was outside filming.

I took my chance. While Baxter was distracted and looking away from me, I grabbed an extra glove I still had in my pocket, reached down with it and swiped the piece of plastic I'd found, and stuffed the whole thing into my back pocket. I pulled down my sweater hem to conceal the tiny bump.

He turned back to me, his expression morphing into one of concern. "You okay? You look flushed. Are you staying ahead of your pain?"

I should have known he'd notice my distress. "Um . . . no. I'm due for another dose of Advil. I'll go in and take it."

"I'll go with you."

I frowned, eyeing the detectives, who were still at the end of the driveway. "Should one of us stay here and keep an eye on Castle and Beckett?"

He snorted. "Yeah, I guess so. Hurry back."

As I hurried to the house, I slipped past the gaggle of Baxters milling around the kitchen and picking at the lunch leftovers and headed straight for Baxter's bedroom. After locking the door, I retrieved my find from my pocket and set it on the desk, carefully pulling back the glove so as not to smudge the object's smooth surface.

I felt terrible for concealing a piece of evidence—especially one that had the potential to point directly to the killer. In my moment of panic outside, I'd weighed the chances and decided that the disposable vape pod I'd found at my feet was most likely discarded randomly by Shawn. I'd witnessed him vaping last night, and this pod looked to be the size and shape that would have fit into his pen.

If I'd spoken up and shown the detectives my find mere feet from the scene perimeter and voiced my theory on the item having been accidentally left by the killer as he or she exited their vehicle, I had no doubt they would have felt compelled to take it into evidence. If Shawn's fingerprints and DNA showed up on the pod, which I whole-heartedly believed they would, that would cast all kinds of suspicion on him. They could use it to help make their case that Shawn had driven his kidnapper out here to kill her. And I'd be responsible for it.

I glanced around the room. I needed to hide this thing somewhere someone like me would never look for it, just in case. The best I could come up with was to tape it to the back of the desk. I wrapped the pod carefully back into the glove, found some tape in the desk drawer, and affixed it to the back side of the desk.

Now my head was throbbing from the stress, so I popped a couple of Advil and returned to where Baxter was standing with the two detectives. I noted some pretty stiff body language between the three of them. I wondered if words had been exchanged.

As I approached, Martin said, "Ms. Matthews, we need to search your vehicle."

I tried to keep my expression passive as I panicked over the fact that I had stashed my used gloves, makeshift booties, *and a blood sample* in my overnight bag, which was unfortunately in my trunk. "Do you have a warrant to search my vehicle?"

Barnes's lips curled into a triumphant smirk. "Spoken like a person with something to hide."

"No, just making sure you're following the rules," I replied.

"As I'm sure you always do."

Well, she had me there. I said nothing.

Martin cut in. "To answer your question, Ms. Matthews, our warrant authorizes us to search all vehicles on the premises."

Hoping to appear much more in control than I was, I shrugged. "It's unlocked. Knock yourselves out."

～

WHILE DETECTIVE MARTIN started his search of my vehicle and Detective Barnes began searching Mr. Baxter's truck, Baxter and I stood watch. It wasn't long before the lone crime scene tech came out of the barn and began perusing the secondary scene Martin had flagged. The guy didn't take much time with it. He did, however, use the proper search method— the strip method, pacing back and forth until he covered the entire area. He didn't collect any samples, not that I'd seen anything I might have collected had it been my scene. He then walked quickly down the driveway, giving it a cursory glance, clearly not expecting to find any evidence.

Out of the corner of my eye, I saw Martin pop my trunk. My stomach clenched. My overnight bag was in there, full of felonious evidence if you knew what you were looking for.

He pawed through my clothes, looked inside my spare pair of shoes, and went through my makeup and toiletry bags. Then he unzipped the side pocket and pulled out a plastic bag.

Channeling all the nerve I could manage, I lied apologetically, "Oh, yeah . . . um . . . you may not want to get too up close and personal with the contents of that bag, Detective. I, uh . . . wasn't paying attention to my monthly calendar and had a little incident with my undies."

The detective's face—and Baxter's face—twisted in horror upon hearing my way too intimate explanation.

Martin slipped the plastic bag back into the zipper pocket. "Thanks for the heads-up." He then slammed my trunk and ripped off his gloves, discarding them on the ground and walking quickly away.

"Nice save," Baxter murmured. "Disgusting, but brilliant."

I let out a mirthless laugh. "That's me."

$\sim$

IT DIDN'T TAKE the detectives long to search the other vehicles. Once they were finished, Barnes came up to me and said, "Time for that follow-up interview I promised you. We'll follow you to the station."

I forced a fake smile. "Is it that time already? I've been so looking forward to it."

Her gaze on me became steely. "Me, too."

Once she was out of earshot, Baxter said to me, "Ellie, don't panic. You've got nothing to worry about."

Sure, if you didn't count my clandestine crime scene investigation, stealing possible evidence, and my reason for making this trip in the first place.

I frowned. "Protecting the other half of the Dream Team wouldn't be seen as a motive to kill or at least cover for you and your family? Barnes isn't too stupid. She sees how close we are. Oh, and don't forget—neither of us has an alibi for last night because we were supposed to be sleeping in separate rooms."

He smiled. "We'll get through this. We've been through worse, right?"

The image of when we found my sister, Rachel, chained up by a madman popped into my head. I winced as a wave of guilt coursed through me. She'd been targeted because of me, and I'd never forgive myself for the pain and suffering it caused her . . . and continued to cause her. Every time my job put me in danger, one of the most difficult parts was having to tell my sister what had happened to me so she didn't have to learn about it on the news or from local gossip. Before leaving last night, I'd told her about getting injured yesterday but had left out the part where I'd been bound and held—essentially having been put in a similar situation as she'd endured. I didn't have time to unpack all that with her before Baxter and I left town. I thought we'd be back by now and I could break the news face-to-face. But given my current circumstances, I didn't know how soon I'd get to see her. And now I had to heap on the fact that I found a body, was a person of interest in a homicide, and had lost one job already today. Oh, and if all that wasn't bad enough, if I actually did end up losing my Ashmore job, she'd lose the family discount on her tuition as well as Nate's free daycare. Sister of the year, I was not.

As if reading my thoughts, Baxter asked, "Have you not talked to Rachel yet?"

"I'll call her on the way."

"Good luck."

~

RACHEL ANSWERED HER PHONE WITH, "How's your head?"

"Not terrible. Advil is taking care of the pain." That was a lie. I didn't want to admit it to anyone, but my head hadn't stopped hurting since I'd gotten injured.

Relief was evident in her voice. "Oh, good. So are you almost home? I've got some studying to do, and our little man is wound up. He hasn't stopped talking for, like, two hours straight."

I longed to spend two straight hours doing nothing but listening to my vibrant, chatty nephew talk. "Uh . . . no. I'm sorry, Rach. Things went really badly here."

Her tone became concerned. "Is Nick's brother okay? Are you guys okay?"

"We're fine, but . . . I think we're stuck here for a while."

"That sucks. What the hell happened?"

"I, uh . . ." I sighed. "I hate to put this on you, Rachel, but I don't want you to find out from someone else." I launched into my story from this morning, leaving out any details she might find upsetting. Which meant I left out a lot of details.

I could tell she was close to tears. "I can't believe all that happened so fast. I mean, at least you've got your school job to fall back on, and based on what you've told me, it's a long shot that you'll actually get accused of this crime."

"Yeah, I'll be fine. Don't worry about me. But I think it would be a good idea to go stay with David for a bit. I'm afraid once this story hits our local news, you'll have media camped in front of the house." We'd had one stepdad who was decent. Even though he'd only been married to our mother a short time many years ago, David still took care of Rachel, Nate, and me like we were his family.

She groaned. "Ugh, not again." She'd had more than her fill of the media over the last several months.

"I'm sorry, sis. I hate that my life is making a whole ordeal out of yours."

"I'm only being mildly inconvenienced. Who I'm worried about is Nick. How's he doing with . . . everything?"

Rachel had become close with Baxter after her kidnapping. He'd gone through the other side of it with Shawn and knew how to talk to her, his empathy making him the person she went to most often with her problems. They'd met on a regular basis until things started going downhill for Shawn and Baxter hadn't had as much free time to meet with her.

I replied, "He's upset. He's worried sick about what this means for his family."

"I'm happy he's got you there with him. But aren't you still not supposed to hang out or work together?"

"We're not, but . . ." Rachel knew Baxter and I were friends, but that was all. I wished I could tell my sister the whole truth, but that was definitely an in-person conversation. I pulled into a parking spot in the sheriff's station lot and gave her my stock explanation. "He's helped us out so much. I wanted to try to return the favor."

"Oh, yeah. We absolutely owe him."

"Uh . . . I'm sorry, but I have to go. I'm getting questioned by the police a second time."

She tried for an upbeat tone, but didn't quite make it. "I'm sure everything will be okay. Let me know how it goes."

I smiled, tears threatening again. "I will. I love you."

"I love you, too." As her voice broke, I almost lost it, yet again.

10

Detective Martin met me at my car and escorted me into the sheriff's station. The building was much newer than the city police station and frankly didn't have the charm. He showed me to one of their interrogation rooms, which was no different than the ones I was used to in Hamilton County. Not that I might ever get to go into one of those again.

They proceeded to ice me for what I assumed was at least fifteen minutes. I had no access to my phone, nor was there a clock in the room. I was past anxious and beginning to get agitated when the door opened and Detective Barnes sailed into the room. She smelled amazing, and there wasn't a single smudge to her eye shadow or a hint of shine to her face after a full day's work. I'd bet the balance of my checking account she'd used the fifteen excruciating minutes I'd been waiting to reapply her perfume and makeup. She'd no doubt taken the time to touch up her hair as well. Every hair was in place, and that wouldn't have been the case after being outside this afternoon in the brisk wind. My hair did not look its best.

"You don't mind if we start over officially, do you, Ms. Matthews?" she asked as she slid into the seat across from me, a folder, notebook, and cup of steaming coffee in hand. The coffee smelled amazing as well—I even detected a hint of vanilla. It was quite the opposite of the bile we had to drink in the station at home, another thing I'd randomly miss if I ended up with a permanent job loss. I wished she'd offer me some of that coffee, but I had the feeling this was going to be more of a suspect interrogation than a person of interest interview.

"That's fine," I replied, working to repress the knot in my stomach.

"What time did you find Marie Collins's body in the barn on the Baxter property this morning?"

"I'm not sure of the time. Baxter and I were about to leave, but he needed to speak to his family in private, so I wandered the property for a while to give them some space. I went into the barn and nosed around, and that was when I found the body."

"Why were you nosing around in the barn?"

"I was in there last night and thought it was interesting. I didn't get to look around much, so I took my opportunity this morning. I've always lived in town, so barns are kind of a novelty to me."

She cocked her head to the side. "I find it odd you'd barge into someone else's barn."

"I'm a guest of the Baxters, and I'd been in there last night. I didn't feel like I was barging into anything. Plus the door was open."

"Why were you in there last night?"

She really was serious about starting over. I gave her the same answer I had earlier today. "Baxter and I were speaking to Shawn about turning himself in for the vandalism he caused at Margo Watson's house."

"Why did Nick bring you into a family matter?"

An interesting deviation. I worried where she'd go with it. I shrugged. "I was a teenage delinquent. He thought I might be able to relate. And with being a college professor, I'm pretty good at talking to young adults."

"That must be so interesting. What do you teach?" she asked, either badly feigning being impressed with me or flat-out mocking me. I assumed the latter, knowing she'd already done her homework on me.

"Criminalistics."

"And you're Nick's work wife."

"I consult for the sheriff's department. We're often partnered together, but not always."

Her gaze piercing me, she added, "And you're in a romantic relationship with him."

There it was—said as a statement, not a question. "That sounds more like gossip than pertinent case information, but I'll clear it up anyway: no, we're not in a romantic relationship." Technically not a lie in the sense that we'd yet to go on a date, hadn't defined our relationship, and hadn't had sex.

"Yet you made a three-hour trip with him to help him with a family matter."

I'd been rehearsing my answer in my head long enough that I was even starting to believe it. "We had a case to wrap up. It felt easier to work in person as he drove rather than trying to collaborate over the phone. Plus, I feel like I owe him. He's saved my life more than once, as well as my sister's."

She sighed, smiling. "Oh, that Nick. He did always love a damsel in distress."

I had to take a beat to cool my temper. She was good. "He does his job. When our team is in the field, the detectives watch out for the criminalists. Sometimes it gets dangerous."

She nodded thoughtfully, her gaze on my injury. "It does. How'd you get that shiner?"

"I got it during our last case. It was one of those times it got dangerous."

"Did Nick not come to your rescue?"

"He wasn't there."

"Bet you wish he had been."

That was where she was wrong. I eyed her. "You keep coming back to the whole romance angle, Detective. Are you just being nosy? Because I don't feel like it has a damn thing to do with your case."

"Oh, but it does. Maybe Nick brought you with him because he knew that you, as his girlfriend, would help him cover for his family."

Having dated Baxter herself, she should have known better than to think that about him. She was going down this road to bait me. "If that's the case, then I did a shit job, didn't I? I found the body, immediately told Baxter, and he called it in. How is that covering anything up?"

She shrugged. "You obviously know your way around a crime scene. Don't tell me you didn't at least take a look at this one with your criminalist eye."

"If you mean I didn't run away screaming like a little girl at the sight of a dead body, then you're correct. I looked. But I know better than to touch."

"I'm sure you do. I bet you also know how to remove evidence without a trace."

I tried not to think about the vape pod I'd hidden in Baxter's room. It wasn't like I could put that horse back in the barn, so to speak, so there was no use narcing on myself for it. "You mean like the murder weapon that's probably still lodged in your vic's skull? If I wanted to tamper with the scene, don't you think I'd start there?"

"Maybe, maybe not."

Swiveling in her seat so she could cross her long legs, she began staring at me. I assumed she was waiting for me to say more, a tactic Baxter and I often employed when a suspect was being less than forthcoming. Little did she know, I was stubborn enough to wait her out.

We stared at each other for what had to have been five minutes. It was excruciating and it started to make my black eye twitch, but I powered through.

Detective Barnes caved first, a smile playing at her rosy lips. "You're good." She snapped her fingers. "You know what I forgot? Your alibi. Where were you between one and three a.m.?"

"Asleep."

"Alone?"

"Of course. Mrs. Baxter gave me the older boys' old room, which meant Baxter had to sleep on the couch." I hoped I wouldn't have to take a polygraph. I'd never pass.

"So you have no alibi."

I rolled my eyes. "*None of us* have an alibi. Hence the reason we're all currently guilty until proven innocent."

Flashing me a shit-eating grin, she said, "I think you have that backward."

"Do I, Detective?"

"Let's circle back around to you finding Ms. Collins. Did you know you'd find her there in the barn?"

"No."

"Were you searching for her?"

"No."

"Did someone tell you to go 'discover' her?"

"No, and that's three times you've asked the same question. Were my answers unclear?"

Barnes chuckled softly. "Forgive me. I'm used to interviewing the normal riff-raff that comes through here. Going up against a seasoned professional such as yourself is a little more difficult."

"Why, because I can count?" I snapped.

She leaned her head back and laughed. "You're funny, too. I can see why Nick likes you."

I sighed. "Okay. Can we just cut the bullshit instead of dancing around it? Are you holding a torch for him and assuming I'm a threat to you? Or do you honestly think a man and a woman can't work together and keep things platonic? I do not get your fixation with this."

She started staring at me again like she had before, refusing to speak. She had a solid cop face: blank, detached, unreadable. She actually reminded me a lot of Vic, at least the old version of him. Since his near-death experience, he'd loosened up and chilled out a lot. But I hadn't forgotten how to deal with the old Vic when he was being confrontational like Detective Barnes. If they were as alike as I assumed, I was confident I could rattle her.

I leaned back lazily in my chair. "So you're a woman and your partner is a man. Am I to assume you guys are a thing? I mean, not that I blame you." I slid her an appreciative glance. "Detective Martin can get it."

Her jaw clenched. She changed the subject. "Had you met Marie Collins before?"

Interesting. Smiling, I went on, "Ah. You and Detective Martin *are* a thing. I guess it makes sense that you're projecting your relationship onto others in your situation. And no, I hadn't met Marie Collins before."

"But you know all about her and had a poor opinion of her."

When I'd mentioned Detective Martin's name, something had flashed in her eyes. Got her.

"Oh, wait . . . you and Detective Martin *were* a thing. Past tense." I clicked my tongue. "That sucks. Nothing worse than having to work with someone you used to bang." Leaning in conspiratorially, I said, "I made one drunken mistake with Baxter's detective partner years ago, and it's still a huge elephant anytime we're in a room together. I can't imagine having an actual relationship go wrong and then having to work with the guy. It must be excruciating. And I'm sure it doesn't help that your partner is so easy on the eyes. I bet you have to watch women flirt with him nonstop."

Her emotions barely contained, she ground out, "Nice try. But you're the one in the hot seat, not me."

I smiled. "You're hot and bothered, though."

"And you're teetering on the brink of obstructing justice."

I wrinkled my nose. "Nah, I'm just being an asshole. There's a difference."

I'd derailed her enough that she'd lost where she was going with her questioning. Grimacing, she asked, "What . . . uh . . . what did you see around the body?"

This, I could answer. "A lot of blood and not much else."

"So you did take a look. How long were you in there taking a look?"

I lied, "Not long." When she didn't seem to believe me, I added, "Come on, Detective. You and I can look at a crime scene for thirty seconds, notice every scrap of evidence, and come up with a theory of who did it."

She sat up in her chair. "So what's your theory on who did it?"

"Someone who wanted her dead."

She shot me a look of irritation.

I added, "I can't get much more specific than that because I'm not privy to any information about the victim or her enemies. And I literally know no one in this town."

"You're privy to the identities and motivations of five of her enemies. Six, if you count yourself."

I shook my head. "I know you don't know me, so if you want to be suspicious of me, that's fine. I get it. But you know the members of the Baxter family. Intimately, in one case, so that means you know all of them better than I do. I assume, since you're one of two detectives assigned to probably the biggest case this county's seen in a decade, you've got a pretty amazing gut when it comes to investigations. Forget the facts. What does your gut say about one of the Baxters being guilty of killing Marie Collins?"

She shrugged. "Anyone's capable of murder, Ms. Matthews. Do you have children?"

"No."

"Then let's talk about your sister—how would you feel if her captor was walking around loose instead of safely six feet under? You of all people should be able to empathize with the Baxters on this one. Say you found him trespassing on your property the very night he was released from prison. What would you assume he was doing there, and what would you have done to keep your sister safe?"

My stomach lurched. I hadn't thought of it that way. What if Marie Collins had come out to the Baxter property on her own not to apologize or pay back Shawn's vandalism, but to hurt Shawn or any one of us while we were sleeping? A shiver ran through me. What if someone heard her out there, went to check on it, and she came at them with the axe? What if they'd had to wrestle it away from her and drive it into her skull to keep from being killed themselves? To keep Rachel safe, I'd do—and had done —incredibly dangerous and stupid things without even a thought about the outcome.

She drawled, "I feel you're having a bit of trouble working this one out, Ms. Matthews. Keep thinking on it."

I hadn't doubted any of the Baxters' innocence before. But now? I didn't know. I did know it wasn't my Baxter. For one thing, he'd been literally next to me all night. The only exception to that was when he'd been talking to his family in the living room, but I could hear his voice the whole time. Plus, if he'd killed or hurt anyone, self-defense or not, he would have called it in on himself. That was one thing I had zero doubt about. The others in that house, though, after the shock of killing someone and seeing that kind of carnage, might have blocked out what they'd done and gone to bed. It wasn't uncommon for people to have that kind of dissociative reaction.

I cleared my throat and said quietly, "What I'd do and what other people would do aren't always the same thing." I let out an unconvincing laugh. "I blame my upbringing."

Detective Barnes softened her tone and looked me straight in the eye. "Look, Ellie—woman to woman—please watch yourself in that house. I have nothing but love for the Baxter family, and I don't *want* to believe one of them is to blame for this act, but . . . for those of us who lived in the after-math of their tragedy . . ." She sighed and ran her hands through her perfect hair. "There's mental illness there borne from old, deep wounds. I'm sure you've seen bad things happen when the balance tips like this—and I assume you've experienced a shift in dynamics in your own household after your sister's experience. I know you want to believe none of the Baxters are capable of inflicting harm, but I also want you to keep your guard up. I truly don't want to see you get hurt."

Her expression, her voice, her eyes—all were sincere. Although she clearly didn't want to believe it could be true, deep down she thought one of the Baxters had killed Marie Collins. It was only a matter of time before she and her partner narrowed it down enough to arrest one of them.

Now I was worried. And that meant I had to do something about it.

11

"Hey, Vic. Does your offer for help still stand?"

I could hear the smile in his voice. "I'm already on the way."

I heaved a sigh of relief and dropped wearily into the driver's seat of my vehicle. If anyone could figure this out, Vic could. And although Baxter's investigative brain was equally amazing, he wasn't in the kind of headspace where he could be objective. Not that I was planning to ferret out evidence against any of the Baxters, but if the path led to one of them, we needed to be impartial in our investigation of it.

As I started my car, I said, "You know me so well that you had no doubt I'd change my mind about investigating, call you back, and beg for your help?"

He chuckled. "That, and I'm bored as hell and in desperate need of a vacation."

Vic was on disability leave from the bureau recovering from injuries sustained as a result of our previous big case together. He was recovering quickly, so the FBI (who'd taken over a portion of our latest case) had invited him to consult yesterday at the scene of Sterling's and my big take-down of our suspect. On the side, Vic had been helping me and our department profile our suspect throughout the case, and when his FBI buddies found out, they jumped at the chance to pick his brain. I knew he'd been thrilled about getting to do what he loved again. It was no surprise to me that he'd wanted to help Baxter and me out, and I knew it wasn't just because he and I were friends or because he needed some time away from home.

I grunted. "This will be no vacation, trust me."

"Are you kidding? I get to live out my dream of being a PI."

Snorting, I said, "Your dream is not to be a PI. Your dream is FBI director."

"My attainable career goal is FBI director. My dream is being a PI with no federal red tape to weed through."

"PIs still have rules they have to follow to keep their licenses. Not to mention laws."

He scoffed. "I'd make a sick PI."

"Yes, you'd be a total Magnum," I replied dryly.

"I would. It's settled—I'm growing a mustache."

"I wish you were here so you could see how hard I'm rolling my eyes right now."

"You can do a reenactment when I get there in a couple of hours."

I laughed, but then sobered quickly. "Seriously, Vic, thank you."

"What are friends for?"

～

I WALKED into Baxter's room and collapsed onto his bed next to him. "I never realized how exhausting it is to have some asshole investigator ask you the same question twenty different ways to try to get you to trip up. We have to quit doing that."

He smiled. "But it's so effective. And thanks for the heads-up. I've got my interrogation appointment in an hour. At least I'll know what to expect."

"Ooh, so you get a second date this afternoon with *Corinne*, too?" Her name even sounded smug.

"No, my date is with Detective Martin."

"Because you and Detective Martin haven't slept together."

"That is correct."

I laughed. "Hey, I don't begrudge the attraction. She's hot."

Baxter's cheeks turned red, which delighted me to no end. "Can we stop talking about my ex now, please?"

"Absolutely not. In fact, we've never talked about any of your exes. I want to hear some dirt. Go."

He shrugged. "There's not a lot of dirt. I've had a few serious girlfriends and several not-so-serious ones. For the most part, my relationships have ended amicably enough. There's really not a lot to tell."

"I still want to hear it anyway, especially after spending so much quality time today with Detective Hottie. Besides, you owe me. You've literally had a front-row seat for the implosion and subsequent fallout of two of my romantic relationships. Three, if you count . . . whatever you'd call what you and I have going on. Just don't call it a 'romantic relationship,' because I've spent the last hour of my life swearing to Barnes it's not that."

He laughed. "Okay, I won't. Besides, things between us didn't fully implode. The last two months have just been . . . a rough patch."

I let out a grunt. "A rough patch? Really?"

"That's what I'm calling it. Because it was worth it to get to here."

"Okay, if you're going to say sweet shit like that, then maybe I won't make you dish on your exes."

"Works for me."

I sat up suddenly. "As much as I'd love to lie here with you and shut out the rest of the world, I think we need to pick your family's collective brain."

Baxter groaned. "I know. I've been thinking about that, too, and finding reasons to put it off."

"I don't think we can put it off any longer. We're all in trouble here."

He nodded and got up. We walked to the kitchen together.

The family, minus Janelle and baby Olivia, who I assumed were somewhere napping, looked up at us from their listless grazing in the kitchen.

Baxter said, "We want to talk to you all about our . . . situation. Ellie and I have been trying to read the detectives as they've investigated this case, and our unfortunate theory is that they're not going to look much past the people in this room for their suspect pool."

Evidently Mrs. Baxter had never dreamed this could happen, because she gasped and cried, "What? They're only considering us?"

Baxter nodded. "We think so. First, we need your help to find out if anyone's been running their mouth around here. Start with the past week or two. I know it's been crazy, but can any of you think of an incident where someone made an odd comment to you about Marie Collins? I know people have said all kinds of things like 'she doesn't deserve to be let out' or 'she shouldn't be allowed back in town' or whatever. I don't mean that. I'm talking about physical threats like 'she doesn't deserve to live' or 'she'll get what's coming to her.' Anyone hear anything like that?"

Shawn scoffed. "Yeah, all the time. In fact, my buddy Scotty said 'Marie Collins doesn't deserve to be breathing fresh air' on live TV."

Tom said, "Most of my friends have said something to that effect at one time or another."

Baxter conceded, "True, but I'm asking about a comment that was enough to set you on edge, regardless of whether or not you agreed with it."

Mrs. Baxter piped up, "My hairdresser said if she ever got Marie in her chair, she'd get out her straight razor and—"

As the rest of us listened in horror, Baxter cut her off, but gently. "Mom, Denita is sixty-five years old and can barely lift a straight razor. Trust me, she didn't swing that axe."

I'd spent plenty of time mulling over what type of person could have enough malice toward Marie Collins to carry out the act of driving that axe into her head. What I hadn't thought about was the type of person who'd be physically able to carry out the attack. The axe had made contact dead center through the side of her head with enough force to split her skull wide open. In my experience, I knew it took a decent amount of force to do that much damage to a body, not to mention accuracy. The surge of adrenaline accompanying the act of the kill could easily cause any initial shot, stab, or punch to go wild. That was not the case this time. Whoever wielded this axe was either a stone-cold assassin (which I doubted) or someone with inherent muscle memory and stellar hand-eye coordination. That stipulation put the perma-buzzed, out of shape Mrs. Baxter in the clear.

Baxter prompted them, "Any other thoughts?"

When they all shook their heads, I said, "What about something Marie Collins had done to someone here in town before she got locked up? Mrs. Baxter, you were friends with her. Did she ever confide in you about any trouble she'd gotten into or about a violent ex or anything?"

Mrs. Baxter frowned. "I don't like thinking about being friends with that woman."

I cut my eyes at Baxter, hoping he'd jump in, which he did.

He said, "Mom, I know you don't want to relive any of that time. But we need to know if she had enemies from before. We need to be able to see the bigger picture. Sure, our family has the newest reason to want her dead, but what if she did something to someone around here before that? Did she steal someone's husband or anything to that effect?"

Mrs. Baxter sighed. "She got around, that's for sure. I felt like in the year I knew her she had a new man in her life every couple of months. Nothing serious, as far as I knew."

I asked, "Do you remember any names?"

"She never said their last names." Letting out a snort, she added, "Probably didn't know them."

Baxter said, "Can you make us a list of any names you remember?"

She shrugged. "I'll try."

"Can you do it now?"

His mom grumbled but obliged, grabbing a notebook from a drawer and sitting down at the kitchen table.

Turning to his little brother, Baxter said, "Shawn, I hate to ask you to relive a moment of your time with her, but did Marie Collins ever tell you anything about herself?"

Shawn's expression grew strained, and I could feel his apprehension. It reminded me of the way Rachel always looked after therapy sessions when she'd have to talk about and process her kidnapping.

Shawn shook his head, eyes wide. "I don't . . . I don't really remember—"

Mrs. Baxter stopped writing to slam her hands down on the table. "Nicholas, don't force your brother to go through this."

Mr. Baxter put a kindly hand on his wife's shoulder. "I think we're in trouble, Elaine. Things are going to get harder before they get easier."

Baxter walked over to envelop Shawn in a hug. "I'm sorry. I don't want to do this, but Dad's right. This will probably be the toughest week yet for all of us."

Shawn clung to him. "I'm sorry. I don't know anything. I was so young, I don't remember much of anything besides being really sad all the time because I thought you guys were—" He cut off with a sob.

Baxter said, "I know, buddy. It's okay."

I had an idea. Maybe he wouldn't remember conversations, but surely he'd remember people. "Not to prolong this, but . . . do you remember if anyone visited her at the cabin? Or did she hide out alone with you all that time?"

Shawn seemed to perk up, letting go of his brother. He nodded. "Yeah. Um . . . a woman visited us fairly often. She'd bring food and sometimes bring me toys. Rita."

I asked, "Did the police follow up on this woman after your release?"

Baxter said, "They did. It was a dead end. They couldn't find anyone named Rita who was a known associate of Marie Collins, and she refused to talk. Probably a fake name so the woman couldn't be linked to the kidnapping."

"Oh. So my question did not in fact crack the case wide open."

Baxter smiled. "No."

"Okay, fine." I asked Shawn, "How about guys? She seemed not to be able to go too long without the company of men, so do you remember any male visitors?"

Shawn replied, "Not unless they came over when I was asleep."

Mrs. Baxter shoved her notebook across the table toward us. "There's what I can remember."

Baxter picked it up and read, " 'Mark, Cody, Brock, Tyrone.' " He looked at his family. "Any of those names ring a bell?"

"Cody Bishop?" Mr. Baxter asked.

Tom made a face. "He graduated a year ahead of me. He would have been eighteen or nineteen at the time. She would have been around forty."

Baxter said, "So that's doubtful. These men wouldn't necessarily have to be from Boonville. She could have dragged them home from anywhere. Anything else?"

The rest of the family shook their heads sadly.

Fantastic. We had a bunch of first names of men, most of them common, who couldn't be identified by one of Marie Collins's supposed closest friends. We had the first name of a woman that had been already investigated and deemed a dead end. Granted, there was a chance Shawn could ID "Rita," but would he really remember a face from fifteen years ago? And that was if we could dig deeper than the investigators on the kidnapping case who'd had access to databases we didn't have.

If we didn't start finding something to go on soon, someone in this room was going to be in jail. And if we kept going in circles, our only option might be to give up and let a sleazy lawyer chip away at the detectives' work, hoping for a mistrial or an acquittal. Baxter and I had been on the receiving end of brutal cross-examinations countless times. It sucked, but if you'd done your job well, you had nothing to worry about. I wasn't convinced Barnes was as good an investigator as she thought she was. At least that was what I kept telling myself.

12

I felt ill watching Baxter drive off in my car to go to his interrogation. I couldn't have felt worse for him. He was such a good man. He didn't deserve to be treated like a criminal.

None of us did.

I went back to his room to start on my investigation. I retrieved the glove containing the vape pod from behind the desk and set it on the workspace. This thing wouldn't do me a lot of good if I didn't know what type of fingerprints Shawn had. And I couldn't go ask him for a fingerprint sample without tipping my hand.

It was time for an overt op. It was one thing to go undercover and coax information out of an unsuspecting stranger. It was something entirely different to lie to people who were allowing you to stay in their home. I was doing this to help them, but it still didn't make me feel much better about it.

Formulating the best plan I could, I headed for the kitchen. The living room was empty, so I'd assumed Tom and his family had left. Mrs. Baxter was in the kitchen alone, hard at work removing clean dishes from the dishwasher. As a polite guest, I should have been offering to help with stuff like this, considering my mere presence in her home was putting more work on her, but I honestly didn't have the energy to deal with the obvious issues she had with me. But now I needed something, so I bit the bullet and steeled myself for a painful conversation.

"Hi, Mrs. Baxter. Can I help you with that?"

The look she gave me was somewhere in between sneer and surprise. "Oh. Yes, I suppose."

I gave her a big smile and began removing the rest of the dishes from the dishwasher while she bustled around the kitchen putting them away. As we worked, I said, "I hope Shawn is doing okay. He seemed pretty upset this morning when we were . . ."

She snapped, "When we were all held hostage in our own home? I hope that's not a tactic you and Nicholas employ when you're the ones doing the investigating."

Ooh. As a person on the other side, Baxter's mom probably wouldn't have approved of a few of the tactics we've used to get information we've needed. I replied, "No, we've never held a whole family hostage during one of our investigations."

She let out a harrumph. "Well, see that you don't, especially now that you know how it feels."

Even though I knew Baxter wouldn't approve, I said, "Nick is the most empathetic law enforcement official I've ever worked with. He's really amazing with victims, witnesses, and families. You'd be proud."

She slammed down a casserole dish on her counter and turned to face me. "Why are you here?"

Mrs. Baxter was a formidable woman. I understood why it was difficult for Baxter to stand up to her at times.

I cleared my throat. "Uh, I . . . I mean, at the moment I'm not allowed to leave, so—"

"I'm asking why in the hell did you come all this way to butt into a family matter? What game are you playing with my son?"

"I'm not playing games. I don't know if you're aware of this, but Nick has been the key to my sister's recovery after her kidnapping. He's been there for her every step of the way. More than anyone, he understands what she's going through and knows what to say to her. When he told me what was happening with Shawn acting out, I could relate. I was a serious hellraiser when I was a teen, and our boss, the sheriff, was the one person who finally got through to me and helped me turn my life around. I offered to come down here because I thought I might have some insight to offer. And I hoped in some small way my help could repay Nick for everything he's done for me."

She eyed me, I assumed trying to determine if I was being sincere. "If all this is true, why did you treat him so poorly?"

"I was afraid we'd ruin our working relationship if we got too close personally."

"So you went behind his back and began dating someone else. You didn't think breaking his trust might ruin your working relationship?"

I sighed. "I knew it might, but I figured it would be less hurtful if I pushed him away before he got too invested in us. I made the decision for both of us, and that wasn't fair."

Her face fell. "So you do care that you broke his heart."

"Of course I care."

"Is Nicholas aware of that?"

I wished we could have told his family the truth, if only for the selfish reason of making myself seem like less of a villain. "I've apologized to him for my many sins. What's important right now is that we all at least try to be a united front in the face of what's happened today."

Mrs. Baxter's expression became grim. "You've investigated enough murders to know—what do you think is going to happen to my family?"

My heart sank. That was a much more difficult question than any she'd asked so far. I decided to be frank with her. "Your family is going to go through a lot. On the personal side, it's going to probably feel a lot like when Shawn went missing. The press is going to start calling—"

She held up a hand. "Dealing with the press and the public is old hat for us. We were already forced to unplug our landline and turn off our cell-phones last week because we were being hounded about that woman's release."

"Oh. Well, on the investigative side, you can expect a lot of unexpected visits from various law enforcement officials and immediate summons to the sheriff's station. If the detectives have a plausible reason to believe one of you could be involved, they can hold you for seventy-two hours on suspicion while they're still collecting evidence."

"What would they consider a plausible reason?"

I shrugged. "Unfortunately, everyone in this house had the means, motive, and opportunity to kill Marie Collins. The means being access to the axe, which was kept in the unlocked barn. Our motives are varied but strong. And any one of us had the opportunity to sneak outside during the night without being noticed."

"Jim couldn't have snuck out without my knowledge. We share a bed."

"Were you awake all night watching him?"

She scoffed. "No."

"Then the detectives would argue that you could have been sleeping soundly and didn't realize he was gone. They could just as easily say you're covering for him or even that you and he did the deed together. None of us are going to be taken at our word as the alibi for another."

Her face fell. "That isn't fair."

"No, it's not, but that's how it has to work, because too many people lie to the cops. It would make my job a lot easier if people always told the truth." Speaking of not telling the truth, I needed to get on with my task, so I changed the subject. I gestured to the full pitcher of lemonade on the kitchen table and asked, "Is that fair game? Would you like me to take Shawn a glass?"

A ghost of a smile crossed her face. "Sure. He loves lemonade. And do come back in a bit—as soon as I'm finished with the dishes, I'll set out some cold cuts for dinner."

～

FEELING LIKE AN ASSHOLE, I knocked on Shawn's door. I reminded myself this little con was about helping him and pasted on a smile.

"Come in," he called.

I opened the door and approached him. "Your mom made lemonade. I thought you might like some."

He gave me a strange look, but accepted my proffered glass.

As soon as I saw all of his fingertips make solid contact, I said, "Oh, wait. That one's mine. I forgot I'd taken a drink from it already." Holding the first glass completely still until he released his grip on it, I then handed him the glass in my other hand. "Here you go. Sorry about that. My brain's kind of fried after . . . everything."

Shawn studied my black eye. "Does that hurt?"

"Not as much as the bump on the back of my head. Our suspect was pretty jacked, and he didn't hold back because I'm a girl." I frowned. "Although now that I think about it, maybe he did. He pistol-whipped my partner and gave him a nasty concussion. I consider myself lucky."

He turned pale. "Does my brother get into trouble like that, too?"

I smiled. "No, he's a little smarter than the rest of us. He's usually the one doing the rescuing. Did you know he shot a guy once to save my life? Dropped him with three shots to the chest. I'll never forget it."

I thought Shawn's eyes were going to pop out of his head. "No," he breathed.

Uh oh. Maybe that was something Baxter didn't want his family knowing. Well, too late now. "Yeah, he's kind of a badass."

I'd thought my comment would have impressed the kid, but he set his glass down on his bedside table and looked like he was going to be sick. "Uh . . . so if he . . . killed a guy to save you . . . do you think he'd . . ." He wheezed out a breath and looked up at me in anguish. "Would he do the same for me?"

I said automatically, "Of course he would. He loves you. He'd do anything to protect—" I sucked in a breath, realizing the real meaning of Shawn's question. "Wait. Let me rephrase that. If you were in danger, he would absolutely do anything it took to . . ." I closed my eyes. I was making this worse. "What I'm trying to say is that while he'd risk his own life to save yours, he absolutely did not kill Marie Collins to punish her for what she did to you."

He choked out, "She was out here on our property in the middle of the night, when we were all sleeping. She wouldn't have come here then unless . . . unless she was going to try to—" His voice broke, but he managed to add, "What if he was protecting us from her?"

Although I knew for a fact Baxter hadn't done the deed, the kid had a point. Nick Baxter wouldn't have hesitated to end anyone he thought was going to hurt any one of us in this house. I understood how it must have been difficult for young Shawn to understand the nuance of the situation.

And unfortunately, I couldn't tell him how I knew beyond a shadow of a doubt that his brother was innocent.

I said, "He didn't kill her, I can assure you. Your brother is an honest man, and he's brave enough to own his actions. He'd never stand by and let the police accuse all of us—like they've been doing all day—of a crime he committed."

Shawn seemed to be mulling that over. He finally said, "I guess that's true."

"Sorry to barge in and shit all over your afternoon. It wasn't my intention."

"Whatever," he grumbled, flopping back onto his bed and grabbing his phone, the universal teenage sign for "this conversation is officially over."

On the way back to Baxter's room, I carefully emptied the glass of lemonade in the bathroom sink. I set it on the desk to dry while I used my phone's magnifier app to study the vape pod for fingerprints. The plastic material's finish wasn't smooth enough to show anything, so I got out my makeshift fingerprinting kit—black eyeshadow and a blush brush. I swirled the brush in the eyeshadow and then gently blotted the brush onto the surface of the vape pod. It was a different technique than I normally used with my professional fingerprinting equipment, but this way seemed to work better with the not-so-professional tools. Some of the eyeshadow powder stuck to the surface of the pod, which meant there was a chance a print had been left behind. Excited, I got out my phone again and used the magnifier app to take a closer look. Sure enough, there was a decent print, a loop pattern.

Now to find out if it belonged to Shawn. With my naked eye, I could see some residue on the glass from Shawn's skin oils, which was the medium that created latent fingerprints. These types of prints, which were not made by a transferred substance like blood, had to be treated with a powder or chemical to become visible. I used the same blotting technique with my eyeshadow and brush to bring the prints to life.

I startled when my phone buzzed in my pocket, sucking in a gulp of air and saliva, which prompted a coughing fit. I turned quickly from my evidence so as not to contaminate it while I calmed myself. Once I was back in control, I looked at my phone and sucked in another breath, causing my cough to come back with a vengeance.

The text message said, *This is Corinne Barnes. I hope you're considering what we spoke about and are staying out of trouble.*

I forgot all about my irritated throat as a horrible thought gripped me. I fought to keep my cool and assured myself there was no way Barnes could know what I was doing right now. It was a ridiculous intrusive thought, and I chalked my flicker of terror up to my worry about Baxter finding out what I was doing.

Dismissing my silliness, I used the magnifier app on the glass to discern that Shawn's prints were all arches. Shit. I took another look at the pod. Definitely a loop. The discarded pod from the area where the killer would most likely have parked his or her getaway vehicle did not in fact belong to Shawn, as I'd incorrectly assumed. I felt sick to my stomach as I stared at my stolen—and now ruined and inadmissible—evidence.

"What are you doing?"

13

For the second time in five minutes, I nearly jumped out of my skin. I thought Baxter would be gone for much longer. Now I was really in trouble. "Uh . . ." I breathed, swiveling in the chair to face him but not being able to fully meet his gaze. "Would you accept 'nothing' as the answer to that question?"

His frown said it all. He wasn't going to let me get away with this.

"Okay, fine. I'm studying a fingerprint." One which quite possibly belonged to the killer. I didn't want to admit to Baxter how badly I'd screwed up this time. Maybe I could at least put it off.

"Why?" he asked.

"Because I'm curious."

"About what?"

"About whose it is."

He glanced at the desk behind me, zeroing in on the vape pod still sitting on the protective glove. "Where did you get that?"

"Um . . . outside."

"*Ellie.*"

I shot back defensively, "Hey, *they* missed it, because they couldn't be bothered to set a proper perimeter. It's not my job to find their evidence for them."

Gaping at me, he griped, "You should have left it and told them."

I shrugged.

"Where outside?" he demanded.

No more putting it off. "Near where we had them look for tire marks."

His eyes flashed. "Where you and I were standing? Were you hiding it so they wouldn't find it?"

I said nothing.

He exploded, "Ellie, what the hell?"

Sighing, I said, "I'm sorry. I . . . I assumed it was Shawn's . . . so . . . I didn't think it would be best for him if they found something of his at the secondary scene that *we* made such a huge deal about and essentially bullied them into processing. I figured he tossed it aside carelessly, like teenagers do, banking on the fact that someone else would clean up after him."

His voice still raised, Baxter snapped, "It's not for you to decide what's evidence and what isn't in this case."

"I know, and again, I'm sorry."

After a moment of hesitation, he asked, "Do you know if the print on the pod is Shawn's?"

I said quietly, "It's not."

"How did you collect Shawn's prints to compare them?"

I flicked my eyes away. "Through trickery and deceit. The print doesn't belong to Marie Collins, either."

"So there's a chance it belongs to the killer."

"Unless someone else in your family vapes."

"They don't."

"It could belong to one of Shawn's friends."

"It's possible." His expression went totally dark. "But it's also possible you may have just destroyed the only evidence that could exonerate my family!"

"Nick, I thought the chances of it belonging to the killer were slim to none." I hung my head. "I admit I wasn't thinking clearly. I was trying to protect your brother."

"That's not your job, either."

I snapped my head up. "If the situation were reversed, would you do what I did so you could protect Rachel?"

He said nothing, staring back at me with those icy blue eyes of his.

I said, "See? You would—or you would have at least considered it. Given the chance, I'd do it again."

He growled. "Like hell. You will *not* mess with any more evidence pertaining to this case."

Without knocking, Mrs. Baxter burst through the door. "Nicholas, do not speak to her like that."

My eyebrows shot up. Mrs. Baxter was defending me? Maybe our little chat had gone better than I'd thought.

Baxter griped, "Mom, this is a private conversation."

"You know there's no such thing in this house with these thin walls." She looked at me with decidedly less disdain than she ever had. "I appreciate the fact that you're trying to protect us, Ellie, even if my son doesn't."

"Thank you, Mrs. Baxter," I said uncertainly.

She eyed her son. "Apologize to your friend." She left us alone and shut the door behind her.

Baxter looked down at me, anger still radiating from him. "I'm sorry for losing it on you. I know you were only trying to help, but . . ."

I frowned. "But I did it so stupidly it warranted calling out?"

He shrugged. "You said it, not me." He sat down heavily on his bed and ran his hands through his hair. "Okay, now what?"

"Before or after you kick me to the curb?" I muttered, only half-joking.

I supposed I shouldn't be surprised—I always managed to screw up relationships. I'd so hoped with Baxter that things would have been different, but I didn't know why I'd bothered to try to fool myself. At least this time my bad choices were made for a good reason, or at least a bad reason borne from a good intention.

He huffed out a tired-sounding breath. "Ellie, I'm not kicking you to the curb."

"You sure?"

Giving me a wry smile, he said, "At least not until you figure out whose print is on that vape pod."

"Ha, ha." I turned my attention back to the pod, giving the tape one last smooth with my finger.

He got up and watched what I was doing over my shoulder. "Wait. You're using household tape, and is that . . . eye shadow?"

"It is."

"That's unusual. Are you channeling MacGyver?" He was trying to keep it conversational, but I detected unease in his tone.

"If you're worrying it's not going to work, don't. I've done this tons of times." I picked at the corner of the tape with my fingernail to loosen it, then started pulling slowly.

"Where? I know you don't do it at work, and I hope this isn't how you teach."

As I carefully smoothed the piece of tape with the transferred print onto a second clean sheet of white paper, I said, "I do a presentation every year for the town elementary schools on how to collect certain kinds of evidence with household items. The kids love it, and some of the techniques actually work pretty well. This is one of them. See?" I held up the paper. The print looked great. It was decent enough that I could see the ridge endings and bifurcations with my naked eye.

"Now I'm impressed. But I never would have guessed you'd want to go to elementary schools and teach that age kids."

"Why? I love kids." I got out my phone and brought up the magnifier app to take a photo of the print.

"You have zero patience."

"I have zero patience with adults. Plus when I'm there, it's not my problem to keep the kids in line. I just talk. And it helps that it's a cool topic." I brought up my phone app and called Amanda. "For my next trick, I'm going to try to talk Amanda into processing this print for me without asking too many questions."

Baxter only shook his head tiredly and plopped back down on the bed.

When she answered, Amanda didn't bother with the pleasantries this time. "So . . . Marie Ann Collins. I Googled her."

Why did I not assume my brilliant and thorough friend wouldn't have seen right through me earlier and figure out something was up? "Amanda,

I'm sorry I didn't tell you the whole truth. This whole thing kind of got away from us."

"Us? You mean you and Nick?"

"Yes."

"Where are you?"

I hesitated. "Boonville."

"You mean, the town where Marie Ann Collins was found dead this morning."

"That's the one."

"I get why Nick's there, but why are you there?"

Amanda knew a lot about me, including all about my former relationship with Vic, but she didn't know about my relationship with Baxter. For her own deniability, I needed to keep it that way. I decided to try to derail the conversation. "I was trying to do him a favor. And for my trouble, I ended up finding a dead body."

Baxter glanced at me, frowning.

Amanda gasped. "Holy shit, Ellie. You found *the* dead body? Are you okay?"

"Yes, and I'm good."

"Where exactly did you find her?"

I hesitated again. "In Baxter's family's barn."

Baxter's frown deepened. I shrugged helplessly. Now that Amanda knew the basics, there was no point in trying to hide information from her. The location of the murder was going to be splashed all over the news if it wasn't already, and it was only a matter of time before the news of Baxter's and my firing got around the station. I wasn't ready to talk about my job situation, so I didn't open that can of worms with her.

She said, "So that makes you guys persons of interest in a homicide. I think that would get away from anyone. You know I'll do whatever I can to help you, right?"

I smiled. "I know. I was trying to keep you out of it as much as I could . . . but I do need another favor."

"Name it."

"I collected a fingerprint, and I need it analyzed and run through AFIS."

"They let you do that?"

"Uh . . . I found something they missed."

Yet another frown from Baxter.

She laughed. "Oh, do they have a Beck in their department, too?"

"Something like that."

"I'd be happy to do it. Send it to me."

"Thanks, Amanda. You're a lifesaver. We'll talk soon." I got off the phone and sent the photo of the vape pod print to Amanda, hoping it would be decent enough quality that she could work with. Normally we used a high-resolution scanner rather than a phone camera to make a digital copy of our prints. Sighing, I said to Baxter, "If all goes well, we could know the killer's identity soon."

He rolled his eyes. "*If* that vape pod belongs to our killer. *If* that photo of your hard-won print is sharp enough. Oh, and the really big if—*if* the print is even in AFIS."

"I thought you were always the positive guy and I was the negative guy."

That got a smile out of him. "I'm always the guy who's most interested in the facts."

I stood and backed up against the desk so he wouldn't see me slide the eye shadow palette, brush, and tape into my back pockets. "Speaking of facts, would you like to go out to the barn with me and find out whether the crime scene techs tried to collect fingerprints from the light switches?"

He stood and moved toward me. "Yes, if only to stop you from trying to collect them yourself."

"You don't know that's what I was going to try to do."

Reaching his arms around me, he plucked the items out of my pockets and set them back on the desk. "Really?"

"Worth a shot."

When we got out the front door, I saw that a different deputy's cruiser was parked outside, this time as close to the barn as the secondary scene's tape would allow.

Baxter frowned. "I guess we'll have to wait until later. Looks like they've sent a fresh deputy out to oversee the scene."

While he was speaking, I noticed headlights swing from the road into the driveway. It was only upon seeing Vic's car that I realized I'd forgotten to tell Baxter I'd called in reinforcements. On a good day, Vic wouldn't have been Baxter's first pick.

Baxter squinted as he watched Vic approach. "What now?"

I said in a rush, "So, funny story—Vic offered to come down and help us make sense of this case. And I accepted. And then I forgot to tell you."

He turned to glare down at me. "You did *what*?"

"I know I'm already at the top of your shit list, so surely this little oversight can't make things too much worse."

"You inviting your ex to wade through my family's dirty laundry and not bothering to clue me in on it until he got here is not what I'd call a 'little oversight,' Ellie." If I was reading him right, he'd returned to nearly the same level of anger he'd reached several minutes ago.

I said evenly, "Look, Nick. After talking with Barnes this afternoon, I'm quite frankly terrified. She's gunning for your family, and I don't think she's going to stop until she has one of you to crucify. That means you and I are going to have to find the real killer. The problem is we're too close to the situation to be impartial. We need Vic's brain. He'll be able to see the bigger picture and come up with a profile on the killer. Since we have no access to evidence or any of the resources we normally have, without his insight we're going to be pulling random suspects out of our asses and end up wasting precious time chasing dead ends. I knew you wouldn't like it if I asked him for help, but I care more about your family than your feelings right now."

He stared at me for a moment, his eyes boring into mine. Then he shook his head. "Okay."

Vic had parked by my vehicle and was just getting out of his car as Baxter and I ended our conversation. I hurried over to him and gave him a hug.

"You hanging in there?" he asked me, taking a step back from me as he noticed Baxter staring daggers at him.

I gave him a rueful smile. "Barely."

"Well, you look like shit."

"You always know what to say to a girl."

He chuckled. "Damn right."

I lowered my voice. "Full disclosure—you may not get a warm welcome around here. In all the chaos, I neglected to tell Baxter you were coming down. And his family thinks I'm the devil for rejecting him for you."

His face fell. "Seriously? You haven't even been here twenty-four hours and—"

"And I've turned the whole town into a shit show? I'm well aware."

Shaking his head, he replied, "You have a gift."

14

As we approached Baxter, I didn't quite know what to expect. After all, just yesterday Vic had invited Baxter over to his home, where I was recuperating after my difficult afternoon, so he and I could have some alone time together. It was in our best interest not to be seen in public or going to and from each other's homes, so that left very few places we could meet each other. That gesture alone should have served to squelch Baxter's ire toward Vic, but there was clearly some residual resentment there.

Vic greeted Baxter, "I'm sorry you and your family are in this situation, Detective Baxter. I know full well how devastating it can be."

Baxter had slipped into his blank cop face again. "Right. Thanks for making the trip down."

"Like I told Ellie, I'm bored as hell. Plus I never really got the chance to thank you for saving my life. So, thank you."

That much was true. If Baxter hadn't shown up when he did and made sure Vic got the emergency help he needed, he would have died from the wounds that had put him on his current medical leave.

Baxter nodded.

I said to him, "We should bring Vic up to speed."

He replied, a little grudgingly, "I guess we should do this in my room so my family doesn't hear too much."

We walked into the house with Vic in tow. The Baxters had convened in the living room for another harried conversation, but once they noticed a stranger in the house, the noise subsided.

Baxter said, "This is Vic Manetti. He's a colleague of ours from the FBI."

The house became painfully silent.

Shawn spoke up first. "Isn't he the guy Ellie chose over you?"

Baxter nodded. "He is also that. But at the moment he's here to help us make some sense of the incident today. Let's move on."

Shawn clearly didn't want to move on. "Why would you even want his help?"

Baxter sighed. "This situation is bigger than any beef I might have had with him."

Mrs. Baxter eyed Vic. "You drove down all the way from Indianapolis for Ellie?"

Vic replied, "Not just for Ellie, Mrs. Baxter. If it weren't for your son, I wouldn't be standing here." He turned on the charm, flashing her a smile. "I'm sorry to have arrived unannounced. It wasn't my intention to barge into your home." He cast me some side-eye, but quickly returned his attention to Mrs. Baxter.

"Oh . . . well, you're welcome here, Mr. Manetti," she said, trailing off as her eyes landed on his broad chest and traveled down.

Vic continued smoothly, "Call me Vic. I'm here to lend my expertise to help in any capacity I can. If you have any questions or concerns, please don't hesitate to come to me."

She smiled up at him. "I suppose my only question is if you're hungry. Would you like a sandwich?"

I had to hold in a snort of laughter. Women of all ages tended to get hot and bothered when Vic was around, especially if he paid them attention and laid a megawatt grin on them.

Vic replied, "I've had my dinner, but thank you for the offer."

Baxter said to his family, "We'll be in my room. We need to discuss the case."

As the three of us trooped to Baxter's room, I got a text from Amanda. She thought she had a possible match for my print in AFIS, but there was an issue preventing her from accessing the person's information. She said she'd look into it and get back with me. I figured that little nugget of noninformation could wait until later. Once we were settled, I launched into the story of the events of today that I hadn't already told Vic, starting at the point of our house arrest.

Vic took in all the information before he addressed Baxter. "I don't mean any disrespect by asking this, but are you positive there's no possibility one of your family members felt the need to defend themselves and the rest of you from a trespasser and ended up in enough shock to repress the whole thing?"

Baxter ground out, "No."

Vic replied, "I'm sorry, but I had to ask. So, I guess aside from the identity of the killer, the big question is why in the hell Marie Collins was out here in the middle of the night. Have you been able to work that one out?"

Baxter told him what we'd come up with as possible reasons for her presence—coercion, trickery, kidnapping, revenge, and amends-making.

Vic frowned. "That's so many varying types of motive for both the victim and the killer. With so little to go on, I say the most plausible scenario is that she came out here for revenge. It's not uncommon for ex-cons to get out of prison and go immediately after the person responsible for their incarceration. As for the killer, I think whoever it was had a fairly fresh dispute with her and couldn't wait to hash it out. They followed her out here either to confront her or to send her a message. Things got out of hand, and they picked up the nearest weapon and swung. They left her here to rot and covered their tracks. Your family doesn't even factor into the equation."

I stared at him, in awe of the way he could dissect a situation and come up with something equally brilliant, plausible, and outside the box. And the amazing part was that he was very often right.

Baxter was evidently less impressed. "Are you saying your best guess is that whoever did this is long gone by now and probably isn't even from around here?"

"It's my initial hypothesis based on what I know so far."

"It sucks, and it doesn't give us anything to go on."

I corrected him, "Vic's idea doesn't suck—the situation sucks. And I think it gives us a lot to go on. We find out who she'd been having issues with in prison—squabbles, fights, whatever. We find out who she'd been running her mouth to. We cross-reference those names to inmates who've been released in the last year or so, and we've got some solid suspects."

Vic added, "We'll also take a look at her visitor logs, phone logs, and copies of any mail or email she received. I'm leaning toward it being someone she wasn't in the joint with or someone who was about to be released, simply because revenge is rarely served cold in prison. You piss someone off badly enough, you generally don't survive the week."

Baxter shook his head. "What warden is going to give the three of us any of that information? You're not active, and Ellie and I are currently disgraced and for all purposes fired."

Vic said, "The warden at Rockville and I go way back. I can get us whatever we need."

After an uncomfortable beat of silence, Baxter finally said, "Before we start a deep dive that will require a three-hour drive, I think we need to speak to someone who was around Marie Collins yesterday to find out what frame of mind she was in so we can nail down her reason for being out here. That will go a long way toward determining whether or not her killer has a connection to my family. Our investigation hinges on the reason she was here."

Even though he was mostly being contrary, he wasn't wrong. I said, "I guess the person to start with would be her sister, Margo Watson. She was kind enough not to press charges against Shawn last night for the vandalism he did to her property. Maybe she'd speak openly to us about her sister and even know the reason she was here."

Vic added, "Plus the sister may know who Marie Collins contacted yesterday. If she came out here with someone or met someone out here, she had to have a conversation with that person beforehand to work out the logistics."

Baxter stood. "Let's go talk to her."

Vic stood as well. "I'll drive. You guys look beat."

～

MARGO WATSON's home was on the opposite side of town from the Baxter farm. The silence inside Vic's vehicle on the ten-minute drive was oppressive. Now that I'd had time to think about it, I wished we'd done more talking and thinking before racing out to our first interview. If I were in Margo Watson's shoes, the last thing I'd want today would be to lay eyes on anyone named Baxter. I felt ill about what our visit might do to this woman's already fragile state of mind.

With her feelings front and center in my thoughts, I ventured, "Um, Nick, how about Vic and I take care of this one?" I turned around in my seat to gauge Baxter's reaction.

It was just as I'd suspected. He looked at me like I was crazy. "Hell no."

"Hear me out—you know she's talked to the detectives a lot today. She's been told where her sister's body was found. And you know Barnes and Martin have asked her enough questions about her sister's relationship with your family that she's got to realize they think one of the Baxters is to blame. Do you think she's going to want to talk to you?" I thought for a moment. "For that matter, I'm sure they've mentioned my name, too." I turned to Vic. "How do you feel about a solo mission?"

Vic chuckled as he pulled to a stop in Margo Watson's driveway. "I was just going to suggest that." Before Baxter could argue, Vic got out of his vehicle and slammed his door shut.

Baxter fumed from the back seat, "This is bullshit. It's my case."

I faced forward so he wouldn't see me roll my eyes, but I couldn't hold my tongue. "What's up with your one-sided pissing contest with Vic? It's not like you."

He griped, "So I should just act like the past never happened because he's suddenly a chill, cool guy?"

I turned back around. "You know, he never actually did anything to you. He didn't know there was anything between us when he asked me out."

"He's always been a condescending asshole."

"True, but—"

"And only two days ago, he had his hands all over you at that party."

"As did you, pal. Only he had an excuse, being undercover as my husband."

His expression went even darker. "I think he's trying to get you back."

I snorted. "Based on what?"

"For starters, you two basically never stopped dating."

Vic and I did go to dinner often and went running together nearly every day, so I could understand how it might have looked as though we were still together. But Baxter knew better. I snapped, "Well, we stopped having sex. Does that not count for anything?"

He glared at me in response.

"Come on, Nick. You know how I feel about you. Do you think I'd throw away what we have to go back to someone I wasn't happy with?"

His glare dissolved into a sad frown. He shook his head as he stared blankly out the window and muttered an apology.

I regarded him for a moment, his haggard face looking even rougher in the shadows. I hated the havoc this situation was playing on my level-headed, sweet Baxter.

It felt like Vic was in that house forever. I entertained myself by surveying the damage Shawn had caused yesterday. He'd overturned some furniture and smashed a few flower pots, but all in all, there wasn't a lot of monetary damage done. The kid wasn't violent; he was just distraught, and from the way this was playing out, things were going to get worse for him before they got better.

Vic finally returned and slid into the driver's seat, saying, "An awkward conversation, not that it's any surprise. She seems . . . lost. She definitely gave off the vibe that she was embarrassed by her sister's crime and thought she was a bad person, but at the same time she seemed ashamed she felt that way. She said she'd only been able to finally break down and reach out to her sister in the past few months."

I couldn't imagine turning my back on my sister like that, no matter what she'd done. "She sounds judgy." When I heard Baxter huff out an angry breath behind me, I added, "Justifiably, of course."

Vic went on, "I've seen it before, especially in relatives of violent criminals. They don't stop loving the person, but they have trouble separating them from their actions. It's a tough spot to be in."

I turned to Baxter. "That's kind of what Sergeant Woods said last night to Shawn about why she didn't press vandalism charges against him. That she felt she owed him something for what her sister did to him."

Baxter nodded. "That all tracks. After Marie Collins was convicted, her sister tried for years to contact my family and apologize. She'd stop my mom in the grocery store and strike up a conversation, but my mother wasn't interested in talking to her. In fact, she told Margo Watson on more than one occasion to go to hell. My mother isn't the most forgiving woman."

I suppressed a laugh.

Vic went on, "As for Ms. Watson knowing who Marie Collins was in contact with yesterday, that's a bust. She said her sister was so keyed up over her freedom she didn't have the focus to carry on much of a conversation. She did manage to demand they stop at the first Walmart so she could get a phone, a box of hair dye, a couple of 'whore outfits' (Ms. Watson's words), and as many bottles of vodka as she could carry. Against her better judgment, Ms. Watson picked up the tab."

My heart sank. If that wasn't a recipe for self-sabotage, I didn't know what was.

Baxter griped, "She enabled Marie Collins to pick up right where she left off being a total delinquent."

Vic nodded. "Ms. Watson was hoping they could start to reconnect on the drive home, but she said her sister spent the whole time with her head in her new phone, texting and setting up social media accounts. They made a little small talk, but Marie Collins made no mention of her plans for that night or the future. Once they got home, Ms. Watson said her sister spent about an hour at the house bathing and primping before leaving on foot."

My eyebrows shot up. "In the heels she was wearing? I find that hard to believe."

He started his vehicle and gestured down the steep driveway. "Odds are she only walked as far as the road, which you can't see from the house. Ms. Watson said that whenever her sister crashed at her place and wanted to hide the identity of who she was spending the evening with, she'd meet her guy at the end of the driveway."

I added, "At least now we know there's a guy involved." I frowned. "She really did slip back into old habits fast. I'm sure she was excited for her first night of freedom, but it kind of feels like she was using her sister."

"Another old habit, according to Ms. Watson. She said once her sister was finished with a bender, she'd come back and apologize and things would be great for a while . . . until a better offer came along."

Baxter asked, "What time did Marie Collins leave here last night?"

"Around five," Vic replied as he put his vehicle in gear and headed for the road.

"Five p.m. to one a.m. is a huge timeframe. She could have come into contact with dozens of people."

Vic nodded. "There's going to be a lot to wade through to establish a time line for her."

I shifted in my seat so I could see both of them. "Since we've hit a wall at the moment with the victim's time line, could we come up with some possible suspects from a different angle? Baxter, didn't you tell me you had an idea of a few people who might have a reason to want to make your family look guilty?"

He hesitated. "I did mention that to you, but . . . ," he shook his head.

Vic said, "At this point, there are no bad suggestions for persons of interest."

Baxter had seemed confident about making headway in coming up with suspects during our house arrest. I didn't know why the sudden change. He said quietly, "There are when they could have bad repercussions for my family."

I asked, "Worse repercussions than one of you being charged with murder?"

"Possibly."

I frowned at him. "At least trust us with what you're thinking. We don't have to act on it."

He blew out a breath and began, "During the course of our search for Shawn, my mom and dad falsely accused a few people of taking him. As you can imagine, that didn't go over very well. The town stood by us, and . . . it turned into an angry mob situation in at least one instance. I believe two of the people we accused ended up having to move away."

"Ooh," I breathed.

"But one of them is still around." He sighed. "And that's why my dad keeps a gun in his nightstand and another in his truck."

Holy shit. I hadn't known what I was getting myself into when I agreed to come down here. The idea of this family living in a constant state of depression *and* panic was mind-boggling.

I asked, "Did you or any of the rest of your family mention this person to either of the detectives today? I feel like they couldn't have brushed that little nugget aside."

Baxter frowned. "Not yet. Dad said not to bring it up."

Vic and I shared a look.

Baxter snapped, "I saw that."

I replied, "Well, then you know we both think it's a shitty idea to cover for some asshole who's clearly terrorizing your family."

"It's complicated."

"Your family is on the chopping block. Pointing the finger at someone else just got uncomplicated."

"Not when that person is my uncle."

15

My jaw dropped. "What?"

Vic flicked his eyes my direction only for a moment, but I saw the pained look in them.

Baxter sighed. "My mom's brother. His name is Benji McDonald."

"Okay . . . damn. So it just got complicated again." I shook my head. "But still, if you of all people believe someone else could be involved in this homicide, why have you said literally nothing? You, of the high horse about me and my ill-gotten evidence?"

He raised an eyebrow. "I don't feel like you have a right to call me out about this right now."

I wrinkled my nose. "I feel like we're even."

"It's not the same."

I said to Vic, "Special Agent Manetti, are there degrees of obstructing justice?"

Vic replied carefully, "Well, technically yes, but generally an obstruction offense is considered a felony classification—"

Crossing my arms, I said to Baxter, "See? We're both guilty of felonies."

Vic flicked a glance at me again. "What's this about ill-gotten evidence?"

I'd purposely left my lapse in judgment out of my report of today's events, thinking it would be easier to confess my sins to Vic without Baxter glaring at me. I waved a hand. "I'll explain later." To Baxter, I said, "Is there an actual good reason we're not on the phone now with our two favorite detectives? I get that your dad is scared of your uncle, but considering you and Manetti are here to defend the homestead, I'm liking our chances."

Baxter seemed too tired to fight. He slumped in his seat. "We've got jack shit to prove my Uncle Benji had anything to do with Marie Collins's death. We sic Barnes and Martin on him without enough to arrest him, and where's the first place he goes after they're forced to cut him loose? It will be painfully obvious who tattled on him, and he'll be hell-bent on payback."

"First of all, it'll be a cold day in hell before we have the clout to 'sic Barnes and Martin' on anyone. All I want is someone on their radar whose last name isn't Baxter. At best, they might entertain the thought of interviewing him. What the hell's wrong with your uncle that you all think any tip to the scales is going to end in disaster?"

"Our whole family turned on him. His wife even took our side against him. He blames us for their divorce and everything else in his life that's gone wrong since. The worst part is he's not wrong."

I felt for him. I was no stranger to that level of family drama. "I get it. That sucks."

Vic said, "It's a good lead for us to follow, quietly, of course. We can easily find out nearly all we need to know about him without arousing any suspicion. Make a list of his vital info and known associates, and I'll get on it. How about the other two people you said had to leave town? Did they move far?"

Baxter thought for a moment. "No, I don't think so. I'll get you their names and info, too."

Vic nodded. "I can get to work on that tonight so we can hit the ground running tomorrow." We'd arrived back at the Baxter property. Vic pulled to a stop next to my vehicle and added, "I think what the two of you need now is some rest. What's the game plan for tomorrow? I don't know about you guys, but Rockville is my number one. If someone's been in the joint, I always make it a priority to talk to the cellmate. Even above family members. It's been my experience that people don't always want their families to know everything that happens on the inside, especially if they think it's going to upset them. Plus it's easier to confide in someone who's going through a similar situation and can relate." To me, he said, "You want to road trip with me? It'll be fun. You can sleep all the way there and I'll only wake you up to stop for snacks on the way."

A road trip with Vic sounded amazing, even though the destination would be a women's prison. On the flip side, would I be abandoning Baxter when he needed me most? To buy time to weigh my options for another few seconds, I joked, "Good snacks or Vic snacks?"

He eyed me. "Aren't you the one who begged me to do keto with you?"

"It's still a fair question."

Baxter suddenly wrenched his door open and announced, "I'm going inside. You guys can stay out here and flirt if you want to."

Vic and I watched him stalk into the house.

Vic said, "Don't go busting his balls over his attitude."

I frowned. "You think I'd do something like that?"

"You did do exactly that to me when I was in his shoes."

"You were being an ass. He's also being an ass. It bears pointing out."

He grinned at me. "I know you'll make the right decision. Text me by seven tomorrow if you want to go with me. Get some sleep."

~

I GOT READY FOR BED, but there was one more thing I wanted to do before I turned in for the night. And it was best done with fewer people up and about.

I snuck down the hall so I could see the living room couch. No Baxter. I tiptoed through the living room and happened to notice him out on the back patio, deep in conversation with his parents. With them occupied and looking the other way, I took my chance to slip out of the house and out to the barn. They'd finally released the scene while we were at Margo Watson's house.

I felt like Baxter and I had been pretty thorough with the barn even though we'd only had a short amount of time in it. It was often the case that we didn't find much of anything in the way of evidence at a scene, especially if the incident occurred outside or in a larger structure like the barn.

In a home, there were generally a lot of items around that could have been touched or used by the killer, and doors were a great source of fingerprints. The splintered wood of the barn door and the rusty latch were of no help in that department. In cases where I had this little to go on, the victim's clothes and the murder weapon often held a wealth of information and could make or break the case. But of course I had no access to those items this time.

I headed for the light switches with only my phone's flashlight to illuminate the way. Given the fact that someone had been brutally killed out here, the barn held significantly less appeal than it had twenty-four hours ago. Tonight it was borderline creepy.

With little lighting, there was no way to try to discern if there were any fingerprints on the light switches. So I went for it. I took out my palette and brush and dabbed eyeshadow across the part of the wide switch someone would have had to touch to turn the lights on. I smoothed tape onto each one and blew out a breath. Moment of truth.

I set a clean sheet of paper on the nearest tool bench and propped my phone up against an old coffee can full of rusty nails, shining its light toward the panel box. I began lifting the pieces of tape and carefully transferring them to the sheet of paper. Once I was finished with the four switches, I returned to the tool bench and trained my flashlight on the prints I'd collected. Three of them were badly smudged, but one wasn't. Unfortunately, it was only a partial print from near the tip of the finger, where all prints looked a lot alike. Without blowing it up, I couldn't begin to discern the pattern on this one, and I wasn't convinced there was even enough pattern on the print to make a solid call.

Dejected, I schlepped back to the house, hoping to reenter as quietly as I'd left. Of course I wasn't that lucky. I could see Baxter's silhouette as he sat on the couch alone, in the dark.

"I suppose I don't need to ask where you've been," he muttered.

I had no energy left to fight. I hoped reason would keep this conversation more positive than a lot of the ones we'd had today. "They released the scene. Even if I'd found a signed confession out there from the killer, it wouldn't be admissible. But not for nothing, they hadn't bothered to print the light switches. Big fail on their part. Or another purposeful omission so they can build their case on speculation and old grudges."

When he made no reply, I headed to his bedroom and turned on all the lights. I studied my lone usable print with my magnifier app. I tried to compare it to Shawn's prints and the one I'd found on the vape pod, but I really needed my giant monitor back at the station. A fresh wave of disappointment hit me in the gut upon realizing I could no longer refer to it as "my" giant monitor, as I no longer worked there. At a loss, I took the best photo I could and emailed it to Amanda for her help.

My heart hurt at the thought of what Baxter must have been feeling. He'd essentially lost his career over this. He'd talked tough, saying it was the least of his worries. And given the fact that it was only a matter of time before one of his family members was taken into custody as a murder suspect, it probably was the least of his worries. But all of his worries compounded had to be more than anyone could bear. And on top of it all, I wasn't exactly being the supportive partner he needed.

Feeling even worse, I went back out to the living room to speak to him. He wasn't there. Maybe he needed time and space. This was one of those instances when my inexperience with healthy relationships was a real handicap. When Rachel and I had a disagreement, I knew to give her a wide berth. When Baxter and I had been only work partners and would disagree, we still had to get our jobs done, so we never got too tripped up with our personal feelings. That, or one of us would get really mad, repress it, and then ghost the other one once the case was closed. This time, there was more at stake. More feelings to be hurt and more emotions involved. Unable to come up with the right answer about what to do, I decided to go to bed and try to fix it in the morning.

～

ONCE I WAS SETTLED into bed, there was a knock at the door. I was too exhausted to get up, so I said, "It's open."

Baxter stuck his head inside. "Can I come in?"

"Um . . . okay," I replied uncertainly, a little worried he was here to gripe at me some more. But when he got closer and I saw how haggard he looked, my only concern was him. I pulled the covers back and patted the bed beside me. "Come here."

As he slid in next to me, he said, "I wondered if you'd still want to hang out with me after today."

"I wondered the same thing about you."

To answer my question, he pulled me close and kissed me.

Worried I'd get too caught up and not be able to control myself, I pulled back gently and asked, "Does this mean you're not still pissed at me? Am I off the hook for calling Vic?"

"He's honestly going to be a lot of help. Sorry I was being a jealous dick. I didn't mean half the stuff I blurted out. I wish I could take it back. I've had a bad day."

I smiled. "On the heels of a bad couple of months. You get a pass. Speaking of passes, what about me allegedly hiding evidence from the cops? You still mad about that?"

"Not allegedly. Actually."

"Like I said, I'd do it all again. But I'm sorry my *alleged* felony caused you additional stress."

He barked out a laugh and shook his head. "What did your late-night trip to the barn net you?"

"One crappy partial that Amanda is going to have to work literal magic on. And of course your disapproval."

He eyed me for a moment but finally relented and smiled. "You're lucky I can never stay mad at you."

I laid my head on his chest and closed my eyes. "I know."

∾

MORNING CAME WAY TOO EARLY, but again, waking up in Baxter's arms made it seem not so terrible.

And then all hell broke loose.

16

"Jim! *Jim!*" Mrs. Baxter screamed at the top of her lungs. She sounded as if she were in the same room with us.

Baxter bolted out of bed and out the door. I was right on his heels. When we got to the living room, we found Mrs. Baxter on her knees, shaking.

"Mom, what happened? Are you hurt? Where's Dad?" Baxter cried, rushing to kneel down next to his mother.

Mr. Baxter burst through the back door. "Elaine? What's wrong?" He hurried toward us, his face white with worry. "Did she fall? I was in the garage and heard screaming."

Mrs. Baxter shook her head and looked up at her husband. "Janelle called. Tom's been—" She broke into a sob.

Her son took her by both shoulders. "What happened to Tom?"

"He—he was . . . *arrested.*"

I blew out an audible breath of relief. I noticed the two men do the same. At first, I'd thought Tom had been hurt, or worse. An arrest wasn't good news, but it was news we could deal with. And news I'd been prepared for since yesterday.

Baxter's relief was quickly replaced with the level-headed calm he exhibited in crisis situations. Helping his mother into a standing position, he said, "Everyone get dressed, and we'll head to the station. Dad, call Jordan Menendez and have him get there as soon as he can to act as Tom's counsel."

Mrs. Baxter croaked out, "Shawn . . . what about Shawn?"

Mr. Baxter patted her on the shoulder and began leading her down the back hall. "If he didn't wake up to all that ruckus, he's sound asleep. Let's let him rest while he can. Today's going to be another hard day for him."

I followed Baxter into his room and shut the door. He stood there staring at Tom's bed, looking utterly defeated. I put my arms around him, and he clung to me. I could only imagine what he was feeling. He and his brother, only two years apart, had been inseparable growing up, and I knew in adulthood that they visited each other every time they got the chance.

I said, "We've already made progress with this case. We *will* prove his innocence."

After a few moments, he pulled away from me and wiped a hand down his face. "I want you to go with Manetti to Rockville today."

"What? No. I want to be here for you and your family."

"To do what? Sit around and wait while those asshole detectives take their dear sweet time processing Tom and conducting a formal interrogation with his lawyer present? We won't be able to talk to him until all that's done. It'll take half the day."

"Sure, but . . . I don't want to abandon you."

"You won't be. As shitty as it is for Tom, I think this is just the department flexing. I know my brother didn't kill Marie Collins, so they can't have physical evidence against him. I'm betting Janelle misunderstood and they didn't actually arrest him, that they're doing a seventy-two-hour hold while they build their case."

I frowned, dread building in my gut. "They have to have something or they wouldn't start that timer. What makes him their best suspect? And please don't say it's because of an old rivalry between your brother and Detective Martin, because I definitely picked up on some kind of vibe between them yesterday."

"It's that . . . and . . ." He blew out a breath. "My brother bats left."

"Bats left?" My eyebrows shot up as the image of the wreckage of Marie Collins's skull filled my head. "Oh, shit. Your brother's a lefty?" I thought back to lunch yesterday, when I'd noted all of us used our forks with our right hands.

"The only thing he does left-handed is swinging a baseball bat. And Patrick Martin happens to be one of the few people who'd realize that, because they were on the team together in high school."

I blew out a breath. "And that's why you didn't answer me when I asked if you knew any lefties with a grudge."

He took my hand. "I wasn't keeping it from you because I didn't trust you with the information. You had no reason to be aware of that fact, and I didn't want you to feel like you had to choose between ratting out my brother and omitting a truth when you gave your statement."

I smiled. "Look at you withholding information to protect the people you care about."

"I'm not going to make a habit of it. There's nothing else I haven't told you. I promise."

I nodded. "Same."

"Now call Manetti and tell him to come pick you up."

"Nick, come on. I'll be of more use here."

Shaking his head, he said, "Sitting around with me and my family worrying about Tom? That's a waste of your time."

"Not to me."

Baxter took out his phone. "If you won't call him, I will." He started a FaceTime call of all things and waited for Vic to answer.

I offered, "If you'd rather I do something to further the investigation, then I'll start interviewing people here in town."

Vic's concerned face appeared on Baxter's screen. No way he'd assume an early morning call from Baxter was anything besides bad news. "Everything okay?"

Baxter replied, "Yes and no. My brother, Tom, got taken in. We're hoping it's a hold instead of an arrest."

Vic frowned. "I'm sorry to hear that."

"Yeah. Since I'll be dealing with that all morning, I think Ellie should go with you to Rockville."

I grabbed his hand and turned the phone in my direction so I could address Vic. "And I told him I can handle talking to people around here by myself. I know what I'm doing."

Baxter said to me, "What if someone doesn't appreciate a question you ask? You can get kind of blunt with people sometimes."

Vic interjected, "And by 'blunt' he means 'shitty.' "

I flipped Vic off and said to Baxter, "Sounds like you think I need a babysitter."

Vic said, "I also think that." Before I had a chance to defend myself, he went on. "Only because we're concerned for your safety as a civilian. You're never allowed to speak to persons of interest alone while you're working. Even when you're undercover, someone is around to monitor the situation. Why should this be different?"

"Because we're on a timetable. And last I heard, you two are civilians as well."

Ignoring my dig, he replied, "Name one time we're ever not on a timetable. Besides, it always helps to have a second set of eyes and ears during any interview. Don't forget, I'm a little rusty. I could use your help."

"Oh, so now you've sunk to patronizing me."

Vic frowned at me. "Get over yourself."

Baxter threw him a glare, but I had to admit Vic wasn't wrong. If push came to shove physically, I wasn't trained to defend myself. I had the injuries to prove it.

I said, "Fine. I'll go with you to Rockville."

"I'll be there in thirty."

～

I GOT ready as quickly as I could. The Baxters, minus Shawn, left minutes before Vic pulled up outside. I hated the thought of what they would have to go through today, and I felt even worse that I was the slightest bit relieved I didn't have to be here to witness it.

As I hopped into Vic's waiting vehicle, he stared at my eye and asked, "Did you not bring any makeup with you?"

"I'm wearing makeup." I reached over and gave him a slap on the arm. "Good morning to you, too, you dick."

Trying and failing to cover a smile, he said, "Good morning, Ellie. I was only suggesting that we not give anyone anything to be suspicious of or to be distracted by as we question them."

I pulled down the visor and studied my eye in the sunlight. It had looked a lot better in the dimly lit guest bathroom where I'd applied my usual modest amount of makeup, which clearly wasn't enough today. "You don't think my badass shiner will give me some street cred at the women's prison?"

He shrugged. "Maybe, but I'd still like to keep it as professional as we can, considering we have no real jurisdiction of any kind."

I looked at what he was wearing—a well-fitting black T-shirt and dark jeans. "Professional like how your shirt is a size too small in a good way?"

Grinning, he said, "Are you slut shaming me?"

"No, I'm saying I've witnessed you cause mass panic by simply walking down the street. You might want to tone down the beefcake in a place where the women are sexually repressed as part of their punishment. You might give one of those poor lifers a heart attack."

He laughed. "I'd planned to keep my jacket on while we're inside. How's that?"

"You may save a life today with that one simple act."

He rolled his eyes and started driving.

~

ON THE WAY, Vic began to fill me in on what he'd discovered about a few of the people Baxter had him research.

He explained, "Besides Benji McDonald, there were two other people the Baxters had accused of kidnapping Shawn. Gretchen Hollis, a childless friend of Mrs. Baxter's, moved one town over to get away from the community's ire against her. Jeffrey Townsend, a mouthy football dad who regularly threatened Mr. Baxter for not giving his son enough playing time, moved to the next county. According to an old article I found, Townsend claimed the move was to get his boy into a different school district with better football teams."

"I hear that's a thing."

"It is, but it's more likely a guy like that already had enough enemies around here even before the accusation and had to get the hell out of Dodge after. And last but not least, I did a little digging on good ol' Uncle Benji himself. He's a bad apple."

My gut clenched. I didn't know if I wanted to hear all of this.

Vic went on, "I saw two drunken and disorderlies, two DUIs, one public intoxication, and five assault charges on his record. And those are only the ones he got caught for."

I frowned. "Holy crap. No wonder Baxter's dad sleeps with a gun in reach."

Vic frowned, too. "I don't love it that you're staying there, especially now that we're poking into Benji McDonald's life."

"Which is why we're going to do it very carefully."

He didn't seem convinced. "I suppose . . . if we're *very* careful, we might be able to glean some information about him at his favorite watering hole. According to a quick phone chat I had with Mrs. Baxter last night, I found out he spends a considerable amount of money at a local bar on a nightly basis."

"Worth a shot."

"I also perused Marie Collins's brand-spanking-new socials. Unfortunately, there are a lot of photos of her primping to go out—in various stages of undress—but not a single post made after leaving her sister's house."

I frowned. "So either she wanted to keep her whereabouts a secret . . ."

"Or the person she was with did."

"In fairness, if I were planning to take someone out on the town and kill them at the end of the evening, I wouldn't want our step-by-step journey chronicled for the world to see, either."

He chuckled. "You make a good point. Now you nap. I'll wake you when we get there."

On Vic's orders, I did manage to get in a catnap. The rest of the way, we discussed topics other than our current investigation, last week's investigation, my job situation, and my relationship with Baxter. It was refreshing to think and talk about things that didn't stress me out.

We arrived at Rockville Women's Correctional Facility all too soon. We went through the standard entry process—sign in, physical search, storing our belongings—and then went straight to meet with the warden. Warden Aparna Kumari was an FBI buddy of Vic's from his first year with the bureau. She welcomed us warmly and gave us a file containing copies of Marie Collins's incident reports, visitor logs, phone logs, snail mail, email, and general prison history. She then had one of the guards escort us to an empty office where we could delve into the thick file.

As we divided up the paperwork, I said, "Damn, your friend hooked us up."

"Yeah, she did." Vic scanned the short list of incidents. "Looks like aside from running her mouth and defending herself a few times, our victim was a decent inmate."

I glanced over at the papers in front of him. "Any juicy quotes from her running her mouth?"

"Let's see . . . 'Bite me, you skanky bitch,' and . . . damn . . . 'Your boyfriend killed himself to get away from you.' "

My jaw dropped. "Whoa. She certainly didn't hold back. Who was the victim of that last gem?"

"Sabrina Alexander. A former guard."

"Prison guard is truly a thankless job."

"No shit." He shook his head. "Fun fact, though, this incident was recent. Two months ago."

I took note of that in a notebook I'd brought. "That's worth looking into. Can we get contact info for Sabrina and the reason she's a former guard?"

He had his phone out, sending a text. "Shouldn't be a problem. Although I'm going to guess the reason she's a former guard is because the fight ended when she punched Marie Collins."

We went back to work with the files. I had the stack of copied snail mail. Not a ton of letters for fifteen years, but with the advent of email, letter-writing in general had dropped off. I separated them by the sender's name, ending up with seven from Jake Sampson, one from John Kocher, one from Benji McDonald, one from "L" (with no name or return address), and one that almost knocked me out of my chair.

I elbowed Vic and held the letter out for him to see. "Check out who sent this."

His eyes widened. "Elaine Baxter?"

17

I scanned the scathing letter from Baxter's mom and shook my head. "Damn. Baxter told me Marie Collins had sent letters of apology to Shawn over the years and that his parents had kept them from him. I guess his mom thought enough was enough and decided to do something about it. She basically makes it clear that she will have no more of it . . . or else. *You send one more letter to MY SON and it will be your last.*"

"That's a threat."

"Uh, yeah it is. I mean, an empty one, since this was from ten years ago. That is, unless she was considering taking out a hit on Marie Collins from the inside."

Vic snorted. "How many contacts do you think Elaine Baxter has on 'the inside'?"

"Zero. That's why I called it an empty threat." I waggled the letter and mused, "But it's still kind of damning considering the events of yesterday. I hope our detective friends don't decide to actually do their jobs and find this. I could see them slapping a conspiracy charge on Mrs. Baxter . . . or even . . ." My stomach dropped as the gravity of my own words hit me and I couldn't finish my sentence.

"I honestly did lose a little sleep over that idea last night."

Fully queasy, I breathed, "I didn't think of it until now."

He laid a hand on my shoulder. "Don't worry. We'll figure this out."

I nodded, wishing I could wake from this nightmare.

I scanned the rest of the letters to get the gist but didn't spend too much time delving into them. Right now we needed to glean the basics from this file so we could interview the right people here and ask the right questions. I'd leave the deep dive for the drive back, which was always my job when Baxter drove us around during an investigation. I got yet another stab in my heart thinking this might be our last investigation together. Even if Tom was the only one convicted, if the two of us didn't come out of this squeaky clean, it would haunt us for the rest of our lives. I pushed those fears aside and got back to business.

Jake Sampson's seven letters started off a couple of years ago as a prison pen pal type of thing and got progressively intimate. John Kocher's was a kiss-off letter. Uncle Benji's was directions on how to go to hell. And the mysterious L's letter was a love note. Aside from the two from Mrs. Baxter and Uncle Benji, none of these letters sounded particularly murderous. I grabbed the visitor logs and phone logs and cross-referenced names. The only letter-writer who'd visited Marie Collins in prison was Jake Sampson, which came as no surprise to me. Same for phone calls—Jake had called here once a week starting two years ago.

I said to Vic, "We need to track down Jake Sampson. His return address is a PO box, but it's in Indy, so at least that's a start. I imagine he'd be at the top of her list of people to hook up with once she got out. Looks to me like he was her boyfriend . . . or something."

"Groupie?"

I shrugged. "Eh. She wasn't a serial killer. She was a kidnapper."

"The type of crime doesn't always dictate whether or not you have fans."

"Crimes against kids usually do."

He replied, "True, but childless moms generally don't get too terribly shamed for kidnapping if there's no violence involved."

As I mulled that idea over in my head, I ran down the visitor logs again, this time looking for names I recognized. No Mark, Cody, Brock, or Tyrone from Mrs. Baxter's list of suitors. The name I thought I'd find but didn't was Margo Watson.

I said, "Her sister never visited her in prison. Not even once."

Vic shrugged. "Like I said, she seemed embarrassed last night. I'm not surprised she refused to drive three hours just to be more embarrassed having to be seen visiting a prisoner."

"Kind of shitty to do to her own sister."

"She did say she was finally able to reach out lately."

"Better late than never, I guess."

"Not everyone has the sibling relationship you have with your sister."

A ghost of a smile crossed my face. "They certainly don't."

I took the phone log and repeated the same search for names I recognized. Aside from Jake Sampson and Margo Watson (at least she'd deigned to call), I recognized no names. I took out a highlighter and compared the phone log to the visitor log. There were some duplicates there—Jake Sampson, Cheryl Adams, Rosaline Suarez, Bill Jamison, and Emily Anders. I jotted down the names and texted Baxter the list, hoping he might have some insight as to who any of them were. He shot me a quick text back that he only recognized Bill Jamison as Marie Collins's lawyer.

Vic was finishing up with the incident logs and Marie Collins's incarceration history as I finished my searches. He said, "I've compiled a list of people I want to speak to here—current cellmate, former cellmate, a few staff members. You have anyone to add?"

"Nope. My list of interviewees should all be on the outside."

He closed the file and stood. "I'll probably neglect to tell the inmates we're not here in an official capacity."

I smiled. "That's not a bad idea."

∼

WHILE THE WARDEN rounded up the two current inmates we wanted to interview, Vic and I spoke to the director of Rockville's reentry program and the director of the culinary arts program. Both confirmed Marie Collins was excited to rejoin society and didn't speak of her planning to exact revenge or having a score to settle. They were in agreement that she wasn't always sweetness and light, but that her overall outlook had been more positive than most of the women there. We also spoke to one of the guards from her cellblock, who spun her story a bit differently. According to him,

Marie turned on the charm when it suited her and held her position among the inmates by being more of an aggressor. It was clear that he thought she was horribly manipulative. To me, she sounded like she was smart enough to figure out how to get ahead here and stay alive in the process. After all, this was prison, not the garden club.

Another guard escorted us to a small room not unlike an interrogation room, with a single table and four chairs. Melia King, Marie Collins's cellmate as of only two days ago, sat waiting for us, a frown marring her face. I clocked her at around fifty, probably quite the beauty in her youth before prison (and whatever she'd done to get into prison) took its toll. I sat across from her, but Vic stayed standing.

Studying her nails, she griped, "I'm missing a cosmetology class for this."

Vic smiled. "We apologize for the timing, Ms. King. I promise we'll be quick. This is Ms. Matthews and I'm Special Agent Vic Manetti of the FBI."

Once she glanced at Vic, as if on cue, Melia's posture and expression opened up. "What do you want from me? Is this about Marie?"

He nodded. "It is. I'm sorry for your loss. I assume the two of you were close, given that you shared a cell for seven years."

Shrugging, she looked away. "I mean, I'd already lost her anyway, right? I'm stuck in here for another dime, so I guess I wouldn't have seen her again regardless."

Moving so he was in her line of sight, he said, "I'm sure it's still difficult for you, so I'm hoping you'd be able to find some comfort in helping us as we try to track down her killer."

A smile pulled at Melia's lips as she looked up at him. "I can help? From in here?"

"Of course. I was just telling Ms. Matthews earlier that I believe the cellmate is the single most important person to interview in a situation like this when a victim has been recently released. Even if you weren't best friends, Marie would have spoken to you the most and would have likely felt the most comfortable telling you things she wouldn't even tell her own sister."

Now Melia was smiling fully. "To hear Marie tell it, her sister has a pretty big stick up her ass. She wouldn't understand the stuff we go through here."

Vic nodded. "Exactly. If we're lucky, you may know who the killer is and not even realize it. We may have this case wrapped up before dinner."

Her smile faded as she eyed Vic and then me. "Wait. Why does the FBI care who killed some random ex-con?"

Figuring it would be best to let Vic keep being the good cop, I said flatly, "We can't tell you that."

My curtness allowed Vic to swoop in with a chummy aside to Melia. "Federal red tape bullshit." Head-nodding at me, he added, "She's a stickler." As Melia gave me the stink eye, Vic went on, "Ms. King, we believe it's likely that someone your cellmate was planning to meet yesterday was the person who hurt her. Did she tell you what her plans were or who she wanted to celebrate with once she was released?"

Her expression grew worried. "Jake," she breathed.

Vic mirrored her expression and dragged the empty chair over so he could sit right next to her. Her eyes lit up.

Vic said, "Jake Sampson?"

She only nodded, clearly wrapped up in Vic's charms.

I prompted her, "Do you know him?"

Shaking her head and keeping her attention on Vic, she replied, "I feel like I do, but no, I've never met him. Marie talked about him nonstop. He's been writing her and calling and visiting for a couple of years." She shook her head again, more violently this time. "I told her it was a bad idea to get into a relationship with some freak who contacted her in prison. You hear horror stories about that all the time. But . . . this guy seemed nice enough. He waited around for her for two years, so I finally figured he must be legit."

Vic asked, "What did she tell you about him? Even things you never considered important might help us."

She thought for a moment. "She always talked about how he treated her like a queen. He brought her things when he visited and put money in her account here. He spouted the usual crap men feed women—how beautiful she was and how smart she was and how she shouldn't have been treated so harshly for simply wanting a child of her own. He promised to give her a better life once she got out."

"It sounds like they were planning to meet once she was released."

"I know her sister was who was picking her up, but she said she'd be with Jake by evening. Personally, I think she was going to roll her sister for some cash and then run off with Jake."

Vic and I shared a glance. That sounded exactly like what she'd done.

Vic said to Melia, "Jake Sampson is looking like a great suspect in my mind, but while we have you here, I want to make sure to pick your brain. We know about an incident between Marie and one of the female guards a few months back. What did Marie have to say about that? Was she worried the guard might retaliate?"

Melia rolled her eyes. "It was a huge deal and did nothing but get us all in trouble with the warden. That guard and Marie always had beef. I don't know what started it, but the guard ended it. After what Marie said to her that last day, I don't blame her for the throat punch. The guard got fired, and Marie got all of her privileges taken away. It ended up more of a punishment for me because I had to listen to her bitch about it day and night."

I asked, "What do you think about the possibility of retaliation from this guard?"

She shrugged. "It's possible. I'm guessing she'll never be able to get another job as a prison guard again, so Marie could have screwed up her life pretty bad."

"Did Marie have issues like that with anyone else in particular? Someone else who was recently released?"

"Yeah, actually. She had mad beef with her last cellmate. I think her name's Amy. They had to separate them. I think she's still here."

Vic nodded. "Is there anything else Marie ever talked about that felt off to you? Did she ever talk about the child she kidnapped or his family?"

Melia squirmed in her seat. "That kid was a weird subject for her. I didn't like it when she talked about him. She still thought of him as hers, and she loved him. She wrote him letters until his parents had a fit and filed a complaint with the warden. She had this crazy idea of reconciling with him one day and being a family again. The way she talked about him was creepy as hell. Sometimes she sounded so nuts I'd wonder why her lawyer didn't go for an insanity plea."

A cold chill skittered down my spine. Was that why she was at the

Baxter property—to reconcile with Shawn? Or worse, to try to kidnap him again? I didn't like this at all, especially since a case could be made that anyone in that family wouldn't have hesitated to stop Marie Collins if she were trying to take Shawn away from them.

Judging from the look on Vic's face, he was thinking along the same lines. "Do you know if she discussed this with Jake? Did she ever mention if they had plans to act on her delusions?"

"She didn't say. But if she talked to me about the kid, she probably told him, too."

Vic reached out and patted Melia's hand. "Ms. King, you've been incredibly helpful to us. I can't thank you enough."

Grinning, she replied, "Maybe you could come back and see me sometime."

"Maybe I could."

I fought an eye roll as long as I could, but finally let it go once he and I were out in the hallway. " 'Maybe I could,' " I said in a low voice, mimicking him.

Vic snickered. "You of all people are going to bust my balls for flirting with an interviewee? Don't even."

"I didn't realize how icky it is to watch."

"Now you know."

～

AMY PRESSLEY, Marie Collins's cellmate before Melia, waited for us in the next room, a carbon copy of the one we'd just been in. We went through the whole process again—Vic turning on the charm and trying to get her to open up, me making a few gruff remarks that allowed him to apologize to Amy to create rapport, and both of us trying to ask the right questions.

Amy was a much tougher nut to crack than Melia.

After fifteen minutes of fruitless back-and-forth, she finally groaned and spat, "Don't you guys get it? I don't give two shits that someone snuffed out Marie Collins. She was a bitch, and she made my life a living hell. Besides, I'm no snitch, and I don't want people to know I've been talking to the cops. We're done here."

Vic sighed. "Look, we appreciate your situation. And judging from what other people have said about Marie Collins, I get that she was a nightmare. All we're asking for is a little insight into her and who she might have pissed off over the years bad enough that they'd want to kill her."

"Here's some insight—everyone who knew her wanted to kill her," Amy said with a smirk.

I slammed my hand down on the table. At least I made her flinch. "Whoever killed her did the world a favor, but we still have to do our jobs. You're sitting in here, rotting away for something you did. Don't you think it's unfair that you're here and someone who committed a worse crime than you gets to walk around free? Why are you so hell-bent on protecting someone you may not even know?"

"I told you, I'm not a snitch."

I stared her down. "If that's your only argument, it's a stupid one. This prison—your cellblock in particular—is not really that tough a place. No one's going to shank you for talking to us."

"Maybe not, but I could end up with a black eye or two, like you."

"Oh, you absolutely could if you don't start talking. My shiner was collateral damage from me having to rough up another delinquent who wouldn't give me the information I wanted. If I were you, I'd be more worried about me than about your cellblock buddies."

As Amy's façade started to crack, Vic pulled out his phone. After scrolling for a moment, he showed her his screen with a mug shot of the suspect from our last case. I'd done none of the damage to his face—that was all courtesy of my colleague, Jason Sterling, who'd had to literally fight for our safety.

Vic said, "She's not exaggerating. This is the guy."

Her eyes bulged, and she blurted out, "Tiffany Clarke. Her and Marie were into it all the time back in the day. They threatened to kill each other on a daily basis. She got out last year."

I smiled. "See? Was that so hard?"

Glaring at me, Amy bellowed, "You better not mention my name to her or anyone else."

I stood and headed for the door, not bothering to turn around as I said, "Oh, honey. I've already forgotten your name."

Vic met me outside and gave me a high five. "That was epic. I guess I haven't had the pleasure of being on the same side of an interrogation with you before today. You're a good bad cop."

"Thank you, I think. One ill-fated afternoon being partnered with Sterling must have rubbed off. Can we get the hell out of here and find something to eat? This bad cop is hangry."

18

Vic and I killed two birds with one stone, grabbing a late lunch at the nearby diner where Sabrina Alexander now worked. It was a nice place, probably a lot less stressful than working in a prison, but it couldn't have paid well. The prices were more than reasonable, which meant even generous tips were paltry.

Sabrina happened to walk past our table after we'd ordered, and Vic stopped her. The poor woman looked exhausted, but she pasted on a smile.

Vic said, "Hi, Sabrina. I wondered if we could have a quick word with you."

Her smile faltered. "Um . . . I think Angel is your server. I can get her."

He said, "No, we're here for you. This is Ms. Matthews and I'm Special Agent Vic Manetti of the FBI. We wanted to ask you about an incident at the prison a couple of months ago."

Her posture stiffened. "I've already been punished enough for my actions."

I still hadn't had any food yet, so there was no way I could make it through another repeat of our last conversation. I got to the point. "Marie Collins is dead."

Her jaw nearly hitting the ground, Sabrina cried, "What?" Then she let out a little huff. "How? Not that she didn't deserve a good shanking, but no one in her cellblock would have the balls. They all have too much to lose."

I replied, "She died just hours after her release."

She scoffed. "Karma's a bitch."

Vic asked, "Where were you Saturday night between two and four a.m.?" Boonville was in a small section of Indiana in an earlier time zone than the rest of the state.

"Here, picking up a double because I need the money. This place is open 24-7 to cater to prison staff and our—" She grimaced and corrected herself. "*Their* crazy shift hours."

I felt for this woman, especially on the heels of losing part of my own revenue stream. I smiled. "Thank you for speaking with us, Sabrina. If you don't mind a couple more questions, could you tell us if you ever came into contact with any of her visitors or heard her speak of friends on the outside?"

She rolled her eyes. "I overheard way more than I wanted about her weird boyfriend. You would have thought he was some studly knight in shining armor. I saw him once when he visited. He looked homeless and super shifty. Probably a perfect match for her."

"Can you think of anyone who would have been waiting around to end Marie Collins's life the day she got out of prison?"

"No one specific. It's just that . . . the woman thrived on picking at people. She was a miserable person and she liked to spread her misery around." Sabrina shrugged. "She put on a bullshit appearance for the rest of the staff, but us guards saw what she was really like. The people I witnessed her torture are still inside, as far as I know. I only worked there for four years, though. I heard she was even worse at the beginning of her stint."

Vic nodded. "Thanks so much for your time, Sabrina. You've been a big help."

As Sabrina left the table, I mused, "I'd love to know if all those letters Marie Collins sent to Shawn were misguidedly heartfelt or straight up terrorism against Mr. and Mrs. Baxter."

"Could be both. This woman wasn't stupid."

"It was kind of stupid to trust a crime groupie."

"True, but we don't know it was Jake Sampson who killed her."

I smiled. "Remind me of the statistics of which category of person is most likely to be guilty of any given murder, Agent Manetti?"

He frowned. "The significant other . . . I'm well aware. But you of all people should know that's not always the case, given what you've witnessed over the last several months. I thought you'd be open to more possibilities."

"I'm trying to convince myself this one can be different. That for once, the simplest explanation can be the right one and it won't take forever to figure out the truth."

"I think the detectives on the case have already assumed the simplest explanation."

He wasn't wrong. "Okay, so I want it to be the second-simplest explanation."

Grinning, he took out the file and his notes. "Me, too. Let's come up with a battle plan."

~

THE BATTLE PLAN Vic and I came up with over lunch sounded every bit as exhausting as an actual battle. We decided to make a few stops on the way back to Boonville to track down some of our persons of interest. First on the list was a trip to Indianapolis, straight east of Rockville. I longed to make a quick stop to see my sister and nephew. Unfortunately, we were only going to the west and south sides of town, still a good forty-five minutes from our home on the northeast side. It would have been nice to grab some extra clothes as well, but we didn't have that kind of time. We were going to be gone all day as it was. I called Baxter to let him know our plan, but he didn't pick up, so I had to leave a voice mail.

As we made the hour-and-a-half drive to our first stop, I began reading Marie Collins's letters with a closer eye and her emails for the first time. I felt a little icky reading some of them, like I was horning in on someone's private life, but it had to be done.

After I had a good grasp on what questions I thought we needed to ask our next interviewees, I said to Vic, "So basically what we've learned today is that Marie Collins was batshit crazy and a real psycho."

"I thought we already knew that," he replied with a chuckle.

"I've heard exactly that from everyone named Baxter for days, but it's helpful to learn it for myself. To be honest, the emails are kind of boring. People tell her what they're doing in their lives, and she tells people what she's been doing in prison to pass the time. These people seem to be old friends of hers or maybe family members who aren't too close. It's hard to tell, because everything's just small talk. The real heartfelt stuff is in the handwritten letters."

"Let's hear them."

I flipped through the file to find the stack of letters. I started with John Kocher's letter. "Okay, this first one is from John Kocher, the Illinois guy, postmarked fifteen years ago, right when Marie Collins went in the joint." I took a breath to start reading the letter verbatim but stopped on the greeting. "Wait. This letter is to *Mary*, not Marie." I took another look at the envelope. "Hmm. He spelled Marie correctly when he addressed it."

"Could be a pet name."

I quickly scanned down the document. "Judging from the number of misspellings, I'm not convinced. Anyway, here we go. *Mary, I can't believe what they say you done, stealing that boy. But maybe it's true. I ain't seen you in a year and a half. Maybe I don't know you no more. You was pretty cold to me, leaving without no tracks.*" I snorted. "He attempted to spell the word *kidnapping* twice, but gave up and crossed it all out and went with *stealing* instead. I also think he means *trace*, not *tracks*. Oh, and evidently he's not familiar with 'i before e except after c.' "

"Quit worrying about the spelling errors, Professor, and get on with it."

I grunted but kept reading. "*I tried for a long time to find you, but you hid good. I guess you didn't want me no more.*" I looked over at Vic. "Aww, how sad. I wonder why she didn't want him no more."

Vic frowned. "Hold up. This sounds a lot like someone creating a narrative to make himself appear innocent. He's distancing himself from her by noting exactly how long it's been since he's seen her, plus he's painting the picture that he, too, was a victim of hers. If you look at her case, I bet a hundred bucks he was a person of interest they didn't have enough evidence on to charge."

"This guy doesn't seem smart enough to think of all that."

"Absolutely not, but his lawyer was."

"Ah." I added, "Oh, there's a little more. *I didn't think you had it in you to take a kid, even though you lost yours. John.* Ouch. He finally hit below the belt there at the end."

"Was there any other contact from him since that letter?"

"No. No emails, phone calls, or visits."

He shrugged. "He may not be worth our time. We can decide later whether or not to make the trip over to Illinois to see him."

I nodded. "Moving on, then. This one is postmarked five years ago from Boonville, but there's no return address or name besides the initial L. Oh, and this one is also not to Marie, but to 'Sunny.'"

"Another pet name."

"Must be. *My Dearest Sunny, I know I turned my back on you, and for that, I'm sorry. I still can't find it in my heart to forgive you for what you did, but as I look back, I wish I hadn't shut you out of my life. I've missed you. I know you've missed me. I read every one of the letters you sent me over the years, at first out of nothing more than morbid curiosity. Lately, though, they've been a comfort to me and have reminded me of happier times. I won't be around when you get out of prison. But know that I still love you, and I always will. Love, L.* Damn, that's one serious love letter."

Vic shrugged. "It could be from a family member rather than a former flame."

I thought for a moment. "Yeah, I guess I could see that."

He glanced over at the letter on my lap. "And the handwriting is pretty girly, too."

He wasn't wrong. "Okay, Agent Killjoy. Forgive me for trying to inject a little sliver of romance into this freakshow."

"Was it not romance that put you at the epicenter of this freakshow in the first place?"

I ignored him. "So who wrote this? The only family member we know of is Margo Watson. She offered, or at least agreed, to house her sister after her release, plus she picked her up. I can't imagine she'd say she wasn't going to be around and essentially say goodbye."

"That was five years ago. Maybe her plans changed. Anyone with the initial L on your other contact records?"

I scanned all of the names again. "Nope. Not one."

"Again, interesting, but not especially murderous. Next."

I got out the stack from Jake Sampson. "These ones from Jake Sampson are long and cringy, and I am *not* reading them aloud. The gist is that he heard her story and felt her sentence didn't fit the circumstances of the crime, so he reached out to her. After the postmark of the second letter, in which he asks if he can call her, his name starts popping up on the call logs. Not long after that, he's on the visitor logs and the letters get progressively more intimate."

Vic chuckled. "Intimate? Give me an example."

I made a face. "He talks about what he's going to do to her once she's out and they're together."

His head whipped toward me. "In a strictly sexual way? Or does he hint at torture?"

"Just sex. Nothing too weird, but if you want the details, you can read them for yourself. What, were you thinking he spelled out the way he was going to kill her?"

"You were being so vague, I wasn't sure."

"Sorry. I don't want to give too much thought to it. I don't want to get any images stuck in my head considering we're going to speak to him soon. Between that and the fact that he's our most likely suspect, I'm looking forward to his interview the least."

"Which is why I'm doing it alone."

I turned to glare at him. "The hell you are. We're equal partners in this."

Shaking his head, he replied, "No, we are most certainly not. You are still an untrained civilian and I will not take you to an interview with someone I believe to be this dangerous."

"Vic," I griped between gritted teeth.

He held up a hand. "Don't try to tell me Detective Baxter would take you with him in a situation like this. If he thinks a person is dangerous, he makes you wait in the car, too. I know this because you've griped to me about it before."

Frowning, I said, "Fine. Let's get on to the murderous-sounding letters, then, both from Baxter family members." I blew out a frustrated breath as I skimmed Mrs. Baxter's letter another time. "I'm telling you, if it were my case, I'd have Baxter's mom in the cell next to his brother's."

Vic winced. "That bad?"

"*You'll regret the day you betrayed me. You'll burn in hell for what you did to my family.* It's all threats all the time."

"You going to hand it over to the detectives on the case?"

I scoffed. "Hell no. I'm not doing their jobs for them."

He furrowed his brow. "You kind of are doing exactly that."

"You know what I mean." I studied Benji McDonald's letter. "This one from Uncle Benji is a little less physically threatening. *You're a terrible person. How could you do this to a child?* And then the standard final damnation, *You'll get your punishment in hell for the devastation you caused all of us.*"

"I'll ask the same question about this letter: you going to hand it over to the detectives?"

"Maybe. Depends on what I find out tonight when I honeypot Uncle Benji at his favorite bar." I'd been batting the idea around in my head all day and had finally gotten up the guts to clue Vic in on my plan. I'd need him for backup.

He frowned. "I thought we agreed we were going to be very careful about him."

"Careful is my middle name, especially when I'm undercover."

Vic snorted. "You are the least careful person undercover I've ever met."

"I get the job done."

"Yes, but you had me and several people in your department in near cardiac arrest during not one but two of your latest undercover ops."

I waved a hand. "You guys worry way too much. I know what I'm doing. And besides, getting losers to talk is my specialty. Uncle Benji will never know what hit him."

"As long as it's not me having to hit him for getting handsy with you."

Shrugging, I said, "I can't promise that. I've incited bar brawls before over that very situation."

Vic said nothing, just shook his head and kept driving.

≈

WE EASILY FOUND Cheryl Adams's workplace, a small insurance agency in a converted house in Speedway.

Cheryl, the receptionist, greeted us as we entered the tiny waiting room. "Welcome. How can I help you?"

Vic flashed her his badge and rattled off our standard introduction. "We're here to speak to you about an acquaintance of yours, Marie Collins. She died Sunday."

Cheryl's face went white. "She . . . what? She was supposed to get out Saturday. What happened?"

"She was killed. Where were you Sunday morning between two and four a.m.?"

"At home asleep. Why are you—"

Vic went on, "Can anyone back that up?"

"My husband."

"And what's his name and a number where we can reach him?"

Lower lip trembling, Cheryl gave Vic the information and then pleaded, "Will someone please tell me what's going on?"

Vic gestured for me to take over while he went outside to call the husband.

I said gently, "Marie was released Saturday. She went to her sister's house, and then several hours later she was killed. The details are . . . sketchy at best. We're running down her friends and family members hoping one of them knows who might have wanted to hurt her. Can you help us?"

Tears spilled down Cheryl's cheeks. "That's so sad. She didn't even have a day of freedom."

"No, she didn't. And that's why her death is complicated—someone was waiting for her to get out so they could kill her. We believe the plan was in the works for a while."

Dabbing at her eyes with a tissue, she said, "I'll do whatever I can to help. What do you want to know?"

"You were her first cellmate, right?" I asked.

"Yes."

"What did she say to you about the boy she kidnapped and his family? Did she speak to you about them?"

She blew out a breath and nodded. "She really loved that kid." Frowning, she added, "Too much, and in a weird way. She talked about him like he was her own child and hated his family for taking him away from her. That's messed up, right?"

I replied, "It is. Did she ever tell you she'd lost a child of her own?"

"Yes. I knew she had some kind of mental illness, but . . . that didn't keep me from treating her badly." She let out a sad huff of laughter. "I was a different person then. I was constantly angry and scared out of my mind. I stabbed people in the back—figuratively—to survive prison. Once I got out, I went back and made amends with all the people I hurt. Marie was one of them." She smiled slightly. "She was no ray of sunshine herself, but she didn't deserve what I did to her."

"What did you do?"

"I turned another inmate against her because someone else ordered me to. The pecking order in prison doesn't make a lot of sense, but when certain people tell you to jump, you do it."

I smiled encouragingly. "It makes sense. Who was the inmate you turned against her?"

"Tiffany Clarke. Those two finally had to be separated on different cellblocks."

"We've heard her name come up. What happened?"

"It was pretty obvious to everyone but Marie that Tiffany had eyes for her. Tiffany was actually a pretty nice person, but Debra, the ringleader of the group I hung with, was homophobic. She hated Tiffany and wanted to see her suffer. So, Debra, knowing Marie was straight, gave me the task of getting Tiffany to believe Marie was into her so Debra could rip the rug out later. I told Marie that Tiffany could use a friend who understood the pain of being separated from her child, which was true, and the two of them bonded over it. Then I told Tiffany's cellmate that I thought Marie was interested in her romantically but was too shy to say anything." She sighed. "Tiffany made a move on Marie, and Marie lost it on her. Turns out Marie was homophobic, too. Tiffany was devastated and embarrassed, but she never figured out Debra and I had intervened. After that, Marie and Tiffany were mortal enemies."

I asked, "Mortal enough that Tiffany might track her down and kill her?"

Cheryl thought for a moment. "It's a fourteen-year-old wound. But I haven't spoken to Tiffany since my release. I don't know if there's still resentment there."

"You've spoken to Marie, though. Did she mention Tiffany?"

"Not for years. Marie seemed to be over it."

That didn't mean Tiffany was. I asked, "Do you have any idea where Tiffany went after she was released?"

"No, I don't."

I wondered fleetingly why Vic hadn't come back inside yet, but I pushed ahead with the interview alone. "What about Marie's life before the kidnapping? Did she share any other personal background with you? Any stories about old flames or enemies?"

Cheryl let out a chuckle. "I heard a lot about 'that son of a bitch John Kocher.' He didn't sound like a great catch. What I remember most is the day she got a letter from him and went on a rampage."

I nodded. "I read the letter. It wasn't kind."

"She'd dumped him long before that. He only wrote the letter to cover his own butt."

"That's exactly what it sounded like. What I don't understand is why he needed to appear so innocent. According to his letter, she'd left him long before the kidnapping and didn't tell him where she was going. Why would anyone think he'd helped her?"

"I don't know."

I asked, "Did she tell you anything else about her life prior to her incarceration?"

"Not much. I always felt like she had her guard up. It was especially noticeable when we met, but I imagine she didn't trust anyone back then. Even now when I'd go to visit her, I felt like she never really let me in." She looked down. "Not that I blame her, especially after I came clean about the Tiffany thing. I wouldn't trust me, either."

I smiled. "I know a thing or two about turning over a new leaf. The hard part isn't your inner struggle of trying to be a better person. The hard part is not giving up when other people refuse to believe you're capable of doing better."

She looked up at me with tears in her eyes. "That's so true. Marie will never have that chance."

In my mind, Marie had had plenty of chances not to be a piece of shit but hadn't taken them. I kept my views to myself. "Is there anything else you can think of that might point us to anyone else who might have had a score to settle with Marie?"

After pausing for a moment, she said, "Marie gloated a little while ago about getting a guard fired."

I nodded. "We'd heard that, as well."

She shrugged. "That's all I know. She made plenty of enemies over the years, but I don't know if any wounds ran so deep that they were worth killing over. Obviously something was worth it to someone."

19

After leaving a weepy Cheryl Adams, I found Vic sitting in his vehicle out front with the windows down. As I approached, I asked, "Whatever happened to not letting the inexperienced civilian interview a scary suspect alone?"

He looked up at me and grinned. "First, that woman was anything but scary. And second, I was going to come back in, but I overheard you two talking and thought better of it. You sounded more like two friends meeting for coffee than a seasoned investigator grilling a perp, so I decided not to rock the boat. I'd already played bad cop, and it didn't sound like you needed my help."

I laughed. "Since when do you—or anyone else we work with—use the word 'perp'?"

"I heard it on TV last night and thought I'd give it a whirl."

I laughed and got into his vehicle with him. "We don't have the time to fit it in today, but we definitely need to talk to John Kocher. My gut says he knows something."

"Good enough for me," he said as he pulled away from the curb.

"We also need to put Tiffany Clarke on our list. Evidently there's an assload of old hurt feelings between her and our victim. I'll fill you in on the way to our next stop."

~

THE CURRENT ADDRESS listed in Vic's database for Jake Sampson turned out to be a men's rescue mission on the south side of Indy. The rescue mission wasn't in the nicest part of town, but it was housed in a well-kept, clean building. I, of course, had to stay in the car like a child while Vic went and did the grown-up stuff of interviewing Jake Sampson.

In my spare time, I called Baxter, but again, he didn't pick up. I assumed he was still dealing with the situation with Tom, so I shot him an encouraging text. I then texted Rachel to let her know how everything was going, and I also checked in with my TA.

As I was finishing up, I got a text from Vic: *You can come in.*

Hot damn. He didn't have to tell me twice. I hurried to the door and found Vic.

"What's up?" I asked as he led me down a nearby hallway.

He grimaced. "About Jake Sampson . . . I don't think he's our Jake Sampson."

"We got the wrong guy?" I couldn't imagine how that happened, considering we had his driver's license number from when he'd checked in at the prison. It wasn't like we'd been flying blind and had taken a stab at choosing a random "Jake Sampson" from a list of many.

"Not exactly."

We entered a kitchen, where there'd just been a serious baking session. The steel table in the center of the room and surrounding floor were dusted with a layer of flour, and a heavenly, sweet aroma wafted from the commercial ovens along one wall.

Several men were hard at work doing dishes. One of them looked up when Vic and I approached and abandoned his task to gesture for us to follow him into the adjoining dining area.

Vic said, "Ellie Matthews, meet the real Jake Sampson."

After what he'd said as we walked in, I didn't follow his line of thinking. I got out my phone and looked at the photo I'd snapped of the Indiana driver's license Vic had pulled up on his laptop during lunch. This guy, age thirty-one, medium build, long dark curly hair, and long bushy beard, looked exactly like his driver's license photo.

I stared at Vic. "Am I missing something?"

After clearing his throat, Jake said in an uncertain voice, "Ma'am, I believe my identity was stolen."

I thought back to the description Sabrina Alexander had given of Jake Sampson: homeless and super shifty. I hated to profile people based on their looks, but this guy checked both of those boxes for me. The prison guards would have checked his appearance against his driver's license photo, and it would've had to have matched for him to be permitted entry.

Vic explained, "There's no way this man could have made monthly trips back and forth to Rockville. According to the staff here, the men have to check in and out when they leave the premises—if someone leaves for more than twenty-four hours and the facility is full, he loses his bed. Jake here hasn't been away for more than two hours at any one time in the past year."

Jake added, "They're good to me here, so I don't have much of a reason to leave. Plus, I'm the resident plumber, so they need me as much as I need them sometimes. Some of these guys can clog a toilet like you wouldn't believe."

Not at all interested in a dissertation on poopy toilets, I changed the subject. "Do you know Marie Collins?"

"Never heard of anyone by that name."

"In the past couple of years has anyone you know mentioned visiting a friend or girlfriend in prison for kidnapping?"

Jake shook his head.

Still flummoxed, I held up my phone with Jake's photo next to real life Jake. "Do you have a twin or a brother or something?"

"Only sisters, ma'am."

I shrugged and said to Vic, "I guess we can call it identity theft. But now what?"

Vic addressed Jake. "Have you had any luck in remembering where and when you lost your license?"

Jake shook his head. "It was a couple of years ago that I had to get it replaced, as best I can remember. I was drinking pretty heavily then. Could have happened anytime and I may not have noticed for a while. It would have happened somewhere here in Indy, though. I've never been one to venture much out of town."

Vic nodded. "That's a start, at least. Thanks for your time, Mr. Sampson."

"You're welcome. I'm sorry I couldn't help you more."

Vic and I made our way back through the building, waiting until we got outside to discuss anything further.

I asked, "Do you believe him? Alcoholics are good bullshitters."

"I do. I think he's legit."

Although the whole identity theft revelation had thrown me for a loop, I hadn't gotten a bad vibe from the guy, either. "This isn't good."

Frowning, Vic agreed, "You're right, it's not. Someone went to a lot of trouble to impersonate this man to get in to visit Marie Collins."

"To protect his identity? And who was he trying to fool—the prison or Marie Collins? Because she referred to him as 'Jake' to her cellmate. Which doesn't mean anything, I guess. She could have been playing along and covering for him."

"If Fake Jake is an ex-con, that would explain him using someone else's identity. Felons can't visit inmates unless they get prior written permission, and then it's generally only granted for family members. Also, if he had any outstanding warrants against him, he wouldn't have wanted to risk using his own name."

I thought for a moment. "I guess it might be easier to impersonate someone with a lot of hair and a bushy beard. This guy's facial features kind of got lost in all his unkemptness."

Vic nodded as he unlocked his vehicle. "A wig and fake beard surely wouldn't have flown with the prison staff. It would have been a serious commitment to grow the hair and beard required to pull it off, but it could be done. Speaking of prison staff, I'm going to send a couple of photos I took of this Jake to Sabrina Alexander and ask if she remembers any differences to whoever she saw in person." He sent a quick text.

I didn't like what we'd learned at this stop. The Jake Sampson impersonator could have been any man in the world, and we had no real place to start looking other than Indianapolis two years ago, which was no help.

I frowned. "This guy—if he's who killed Marie Collins—was in it for the long haul. He'd been courting her for two years and had been risking getting caught with a fake ID by the prison staff on a monthly basis. It was important to him to play this out. Turn on your profiler brain and figure out why."

"Yes, ma'am."

∼

I TOOK over driving to our next stop in Bloomington so Vic could spend the time starting to profile Fake Jake and researching Tiffany Clarke's whereabouts on his laptop. She lived in Berea, Kentucky, a three-hour drive southeast of Boonville. We didn't have time to add that to our trip today, so she would have to wait. I knew, given the volatility of her relationship with Marie Collins, that neither Vic nor Baxter would want to interview her over the phone or over video chat. One of them would be making the trip.

When we got to the Bloomington address listed on Rosaline Suarez's driver's license, an older woman answered the door to the apartment. She informed us she'd moved in last month, which meant Rosaline hadn't gotten around to updating her new address at the BMV.

His expression stuck in a frown, Vic got back into his car and got out his laptop. Something was bugging him, but he'd yet to voice it. While he worked, I checked for a reply from Baxter. It was nearing dinnertime and he still hadn't responded to my voice mail or my text, which wasn't like him . . . unless things weren't going well, which I couldn't imagine they were.

Vic finally said, "Just as I suspected. Rosaline Suarez has a couple of old misdemeanors—petty theft and disorderly conduct. And she didn't bother changing her address with the USPS, either."

"What made you suspect all that?" I asked.

"The fact that I assumed she was friends with our victim since she called and visited her in prison."

"Oh. Profile much?"

He snickered. "Like it's my job. Plus she's from Bloomington, where Shawn was held, so that was a red flag for me from the start."

A thought struck me. "Wait. If this lady is a friend of Marie Collins and is from Bloomington and is kind of sketchy . . . she might have helped her out while she held Shawn."

"It's very possible."

"Shawn remembers a woman named Rita who would bring him toys. Baxter said the police followed up on several Ritas in the area, but none of them could be connected to Marie Collins at the time."

"You think Rosaline is Rita?"

"I mean, worth a shot, right? We could show her photo to Shawn and see what he thinks."

Vic nodded and got out his phone. He texted Rosaline Suarez's photo to Baxter along with a short message. "She's a dead end for now because it'll require some digging to track her down. I'm thinking she may not want to be found at the moment. But if Shawn can ID her, that'll make her pretty important to find." Closing his laptop, he asked, "What's next?"

For a much-needed mental break, I made Vic go with me to the Bloomington Walmart to buy an outfit to wear to try to pick up Baxter's uncle. Vic had finally gotten on board with my plan, but informed me I'd have to play by his set of rules. For all my bravado, the thought of flirting with Baxter's uncle bothered me, which I assumed Vic sensed, because he kept me laughing as he suggested one terrible piece of clothing after another. We finally settled on a denim miniskirt and a fairly pretty tank top with ruffled straps—an ensemble that was cheap and revealing enough to pick up a sleazebag but cute enough that I didn't look like a common whore. Vic made a purchase for himself as well. Hoping to blend in with the regulars at the bar enough that he could sit near me and listen to my conversation with Uncle Benji, Vic picked out a plaid flannel shirt and a trucker hat to wear. He then insisted we get something to eat, pointing out that I seemed "hangry" again and that he didn't want to be cooped up in a vehicle with a ticking time bomb for two more hours.

After we ate a quick dinner, I continued driving to allow Vic to keep doing his thing. The trip back to Boonville gave me some time to think about the different puzzle pieces we'd unearthed today. We'd learned a lot, but the problem was that none of the pieces were fitting together. I felt like every new bit of information we'd gleaned opened up exponentially more questions. From the moment I'd found out Marie Collins had a boyfriend, he was who my money had been on as her murderer. But now I hoped I was wrong, because finding Fake Jake sounded like an impossible task.

As we were approaching town, Vic looked over at me. "You okay? I don't think I've ever heard you be quiet this long."

I frowned. "I'm concerned about Fake Jake being a ghost. This has gotten way more complicated than I imagined it would be."

Grinning, he replied, "Good thing you have me around. I researched the PO box address from his prison letters. It's rented to a Samuel Wiggins, who bears a striking resemblance to Jake Sampson. Take a look." He held out his phone so I could flick my eyes toward it for a moment and still keep my attention on the road.

The two men looked a lot alike: beard, long dark hair, skinnyish. "I could be fooled into thinking they're the same guy."

"Their height and weight are similar as well. I sent it to Sabrina Alexander for her to take a look."

Hope bubbling up inside me, I relaxed a bit and smiled. "So you figured out Fake Jake's real identity that easily? I guess it *is* a good thing we have you around."

Vic chuckled. "Considering all the hoops he jumped through to impersonate Jake Sampson to get into prison to visit Marie Collins, I'm going to go out on a limb and say he didn't get sloppy and blow his real identity with a return address."

My smile, as well as my hope, faded. "Oh. Fair point." Because why could something have been easy for once? "So who's Samuel Wiggins? Another unsuspecting victim of identity theft or an accomplice?"

"I'm going to say identity theft considering he filed a police report four years ago for that very crime."

Any lingering hope I had was erased. "Our guy isn't a ghost. He's a shape-shifter."

He nodded. "You got it."

I groaned. "That is so much worse."

～

Vic dropped me at the Baxter farm and went back to his Airbnb to change for tonight's festivities.

The moment I entered the front door, Mrs. Baxter's voice slurred, "I didn't expect to see you again after you ran off with your boyfriend this morning."

I briefly considered defending myself, but it would have been breath wasted. She was drunk as hell and clearly in pain. She was sprawled out on the couch alone, her eyes glazed and struggling to focus on me. A bottle of gin sat on the coffee table in front of her, no glass in sight. Remembering the times when I, too, couldn't be bothered to waste the time or effort on a glass, I considered cutting her some slack. But that wouldn't help her. What she needed was tough love.

I replied, "I know you've had a hard day. Can I bring you a glass of water? Or maybe something to eat? You need something to soak up and dissipate all that gin."

"I don't need your help, and don't touch my gin," she muttered as her eyes fluttered closed.

"You may not want my help, but you're getting it. Your drinking is out of hand."

Her eyes flew open, flashing. "How dare you say that to me?"

"Because I care about your son, so that means I care about you. I've been where you are, and your son is the one who called me out on it. It's pretty clear to me that every man in this house is too scared of you to call you out. I'm not."

It took her a couple of tries, but she hoisted herself into a sitting position. "Get out of my house," she growled.

"I will if you let me take you to an AA meeting."

Her shoulders began swaying and she muttered something incoherent as she collapsed back onto the couch, passed out.

I grabbed the bottle of gin and buried it in the kitchen trash can. I bet she had another bottle stashed somewhere, but at least she'd have to sober up enough to get off the couch to retrieve it. Not exactly the full intervention she needed, but anything to keep her from getting blackout drunk tonight was better than nothing. I then headed for Baxter's room. I found him at the desk, hunched over his computer. When he looked up at me, his haggard face broke into the sweetest smile. He stood and swept me into his arms, holding me tight, his welcome more than making up for the one I'd just received.

I relaxed for the first time all day and leaned into him. "I missed you. How did everything go with Tom? Is it a hold or is he really arrested?"

"I missed you, too," he said, not letting go. "The next time I decide to overstep and tell you what to do, please punch me."

"What?" I asked, pulling back so I could look up at him.

"I made a huge mistake insisting you leave today. You were right—I needed you. Call me selfish, but I spent a lot of time wishing you'd wasted your entire day coddling me."

I reached up and cradled his cheek with my hand. "I'm sorry you had such a rough time. Is Tom hanging in there?"

"I'm supposed to be the one apologizing here."

He'd ignored a second question about Tom. I didn't call him on it, hoping he'd eventually spill it. "And I was getting ready to tell you I'm happy you pushed me out the door, because Vic and I uncovered a lot of crazy stuff. I really think we're on to something."

He sighed. "Thank you. I want to hear all about it. But while I'm apologizing, I'm sorry I didn't get back to you. And I apologize on Shawn's behalf, too, because I only texted him that photo Manetti sent me a few minutes ago. It wasn't a good day. We spent until mid-afternoon at the station, and then I ended up taking care of Olivia because Janelle had a panic attack followed by a migraine and the rest of my family flaked on her."

"Again, no apology necessary." I gave him a pointed look. "And it's also not necessary for you to keep evading my questions about Tom. I can tell something's off. What's up?"

Baxter's face fell. "He's arrested."

My heart sank. "Oh no. What do they have on him?"

"His prints are on the axe." His voice broke on the last word, and I drew him to me.

This was bad. And as much as I didn't want to push Baxter to have to dwell on the topic, my criminalist brain needed more information. I let him go but kept hold of his hands. "Where on the axe? Swinging position or a random position?"

"His lawyer was told there was a good print and some smudged prints in . . . swinging position. And then there were random prints and partials in other locations as well."

I frowned and released his hands so I could pace the room and detach myself from the emotional part of this issue. "I was worried the killer had used gloves or wiped the handle. Gloves would account for there being a bunch of smudged prints and only the one good print of Tom's in the proper position." Shaking my head, I added, "I don't suppose they would tell Tom's lawyer if they'd found prints belonging to anyone else."

Baxter said quietly, "They did. Um . . . my dad's prints are on the axe, too."

I shrugged, staring out the window as I tried to create a mental image of the axe and the possible placement of all the fingerprints. "Of course they are. It's his axe."

"That's evidently enough to hold him for conspiracy around here."

I whirled around. "What?"

He nodded, a tear escaping one eye. "Dad's in jail, too."

I rushed over to console him once again, feeling more helpless than I had in a long time. No wonder his mother was drinking herself into oblivion out there. I feared I might have been right there next to her had the same fate befallen my Baxter today. I also feared this last straw could be more than he was able to handle.

I steered him toward his bed and sat him down, then kneeled in front of him to keep his attention on me. "I know this feels impossible and you're overwhelmed, but I'm not giving up until we have them both exonerated. Neither will Vic. You do whatever you need to do to stay sane and leave the rest to us."

He said sadly, "I can't sit by and watch you guys do the work for me. This is my fight."

"It's *our* fight, Nick."

"You don't have to stay. Especially not now. You could go home . . . back to your life."

I took his face in my hands. "My life is right here. I'm not going anywhere." I glanced at the clock at his bedside. "Except right now I'm going to a bar to flirt with your uncle."

I tried to stand, but he grasped my hands. "The hell you are."

I said evenly, "Name one person you know who can talk to your uncle and find out what he was doing the night of the murder."

Baxter shook his head. "I can't name a single person, and that includes you."

"Wrong. He doesn't know me."

"I'm not putting you in that situation. He's dangerous."

"That's why I'm going to play the part of a new-to-town loser looking for love while he's getting liquored up at his favorite bar. He's not going to hurt a flirty thirty-something."

"You'd be surprised."

I shrugged. "Well then he's not going to run the risk of hurting a woman somewhere he goes every night. I can't imagine he would risk getting banned."

"How do you know where he goes every night?"

"Vic talked to your mom."

His expression darkened. "I don't like this."

"You never like it when I'm undercover."

"Especially in this instance because I can't show my face in that bar without blowing your cover. I'm going to have to wait outside helplessly and hope you don't start a bar brawl."

I smiled. "Like I would do that."

"I've seen you do that."

Waving a hand, I joked, "It was one time. Besides, Vic is going with me, and he'll be posing as a good ol' boy. He bought a trucker hat and everything."

Baxter frowned. "Fine, but I'm sitting outside and listening in. We'll rig up something with our phones."

I pointed out, "If we're doing the listening via phone, you could do it from here."

"What if you need backup?"

"That's what Vic's for."

"He's still not at one hundred percent, so I'm going."

Truth be told, as much as I trusted Vic and could count on him in any situation, having Baxter there put any fears I had to rest.

20

While I curled my hair, I filled Baxter in on what we'd learned today. I also popped some more Advil. Even though I was trying to be gentle with myself, the little bit of tugging I did on my hair had my whole head throbbing.

As I was considering whether to pull my hair back from my face or leave it loose, I said, "I hate to ask this, but . . . is there a certain type of look that would get your uncle's attention? Should I overdo the big hair and makeup to make myself look older and rode hard, or would he . . ." I hesitated as I felt a gag coming on. "Would he connect more with a fresh-faced girl-next-door type?"

Baxter winced. "I guess go for the first one. According to Mom, he's not above paying for women's company, if you get my meaning."

My eyebrows shot up.

He added, "But that's probably her being a judgmental sister. I'm assuming the people in his circle are like him—addicts, ex-cons, and others who are down on their luck."

"Got it." I sat down at the desk and started applying makeup with a heavy hand. "I know you'd said he went off the rails when Shawn went missing, but was your uncle always kind of a bad dude? Why did your parents think he'd taken Shawn? I didn't press you before, but I kind of need to know now."

Baxter explained sadly, "Uncle Benji was the best. He was our favorite family member. Always the fun guy. He and my aunt never had kids, so they doted on us. He was absolutely over the moon when he found out Shawn was on the way. Tom and I were teenagers, so we didn't have as much time to hang around with him anymore. Shawn was his little buddy. He watched Shawn on his days off and often picked him up from preschool." He paused so long I thought the story was over.

I asked, "Did your parents mistake his affection for something else . . . like envy?"

"No, it wasn't that. When I said he was the fun uncle, it was because he used to be a free spirit. He'd try anything, and he'd let us do anything. He'd come get Tom and me early from school or from sports practice and take us fishing or out for ice cream. My parents—especially my dad, being a teacher and a coach—didn't approve of us ditching class and practice. Worse, Uncle Benji never cleared it with them ahead of time, mostly because he knew they'd say no. They'd get pissed when they came to pick us up and we were already gone."

"I get it. Rachel would come unglued if I did that with Nate."

Baxter nodded in agreement. "He started pulling that same stunt with Shawn, and my parents finally put their foot down. My uncle didn't understand why they made such a deal out of it, and he was really hurt when they took his name off the list of people who were allowed to pick up Shawn at his preschool."

I said, "He considered it a slap in the face."

"Exactly. And it happened the day Shawn turned up missing at the football game."

My heart sank. "Terrible timing."

"The worst. When Shawn's babysitter admitted to my mom that night at the game that she couldn't find him, the first thing my mom did was call my uncle and tear him a new asshole. When my uncle swore he hadn't picked up Shawn, that was when my parents realized the situation was serious and called the police."

"Wait, so your uncle is still butthurt because they accused him of doing something he did on a regular basis?"

He shook his head. "It gets worse. Uncle Benji really took it hard that Shawn was missing. Personally, I think he was afraid Shawn was dead. He'd take off for hours, sometimes days at a time, and not tell my aunt where he was going. He'd call my parents at all hours, drunk, muttering gibberish about Shawn. Finally he said something coherent enough that made them worry he'd actually done something to him. My parents told the investigator on the case, and he picked up my uncle and held him for a few days. Once my uncle sobered up, he was able to explain that he'd been out searching for Shawn himself because he didn't think the organized civilian searches were getting the job done. He'd gone around threatening people and beating information out of others. The cops were able to track his movements and decided he was telling the truth and wasn't holding Shawn anywhere. And of course they couldn't charge him with murder because there'd been no body found. But it was too late to repair the damage to the relationship between my parents and my uncle. To make matters worse, my aunt sided with us. She'd had a front-row seat to my uncle's meltdown and truly believed he'd lost it and hurt Shawn." He sighed. "My uncle blamed us for everything. It didn't even help his mental state when Shawn was found. He became a raging alcoholic and has spent a considerable amount of time in jail for various assault charges. It's incredibly sad, and my family lives in fear because of it."

I frowned. "If it's common knowledge—or at least police knowledge—that your uncle went vigilante to try to find Shawn and later spiraled into a life of alcohol-fueled crime, why have the detectives not taken a look at him in this case?"

"We don't know that they haven't. I really hate investigating from the other side and not knowing what the detectives are doing behind the scenes. I would never want to be a PI." He added quietly, "Although if this case drags on for much longer, it might be my only option."

Hoping to pull us both out of the dark mood that filled the room, I waved a hand and joked, "Don't hang your shingle just yet. I'm living proof that Jayne's firings don't stick. She already fired me once this year."

Not cracking even a ghost of a smile, he said, "That joke doesn't get funnier the more times you tell it."

Ignoring his jab, I said, "We're going to figure this out." I stood, happy that my borderline ridiculous makeup job completely covered my black eye. "Now drive me to the bar so I can cupcake your uncle."

He looked ill. "I didn't think this day could get worse, but I think it's about to."

～

As BARS WENT, The Depot wasn't one I would ever have frequented. Even as a practicing alcoholic, I'd had standards. The place was grimy and smelly, and my shoes stuck to the floor as I walked. In fact, it reminded me a lot of the last bar where I'd done an undercover op, which was the one where I'd incited the bar brawl. Surely I wouldn't repeat history here.

Vic was already in place, seated at the bar a few seats to the right of a man in his fifties. He caught my eye and gave a slight nod in the man's direction. Luckily, the bar wasn't terribly crowded, and there were empty seats on the man's left. I left a seat in between myself and Uncle Benji and hoisted myself onto the barstool with a sigh. Uncle Benji looked over, as I'd hoped he would, and I glanced his way for a moment to flash him a sad smile.

But when I laid my eyes on him, I had to use every bit of willpower I had not to stare. I set my purse on the bar top and practically buried my head in it, pretending to hunt for something. It was part of my evil plan anyway, but I needed a minute to settle the hell down. When I'd initially met Baxter's parents, I'd noticed the resemblance between Baxter and his father rather than his mother. He'd gotten his eyes, sense of humor, and kind demeanor from his dad. However, everything else had clearly come from his mom's side. Uncle Benji was Baxter, just twenty years older and rougher around the edges. To put it bluntly, Uncle Benji was smoking hot.

I snapped back to reality when Baxter's voice in my AirPod said, "Did you find him yet? Remember I said you'd note the family resemblance."

Understatement of the year. The music was loud enough I could turn my head and say "yes" without Uncle Benji or the bartender hearing me.

"Okay, good luck."

I was going to need it. Loud enough that Uncle Benji could hear me, I let out a sigh and huffed, "Son of a bitch." I plucked a crumpled five and a dollar out of my purse and slammed them on the bar.

Uncle Benji looked over at me but didn't say anything.

The bartender walked over and leaned toward me over the bar. "You okay, miss?"

I sighed again. "It depends on how much liquor six bucks will buy me."

"Tonight it'll get you the Monday special: two well drinks."

The way I got around consuming alcohol while pretending to drink was by pouring it on the floor or even on my clothing while no one was looking. Well drinks were a no-go. I couldn't hide that much liquid.

I replied, "Well drinks are a waste of time. How many shots will it get me?"

The bartender tipped his ball cap at me. "A lady who doesn't mess around. Six bucks will get you two shots."

"Two shots is not enough to make me forget how my asshole ex-boyfriend stole my wallet as I was kicking his sorry ass out of my house today."

"Does that mean you don't have ID?"

Shit. Didn't think about that. It had been a while since I bought a drink. In fact, the last time I'd done so was when Baxter sprang his life-changing intervention on me. I smiled at the thought, but quickly returned my attention to the bartender.

I huffed out a laugh. "Come on. I'm flattered, but I'm clearly in my thirties."

Shrugging, the bartender replied, "I can't know that for sure without ID."

Uncle Benji piped up, "Aww, come on, Charlie. The lady's had a rough day. Besides, I haven't seen you card anyone in months."

Charlie shot him a look. "Because I grew up with everyone in here and know exactly how old they are. Her, I don't know."

I could feel Vic eyeing me, but I didn't dare look at him. Plus I was busy whipping up some tears to try to tug at the unwavering bartender's heartstrings.

Taking in a hitching breath, I said, "It's okay. You're just doing your job. I'll . . . I'll just go home—" I broke my voice and looked down. "You know, it's a lot harder than I imagined to start over in a new town. Maybe I should have picked a bigger city where . . . I wouldn't feel like such an outsider." I sniffed and wiped at my eyes.

Charlie was unmoved by my show of fake emotion. I was impressed by his bullshit meter. He could do well in law enforcement. I had one shot to get Uncle Benji's attention. I closed my fist around the two bills in front of me and slid off the barstool. I sidled up to Uncle Benji and put my hand on his arm. At my touch, he smiled that same sweet smile his nephew used to melt my heart.

I removed my hand from his arm and cleared my throat. "Thanks for going to bat for me. At least now I know one nice person in this town. I'm Ellen, by the way."

"Benji. Good to meet you, Ellen." He slowly looked me up and down—something his nephew did *not* do—and murmured, "You need someone to talk to?"

I broke into a smile. "More than anything."

"Let's find a quiet place."

Baxter, who'd been silent for a while, said, "Do *not* leave with him. I want you in Manetti's sight."

When I'd arrived, I'd scouted out the room and found a couple of empty booths in Vic's line of sight. It was always my plan to get Uncle Benji to move to one of those booths so we could have an unobstructed conversation. It was especially necessary now that I seemed to be on the bartender's radar. From his vantage point, I needed to be nothing more than a lonely woman trying to pick up a random guy in a bar. Him hearing me trying to pump Uncle Benji for information would give him a real reason to suspect me of something.

Once we slid into the booth across from each other, Uncle Benji offered me his drink. "You need this more than me."

Out of the corner of my eye, I saw Vic's posture straighten up. He was probably as worried about my mental health and sobriety as my physical safety. I hadn't been worried until now, having felt relief that the bartender refused me service even though I'd had to switch tactics as a result. It didn't dawn on me that Uncle Benji would try to slip me something while Charlie wasn't looking. I had to pivot fast.

I smiled. "I appreciate it, but full disclosure . . ." I stopped to heave out a sigh. "I'm an alcoholic. And I'm trying so hard to make a fresh start—sober —and . . . I don't know what I was thinking coming here. I mean, I *do* know what I was thinking, and it was pure self-destruction. I think getting denied service was a sign from the universe that I need to stay on the wagon and work on getting my life back on track. I'm a hot mess when I drink, and I get myself into lots of trouble. Right now, I can't afford a lawyer to get me out of another assault charge."

He frowned at the drink in his hand. "I feel you. I've been on and off the wagon myself, and I'm no stranger to assault charges."

I leaned toward him, sliding a hand across the table to be within his reach. "You seem very sweet. I can't imagine you assaulting anyone."

Smiling, he leaned toward me as well. "I could say the same thing to you. I'm sure whoever you assaulted had it coming."

Looking down, I said quietly, "Actually, no. I took my anger out on an innocent person. A girl snapped at me for spilling my drink on her in a bar and I clocked her. Knocked her front tooth right out onto the floor."

He winced. "Ouch."

"It was very unsatisfying to take my anger out on the wrong person. And harder to beat the charges, but I got lucky. How about you? Did you manage to beat your charges?"

Taking a drink, he said, "I didn't. I'm not that lucky."

"Oh, sorry. How long was your sentence?"

"Sentences. I've been in the joint more than once."

I shook my head. "Yeah, once you have a record, they don't show you much mercy. That's why I don't want to repeat past mistakes. Next time they won't go easy on me." I shrugged and started spinning a story, hoping Uncle Benji was drunk enough to buy into it. "But maybe I can keep my anger in check now that my sister has learned her lesson not to get mixed up with another psychopath who thinks it's fun to tie up his girlfriend for days at a time and refuse her access to her phone."

It sounded dumb when I said it out loud, but Uncle Benji bought it. His eyes bulged out. "Your sister was held captive?"

"Multiple times. She kept going back to the guy."

"Did you tell the police?"

"I tried. They'd go question her and she'd deny it every time. His family has influence in town, so I'm the one who'd get in trouble with the cops for making false accusations." I sighed. "I probably should have quit worrying about her if she wouldn't worry about herself, but I couldn't. The only way I could sleep at night was to get blackout drunk."

He covered my hand with his. "It's not easy trying to watch out for family when they don't seem to want it."

Bingo. I could hear Baxter's breathing get louder in my ear. He wouldn't take this well, but I needed Uncle Benji to spill as much of his story as I could.

"Right? I mean, why can't people see how wrong they are sometimes? I know when I'm being a screwup. Not that I don't sometimes decide to lean into it, but my sister seems totally in the dark that she makes terrible decisions. And . . . the more I try to help her, the more she turns on me."

Shaking his head sadly, he replied, "Sisters can be real shitty sometimes."

"Ah. Spoken by someone with a shitty sister." I heard a grunt from Baxter, but he didn't make a comment. I pressed on, "What's your sister's problem?"

His grip tightened slightly on my hand. "She sits in a glass house and throws stones." He wasn't wrong in his assessment.

I nodded. "Yeah, that sucks. I, um . . . I wasn't fully truthful about the main reason I moved here. Sure, I needed a fresh start, but . . . what really drove me away was that my sister shut me out of her life. Worst of all, that means I'm not allowed to see my nephew anymore." I got out my phone and scrolled to a selfie I'd taken of my nephew and myself a few weeks ago and showed it to Uncle Benji. "His name's Nate, and he was my world." I let my voice crack again and tried to imagine what it would have been like to actually lose Nate like "Ellen" had. "His birthday is coming up. He'll be four, and I'm going to miss it."

Damned if an actual tear didn't escape and run down my face. Being barred from seeing Nate was a devastating thought even though I knew Rachel would never do that to me. At that moment I had a major flood of sympathy for Uncle Benji for losing Shawn like he had. Months after the abduction, when Shawn was reunited with his family, Uncle Benji was already out of the picture. After that, he probably only saw Shawn by chance around town. I didn't blame him for turning to alcohol to numb that type of pain. I'd done it over far less heartache than he'd had to endure.

He gripped my hand with both of his. "Never stop fighting for that kid, Ellen. Just because his mom won't let you see him doesn't mean you give up and leave him. You need to move back home and look out for him. It doesn't sound like his mom is strong enough to get the job done."

Was he speaking from experience, and did he still think he was protecting Shawn? A chill crawled up my spine.

I furrowed my brow. "But what can I do? She won't let me anywhere near him."

"Watch them. If she takes him to the park, be there and make sure she's paying attention and not letting him run off. Drive by their house every night and make sure she's not inviting over the wrong kind of company."

"What you're describing is called stalking, and it's a crime."

He frowned. "What's more important? The law or your nephew?"

Spoken like the Uncle Benji I'd heard so much about. "My nephew, of course. But if I do see something I think shouldn't be happening, how do I intervene without my sister knowing I'm stalking her?"

"Call CPS on her ass."

Baxter griped in my ear, "That explains a few things."

I wasn't quite sure what Baxter meant by that, so I asked Uncle Benji, "Can I call CPS for her generally being a shitty mom or does it have to be textbook abuse?"

The corner of his mouth pulling into a grin, he replied, "Well, if you do an anonymous tip right, it doesn't really matter, now, does it?"

That definitely explained a few things about his relationship with Mr. and Mrs. Baxter.

Shaking my head, I said uneasily, "Hey, I was in the system for a while, and it sucked. I wouldn't wish that on my nephew even if my sister wasn't at her best. What else you got?"

"Well, if you see someone doing something to him you don't like, you take care of it."

Another chill gripped me, and Baxter said, "I don't like this, Ellie. I'm texting Manetti."

I blurted out, "Wait."

Uncle Benji gave me an odd look.

I went on, "Uh . . . I mean, are you saying if some little kid picks on him at the park that I should go slug the kid or something?"

Uncle Benji chuckled. "No, he needs to learn how to handle dealing with other kids himself. I'm talking about adults—your sister's friends or boyfriends, teachers, and other kids' parents. Even random strangers who might want to do him harm. You never know who's a wacko out there."

Baxter muttered, "Yeah, you never know."

I said, "That sounds like a full-time job."

Uncle Benji shrugged. "Once they're in school there's not much for you to do during the day. Besides, I assume you don't have kids of your own if your nephew is your whole world."

"That's true."

"So you probably have a lot more free time than most adults. Or at least you have the time if you want to spend it doing your duty to protect your nephew."

Damn. Uncle Benji was kind of preachy.

I smiled. "Sounds like you're pretty adamant about this. Is it from experience?"

"Of course. I've looked out for my youngest nephew his whole life." He hung his head. "Except for . . ." He looked up and shook his head. "Never mind. The answer is yes. He's nineteen and I'm still looking out for him. Like you, I'm not allowed near my nephew, but I still manage to keep him safe."

Baxter said, "That sounded a lot like a confession. I'm texting Manetti to pull the plug."

I couldn't risk blurting out my reply again. But I could distract Uncle Benji for a second. "Do you have a photo of him?"

Uncle Benji nodded and pulled out his phone. While his attention was on the screen, I looked over at Vic and shook my head slightly. Vic raised his eyebrows at me, and I shook my head again. He broke our gaze and took out his phone. Hoping Vic understood my plea, I returned my attention to Uncle Benji as he turned his screen toward me and showed me a fairly new photo of Shawn.

He said with a smile, "This is Shawn. I love this kid. He's had a tough time, and I wish there was more I could do to make life easier on him." He put his phone back in his pocket and said with an air of sadness, "I do what I can."

Again, not exactly a confession. He didn't appear to be taking any kind of credit for ridding the world of Shawn's nemesis. And he didn't seem nervous in any way that our discussion was veering toward the topic of a woman he'd murdered. I didn't get the feeling he was trying to hide anything, but I still hadn't been able to get quite close enough to ask a question that would make him flinch.

Out of the corner of my eye, I noticed Vic settling up with the bartender. Damn. Evidently he'd taken Baxter's side on this one. I had mere minutes to get something we could use.

I said, "You know, what you've said has given me a lot to think about. I appreciate you being so open with me, someone you just met. I'm thinking that sucking it up and moving back home is looking like the right choice."

Uncle Benji took my hand again and nodded. His expression suddenly changed to one I recognized on Baxter. "Before you leave—"

I knew exactly where this was going and butted in to change the subject. I went on like I didn't hear his interjection. "Especially since this town seems to be way more dangerous than I ever imagined it would be. Did you hear that a woman was murdered yesterday? I think she was new to town or back in town or something? It makes me nervous about my own safety here. Do you think I should take any extra precautions?"

Shaking his head, he grumbled, "You'll be fine. That woman had it coming."

Again, not even close to a confession, but evidently enough of one for Baxter. He snapped, "Ellie, get out of there. Now."

I saw Vic coming my way and knew I wasn't going to be able to stall this thing any longer. To leave things well enough to have another shot at speaking to him in the future, I squeezed Uncle Benji's hand and said, "Hey, thanks for talking to me tonight . . . and for not hitting on me. I needed a friend and some good advice." I slid out of the booth. Before I turned to go, I added, "I hope you can patch things up with your nephew," and meant it.

21

After hopping into Vic's vehicle to give him a quick rundown of my conversation with Uncle Benji and thank him for his bodyguarding, I got into my car, where Baxter was sitting there fuming.

I huffed. "Would you settle down? I didn't go to a second location with our mark, and I didn't cause a bar fight. You should be happy. I did nothing stupid this time."

Baxter's frown deepened. "You disregarded multiple requests to get the hell out of there."

"Because I'd yet to get any useful information out of your uncle. I'd call this op a bust because you forced me out too soon."

"He practically told you he killed Marie Collins. What more did you want?"

I stared at him. "Were you listening to the same conversation I was? He absolutely did not confess to anything besides stalking your brother and calling CPS on your parents."

"He said enough to make him our prime suspect."

"He said enough to piss you off real good and put your blinders on."

His expression darkened even more. "Why are you defending him?"

"I'm not defending him. I'm saying his demeanor was not consistent with having cracked his nemesis's head open in the last forty-eight hours. He wasn't sitting there twirling his mustache when he told me how he watched out for Shawn. He mostly seemed sad. The murdery vibe I got from him was lukewarm at best."

"Because you allowed yourself to connect with him and bought his bullshit."

"That man would do anything for your brother."

"You're right. Anything. Including murder."

Maybe Baxter had a point. Maybe I was so blinded by Uncle Benji's love for Shawn and his motivation to protect him that I wasn't willing to consider him a viable suspect. If he had in fact killed Marie Collins believing his actions were fully justified, it wouldn't warrant him being overly emotional about having done the deed. I thought I'd read him right, but I didn't know the man. Baxter did. And even though they were family, he still believed his uncle could be a killer.

Baxter must have realized my dilemma, because he reached over and took my hand. "Hey, I'm sorry I snapped at you. We're conditioned to think of our suspects as bad people, and most of the time they are. When they're good people who do bad things acting out of love, it's hard to want to see them punished for it. And even though for the first time I could not care less if a victim gets justice for her death, it still isn't fair for two innocent men to go down for someone else's crime."

I slumped in my seat. "I know. This would be so much easier if Marie Collins hadn't been such a piece of shit."

"If only." He let go of my hand to caress my cheek. "You look exhausted. Let's get you some rest."

～

THE NEXT MORNING, after Mrs. Baxter angrily accused both of her sons and me of swiping her alcohol for our own use, Baxter and I went to Vic's Airbnb to go over our game plan for the investigation. I'd had a lengthy conversation with Baxter the previous night to bring him up to speed on everything Vic and I had uncovered on our trip to Rockville and all the stops on the way back so we could hit the ground running this morning. Vic's Airbnb was a lovely loft above one of the many shops circling the quaint town square. When we entered the bright, high-ceilinged living room of the apartment, I saw he'd brought along a whiteboard.

"You nerd," I said, walking over to admire the notes he'd already made alongside several photos of potential suspects and persons of interest he'd printed out and taped to the board.

Vic snorted. "I'm the nerd? You, my friend, used your evil science powers to vandalize a crime scene, or so I hear. Twice." He thought for a moment. "Wait, no. Thrice."

I shot a look at Baxter, who shrugged and said, "No part of that statement is inaccurate."

Not wanting to revisit this with either of them, I said, "Maybe we should get to work." I then caught Vic staring at me and demanded, "What?"

He said, "Your eye. It's pretty nasty today. Significantly darker."

I snapped, "Is it, Dr. Manetti? I hadn't noticed."

Hands raised in a gesture of surrender, Vic took an armchair and gestured for Baxter and me to sit on the small couch.

Baxter said, "First, I wanted to let you know Shawn finally got back to me about the woman you wanted him to ID. Rosaline Suarez is the woman he remembers as 'Rita.' "

I blew out a breath. I'd seen Baxter pull his little brother aside for a serious conversation this morning before we left, but he hadn't shared with me what it had been about. "That's great. Once we find her, she's going to be looking at some jail time for conspiracy and obstruction."

"Yeah, she is," Baxter said, probably a little louder than he intended to. He didn't seem to be happy about this new information. It was always disconcerting to find out about people covering up crimes, but this one was particularly vile.

Vic said, "I'll work on locating her today. Speaking of positive IDs, I wanted to tell you I got a text back from Sabrina Alexander last night. I sent her a photo of the Jake Sampson we met and also the photo of Samuel Wiggins. She said the man who visited Marie Collins resembled both men but definitely wasn't either of them. She said Fake Jake was younger, had significantly shorter hair and beard length, and was far more attractive than both of them. She remembered that because she didn't understand how Marie Collins had managed to land someone so far out of her league."

"So if we actually manage to figure out this guy's real identity, she should be able to positively ID him for us?" I said.

"Yes."

Baxter said, "Except you've hit a dead end with that, right? He stole two identities in Indy and that's all you have on him."

Vic shrugged. "As of now, yes. I called in another favor to the warden to get the IP address from the emails he'd sent to Marie Collins. Unfortunately, all we know is that it's from Louisville, Kentucky, but that doesn't mean Fake Jake sent the emails from there. It only means his Internet service provider has a router located in Louisville assigning IP addresses to its customers. Another dead end, but it would have been lazy to not pursue it."

Frowning, Baxter said, "I think we should shift our focus to Benji McDonald."

I didn't agree, but I kept my mouth shut and hoped Vic had been mulling over his opinion of Uncle Benji as the killer.

He had. "I agree your uncle should be on our radar. If you want, I can run point on looking into him and you two can keep grinding on what we learned yesterday." I was touched by his diplomacy, acknowledging Baxter's hunch while making sure we didn't put all our investigative eggs in one basket.

Baxter nodded. "That's a good plan. I have to admit, I'm really stumbling on this investigation. I think a big part of my problem is that we're missing the time line for Marie Collins's movements between the time she left her sister's house until her death. I think that should narrow down our interview pool significantly. If she stayed in Boonville to celebrate her release and bar-hopped her way through town, there aren't many places she could have gone. There are only four bars. If we can find out who she interacted with, we might learn all we need to know."

I knew what he was getting at—Uncle Benji was a regular at the bar we visited last night, and it was the cheapest and seediest one in town. It stood to reason that Marie Collins, having had no revenue stream for fifteen years, couldn't afford much of a night on the town and would have found a place she could get more drunk for less money. If she happened to run into Uncle Benji, I imagined a fight would ensue. And that would make him a great suspect in her death. However, wouldn't the detectives have already looked into that angle? We would have in a normal investigation. I had to admit as well that this case had me turned around and not following the usual succession of investigative tasks. Plus we didn't have the luxury of Jayne coordinating the investigation, a team of several other brilliant minds working alongside us, and access to practically any information we needed. I agreed with Baxter's assertion that it would be no fun to be a PI.

Vic said, "About that, I went back into the bar last night and spoke to the bartender. He said he didn't see anyone fitting Marie Collins's description in there on Saturday night."

"Well, crap." I frowned as I watched Baxter visibly deflate over this news. "What now?"

Vic said, "We keep going. Aside from deep diving into Benji McDonald's life and getting ourselves a time line leading up to the murder, we need to make a couple of trips. We've got Muddy, Illinois, to meet Marie Collins's ex, John Kocher, and friend, Emily Anders, and Berea, Kentucky, to meet her former cellmate-slash-enemy Tiffany Clarke. They're in different directions, so I thought we could split them—"

My phone started buzzing. "Sorry. Hang on a sec." When I got it out, I saw I was getting a FaceTime call from Corinne Barnes.

My face must have registered some sort of panic, because Baxter asked, "What's wrong?"

I murmured, "Ooh . . . it's Barnes."

At the same time, Vic said, "Answer it," and Baxter said, "Don't answer it."

I had an idea. I ordered Baxter, "Make yourself scarce." His response was a nervous frown, and while he was leaving the room I turned to Vic. "You up for some improv?"

Vic's eyebrows shot up. "Why do I feel like this is a bad idea?"

"Because it could so easily go wrong and bite me in the ass."

I hurried over to Vic's chair and plopped myself down on his lap as I answered the call with a smile. "Good morning, Detective! How did you sleep last night? I hope you weren't awake worrying about how much emotional damage you've caused, especially to a new mom, a baby, and a teenage boy already struggling with his mental health."

Barnes's pretty face twisted into a smirk. "I hope *you* weren't awake all night trying to come up with witty remarks to throw in my face, Ms. Matthews. Tell me, how was your trip to Rockville yesterday?"

Son of a bitch. She was tracking my phone. I had to work not to let myself visibly react. No wonder she FaceTimed me. "As fun as a trip to a women's prison can be."

"I thought I told you not to leave town."

"I thought you had not one, but two suspects you're convinced are guilty, case closed. I figure that means I'm off the hook and can do whatever the hell I please. I could even go home and forget this all happened."

She seemed to be studying my surroundings. I'd shown just enough of Vic's shoulder to let her know I wasn't alone. "Where are you? That doesn't look like the Baxter house."

"It's not. I'm at my friend Vic's B&B." I tilted the phone so she could see Vic as well. He smiled and waved as I explained, "He came down to keep me company during my town arrest. Isn't he a sweetie?" I reached over and trailed a finger down his cheek.

As I'd hoped, she was too consumed with trying to figure out what was going on between the two of us to respond. Perfect.

I went on, "Vic, this is Detective Corinne Barnes. Corinne, Special Agent Vic Manetti of the FBI."

Vic said smoothly, "Nice to meet you, Detective."

Barnes had regained control. "You too, Agent. So the two of you are . . . ?"

I looked over at Vic with a flirty smile. "We're *friends* . . ."

Always quick on the uptake, Vic added, "Yeah, we're pretty friendly," as he winked at me and made a show of squeezing my shoulder.

Seeming puzzled, Barnes said, "So you're not dating Nick?"

I laughed. "No. I've only told you that twenty times."

She said, "Agent Manetti, how do you feel about your *friend* there accompanying Nick Baxter to his home to help with a family matter?"

Vic shrugged. "Proud that she wanted to help her partner out of a jam. I'd do the same for my partner. Wouldn't you, Detective?"

Her face fell. Damn, Vic was good, and I'd yet to fill him in on the Barnes and Martin dating debacle. He didn't know how perfect his comment had hit home.

I turned the phone so it only showed my face. I'd played with her long enough, and now I needed to get down to business. "So, do you have some new information to share with me? Or was the purpose of your call to scold me?"

Barnes replied, "It was to warn you to watch yourself. You have no jurisdiction over this case and no right to go poking around in it."

"True, I have no jurisdiction, but I can poke around all I want. And I'm not going to stop until you get your head out of your ass and find the actual killer. That is, unless I beat you to it, which I probably will."

"We have enough evidence to hold our suspects."

Wrinkling my nose, I asked, "Ah, but do you have enough to charge them? In a high-profile case like this one, I doubt it. Our DA would never agree to go into court with nothing but a few fingerprints on the murder weapon and a half-cocked theory. The man loves his evidence."

"We have more than that."

"Oh, right. You have the fact that your partner has an old beef with your suspect—probably over some girl from high school or a spot on a sports team."

Frowning, she said, "We found something belonging to Marie Collins in Tom Baxter's home."

I froze, and Vic's grip on my shoulder tightened. "What?"

She looked like she was about to say something sarcastic, but then her expression turned to one of worry and possibly even pity. "I wasn't joking around when I told you to be careful around that family. Maybe your *friend* can convince you to go home and put this behind you. You're free to leave anytime."

As unsettling as her comments were, I wasn't going anywhere, and I wasn't going to stop looking for the real murderer. However, the fact that Barnes had made several attempts to warn me about my safety made me finally realize she wasn't the enemy here. She seemed like a decent human being (our ongoing pissing contest aside), and we needed all the help we could get from wherever we could get it.

I got up from Vic's lap and stood, disinterested in continuing the charade. "Look, Detective, my take on this case is biased. I know that. But I also believe there are a lot of people out there who wanted Marie Collins dead. And unless you've turned over every possible rock—which I know you haven't had time to do—there's a good chance a killer is out there getting away with murder. I know the evidence is stacked against the Baxters and you're up against a time crunch." I sighed, steeling myself to do something I hadn't planned to do. "But if I share some info we've gathered, will you at least consider a couple of our suspects?"

Her brow had been furrowing deeper and deeper as she listened. After a pause, she said, "Okay. Give me some names. I promise to look into them."

I waited, thinking she was going to add some type of stipulation like that we had to step away from our investigation or that I had to go back home. She didn't.

I let out a sharp exhale. "Great. Thank you so much, Detective."

She smiled. "You can call me Corinne if we're going to be on the same side now."

I laughed. "Let's not get ahead of ourselves."

She rolled her eyes. "When can we meet to discuss this information?"

I had another idea, this one much more brilliant than my previous ones. "Um . . . I'm going to be away for a bit today, so . . . how about you meet Vic for lunch and he can fill you in?"

"Sure," she said, without a hint of hesitation.

"I'll have him text you."

I ended the call and turned to Vic, who was sitting there looking stunned. He said, "What did you just do?"

"I just got you a lunch date with a hottie detective. You're welcome." When he furrowed his brow at me, I added, "In all seriousness, Vic, thank you again for dropping everything to help us. We couldn't do this without you."

A smile tugged at the corner of his mouth. "I should be thanking you— who wouldn't want to be the third wheel in an off-the-books op with his ex and her new boyfriend? This is super fun for me."

I gave him a mock slug in the arm. "It's not like that. Besides, as far as the world knows, he and I are nothing more than colleagues."

"Then he needs to quit staring longingly at you like you're the only woman in the world."

I couldn't hold back a smile. "He does that?"

Vic rolled his eyes. "Enough girl talk. Let's get to work."

22

Baxter, Vic, and I reconvened our meeting and divided up tasks, and Baxter and I headed first to the nearby town of Evansville to track down Jeffrey Townsend. An overbearing football dad openly belligerent toward Mr. Baxter, Townsend had found himself the subject of police attention when Shawn had first gone missing. I wasn't looking forward to this conversation, especially since we were blindsiding him at work. I assumed his son had lost playing time to both Baxter boys, which always hurt worse when it was the coach's kids, regardless if they were better players.

Townsend worked as a loan officer in a small bank branch, so it was only too easy to gain access to him with a request from a smiling couple to take out a mortgage for their first home together. But when Townsend looked across the desk and recognized who'd just waltzed into his office, things got kind of dicey.

Townsend sneered, "Well, if it isn't the Golden Boy. You slumming it back in Boonvegas? Or are you just here to grease the local cops into letting Daddy and Brother off the hook?"

Ouch.

Baxter said calmly, "It's good to see you, too, Mr. Townsend. My partner and I are here to ask you what you know about Marie Collins's death and if you've had any interaction with her in the last fifteen years."

Townsend replied, "What I know is that I'm thrilled your dear old dad is getting his karmic reward for ruining my kid's football career and my life."

I said, "I heard you moved to get your son on a better team. Sounds like that would have helped his football career—unless he wasn't really as good at football as you thought and he ended up with even less playing time."

He snapped his head toward me. "Who are you?"

"Ellie Matthews. I'm a criminalist from Hamilton County." A true statement. And now for a little white lie that only cost me humbling myself before Corinne Barnes and pimping out my best friend to her. "I'm cooperating with local law enforcement to tie up a few loose ends on the investigation. If we could get your alibi for Sunday morning between one and three a.m., it could help us cross your name off the list of potential accomplices to Marie Collins's homicide."

Townsend's eyes bulged out. "You think I'd lift a finger to help those pompous asshole Baxters do anything?"

"I think you'd lift a finger to help those pompous asshole Baxters look guilty of murder. Maybe you lured Marie Collins out to their property so one of them would find her and get into an altercation with her, then you could sit back and watch the circus unfold."

He barked out a laugh. "I'd love to take the credit for that, but I was in Nashville this weekend visiting my son. Check whatever you need to check to prove it."

I nodded. "Thank you. We will. Have you had any interaction with Marie Collins since she left Boonville over fifteen years ago?"

"No. I've never even met her."

I felt like this guy had something to say, so I baited him. "If you had to guess who might have wanted to hurt the woman who kidnapped Shawn Baxter on the first night she was released from prison, who would you say it is?"

Townsend scoffed. "Exactly who the police say it is. Those two—" He stopped to point an accusatory finger at Baxter. "And you—have hid behind the goody-two-shoes act long enough. Now everyone can see you're no better than the rest of us."

Baxter stood and was about to say something I imagined he'd regret, so

I took him by the arm and ushered him out of the office, calling, "Thanks, Mr. Townsend," over my shoulder.

Baxter managed to keep his cool until we were in the parking lot. "That jackass is still holding onto old grudges?"

"Well, considering he blames the loss of his kid's NFL career on you, your brother, and your dad, then yeah. And he doesn't seem to be the only one around here with a grudge."

A smile pulled at the corner of his mouth. "Okay, fine. Point noted." His eyes suddenly narrowed. "What was that about you working with local law enforcement? Barnes will arrest you, too, if she catches wind of you saying that."

I winced. "True, she's not going to like the phrasing, but it's not untrue that I'm cooperating with her."

"What?" he demanded.

"Not against your family. I asked her for her help." I'd been putting off telling him this, hoping I could come up with a way to frame it so our conversation wouldn't be as uncomfortable as it was fast becoming. I hadn't been able to come up with anything, so I'd changed the subject every time Barnes had come up on the ride to town.

"You said that call was nothing and that you'd tell me about it later. I think it wasn't nothing, and it's later. Spill."

While he was already upset, I started with the worst part. "Barnes said they found something belonging to Marie Collins in your brother's home."

His face went ashen.

I said, "Look, the only thing this means is that whoever killed her really wants Tom to look guilty and went to the trouble of breaking into his house to plant some evidence. I think it wouldn't hurt to start compiling a list of his enemies."

His voice barely above a whisper, he choked out, "Everyone loves Tom."

"Detective Martin doesn't." When his response was looking at me like I was crazy, I held out a hand and said, "By that, I don't mean I think Martin planted evidence. I only mean that if he doesn't like Tom because of old jealousy, he's probably not the only one. Some people hang onto high school drama forever."

Baxter nodded, and I managed to get him settled into my car. As I drove to our next destination, I explained my reasoning for showing our hand to Barnes.

When I got done, he was no longer frowning quite as much. "I'm glad you did what you did, especially since they now seem to think they have Tom dead to rights. I think we'll get farther with this the more transparent we can be with Corinne. Did you tell her about the evidence you collected?"

I huffed out a nervous laugh. "Are you crazy? A little of the Ice Queen's frostiness might have melted toward me, but I'm not that confident of our new common ground, nor of Vic's powers of seduction."

He shot me a look. "His what now?"

"I'm pretty sure Barnes has the hots for Vic . . . probably because he and I made her think we were more than buddies while I was trying to convince her you and I are nothing more than partners. It's become clear to me that if she thinks something's mine, she wants it. So I managed to set the two of them up on a lunch date."

He groaned. "Poor Manetti. She's a lot."

"He survived dating me, so he should be fine."

A ghost of a smile pulling at the corner of his mouth, he replied, "Fair point."

～

THE DRIVE to Gretchen Hollis's workplace didn't take long. She, too, was easy to access, working at a lovely family-owned jewelry store with more sparkly things than I'd ever seen in one place. We didn't have to pretend to be a couple looking for a ring, thank goodness, to speak with her, because she caught us the moment we walked in the door.

Smiling, she said, "Good morning. I'm Gretchen. Can I help you find something special?"

Evidently she hadn't recognized Baxter. Maybe we could keep it that way. I said quickly, "Um . . . no. We came to see you, Mrs. Hollis. I'm Ellie Matthews, and I'm working on the Marie Collins homicide."

Gretchen's face fell. "Oh. Are the Baxters going to accuse me of having a hand in that, too?" She flicked her eyes toward Baxter and suddenly blanched. Her voice shaky, she said, "Wait . . . *you* . . . I haven't seen you in . . ." She took a step back from us and shook her head, muttering. "No, it can't be . . ."

The woman seemed frightened of Baxter. I couldn't imagine she had a reason to be, so I said, "This is Nick Baxter. He's cooperating to help me with some insight into the situation. Please don't be afraid, Mrs. Hollis. Neither of us mean you any harm."

Her expression showed relief but still harbored apprehension. "I thought . . ." She cast another glance at Baxter and said to me, "He looks so much like . . ." She shut her eyes and shook her head.

I supplied, "Benji McDonald?"

"Yes," she breathed.

"Did Benji McDonald do something to you?" I asked.

Gretchen huffed out a breath. "He stalked me for months after the family accused me of kidnapping Shawn. The police did nothing about it."

Baxter said, "I'm sorry for what my family and my uncle put you through, Mrs. Hollis. I wish they'd handled it differently." I could tell by the defeated tone of his voice he was still worrying about the new development with the alleged evidence found in Tom's home. He wasn't himself.

Shaking her head, she replied, "You were a boy at the time. I don't blame you. I wish your mother had had a little more faith in me, though."

I asked, "You and Elaine used to be friends?"

"Good friends."

"Were you also friends with Marie Collins?"

"Not exactly. I knew her through Elaine. I met her a few times at Elaine's home." She said to Baxter, "Your mother was always throwing a party of some kind back then—bonfires, scrapbooking parties, holiday open houses." She cleared her throat. "How is your mother these days?"

Baxter's expression clouded even more. "She's . . . not too well. Shawn's kidnapping took a toll."

Gretchen nodded. "I imagine it did. I tried to do what I could for her, but once she . . . well, I was hurt and didn't bother to contact her after that."

I said, "I don't blame you. And I know you relocated to distance yourself from . . . everything, but we wanted to ask if you have any insight on Marie

Collins's death. Had you been in contact with her since she left town with Shawn?"

"No, like I said, I only ever spoke to her at Elaine's parties."

"What was she like?"

She shrugged. "Kind of odd. I hate to be snooty, but she was very much unlike most of Elaine's friends. They were all well-off and for the most part pillars of the community. Marie was . . . kind of downtrodden. The rest of us . . . well, everyone always assumed she was Elaine's latest charity project. Elaine was always a fixer and never passed up an opportunity to help someone. She could take any disaster and turn it around." To Baxter, she said, "Do you remember when Kate Darden went into labor two months early and your mother had to take over the big library fundraiser with only a week's notice?"

Baxter brightened at the memory. "Tom and I were pretty little, but I do remember that. What I remember is that we got to stay with Uncle Benji and Aunt Lucy that whole week because Mom basically lived at the library and Dad was in the middle of football season."

I said, "Mrs. Hollis, do you remember anyone—aside from the Baxters —having a particular grudge against Marie Collins?"

"Are you considering Benji McDonald one of them?"

"Yes. We know about his issues with her."

"Well, none of Elaine's friends were fans, but I don't know of anyone with what I'd call a grudge. I admit none of us made much of an effort to get to know her. She kind of clung to Elaine or played with Shawn while all of us were around. She didn't try to mingle. We probably weren't the most welcoming bunch." She frowned. "I learned the hard way that our little circle could be cliquish and it was no fun being on the outside of it."

I smiled sympathetically. "I'm sure it wasn't. Did Marie ever mention anything about her personal life or her past to you? Did she ever say anything that struck you as unnerving or strange?"

"Not really. It was all gossip and small talk at those parties. Marie didn't chime in much." She thought for a moment. "Although . . . I do remember overhearing her on a phone call once. I haven't thought about this in forever. I heard her arguing with someone on the other end . . . she called him . . . Corey, I believe, and—"

I elbowed Baxter as I interrupted her. "Cody?"

She nodded. "Oh, yes. Cody, not Corey. She said she'd made a mistake falling back in with him. That he ruined her life once, and that was enough. I felt bad for eavesdropping, so I snuck away before she saw me."

"That's all you heard? She never mentioned Cody to you?"

"No, that's all."

Baxter smiled. "Thank you for your time, Mrs. Hollis."

She smiled back, but then her face fell. "Tell your mother I hope she's . . . okay."

He nodded. "That means a lot. Thank you."

As we left the jewelry store and got into my car, my phone rang. I was surprised to see the caller was Jason Sterling. Before I could say hello, he demanded, "You with Baxter right now? Put him on the phone. He's not answering my calls."

Good old Jason Sterling, sounding like his usual self, barking demands while he was supposed to be taking it easy and recuperating.

I said, "Hi, Sterling. I'm good, thanks for asking. How's it going with you?"

He barked, "How do you think it's going, Matthews? I have a damn concussion thanks to you."

I rolled my eyes. I'd hoped after what we'd gone through that our relationship would be a little smoother, but maybe that was wishful thinking. I transferred the call to my car's speakers so Baxter could listen.

Amanda's voice called from the background, "Don't take it personally, Ellie. Someone's being an angry child right now because his screens got taken away."

I snickered. "Ah. Sorry, Sterling. That sucks."

He griped, "It certainly does. And I wasted the few minutes I was allowed to use electronics this morning to run Nicky a background on a name he sent me. Email's on its way."

"Aww, that's so sweet of you."

"Don't patronize me, Matthews."

I did appreciate the gesture, but evidently my tone didn't convey the sentiment. "Old habits."

Baxter said, "I'm here. I appreciate your help."

Sterling griped, "And I'd appreciate it if you got your dumb ass out of hot water and came back and did your damn job. There's no telling who they'll partner me with if you're out much longer."

Unable to hold my tongue, I said, "Well, it's good to know you're not making this all about yourself."

"Shut up, Matthews."

I shot back, "*You* shut up, you—"

Baxter gave me a pained look. "Okay, you two, enough. You're not allowed to speak to each other until both of your head injuries are completely healed."

"Fine by me," I grumbled as Sterling grumbled pretty much the same thing.

Baxter said, "We appreciate you guys."

Amanda said, "Ellie, I'm sorry to admit I haven't been able do anything with that second print you sent. There's not enough of it."

"Don't apologize. I knew it was a long shot," I replied.

She added, "And I'm still waiting to hear back about that first print. My request for more information is not being fulfilled with any urgency."

"No problem. Thanks for staying on it," I replied.

I'd run into similar issues in the past. Since every law enforcement agency in the country, big and small, fed into AFIS, the information attached to each fingerprint wasn't always uniform or properly entered. That was especially true if the print had been collected many years ago or had been entered years later from a batch of old paper files. Then there were myriad other reasons for missing or redacted information like military or government ties, sealed juvenile records, witness protection, and undercover officer protection. Requests for more information didn't always produce a result, so I wasn't holding my breath with this one.

Amanda and Sterling said their goodbyes, and I ended the call. I asked Baxter, "Who did he run background on?"

"Brock Lovell, the Brock from my mom's list," he replied, taking out his phone to check his email.

"How'd you figure that one out?"

"Last night I sent the list to Joe Finnegan, and he knew the guy. Joe questioned Lovell when he worked Shawn's case because Marie Collins had been seen with him shortly before she left town. Even better, our next stop is to meet Joe for coffee so we can pick his brain. He's also going to loan us his case file."

I smiled. "That's great. How long has it been since you've seen him?"

"A couple of months. I try to catch up with him most times I come down here."

Joe Finnegan was Baxter's earliest mentor and the reason he became a detective. Joe had taken over Shawn's kidnapping case after the initial detective assigned to the case switched departments. He'd been a blessing to the family, treating them like real people rather than victims and taking the time to get to know them to better figure out who would have wanted to take Shawn. He let Baxter shadow him at the station and inspired him to spend his life helping people get justice and closure.

Thinking back to our earlier conversation with Gretchen, I said, "I know Joe spurred your interest to protect and serve, but I'm guessing you got your thing about caring for people from your mom, huh?"

"I did. I wish you'd met her before . . ." He shook his head sadly. "You would really have loved her."

My heart ached for him. I understood his pain. My mother had been for the most part horrible, but during the time she'd been married to our step-father David, she'd been sober and had actually been a decent mom. It was heartbreaking for Rachel and me when she fell off the wagon and returned to her old habits.

As the silence inside the vehicle got too quiet, I had a horrible thought. Did Baxter wonder if I'd fall off the wagon at some point and end up like one of our mothers? He'd spent his adult life saddled with an alcoholic mother. Why would he allow himself to gravitate toward me knowing there was the possibility of being dragged through that same hell all over again? I was doing well now, but what if things changed? I would never forget the look he had on his face when he told me I was out of control. It was a lot like the one he wore now, thinking about how much his mom had changed. Could I live with myself if I made him feel that way about me again?

I reminded myself of how far I'd come and shoved my worries off to the side, concentrating my thoughts back onto the case.

23

Baxter and I met Joe Finnegan at a charming coffeehouse downtown. Joe was already seated, but rose to give Baxter a bear hug, slapping him heartily on the back. "I hope you're keeping your chin up, kid. I know this is tough, but so is your family. I'll do whatever I can to help."

"Thanks, Joe," Baxter said as they broke apart. "This is Ellie Matthews. Ellie, Joe Finnegan."

Joe shook my hand. "I've heard a lot about you, young lady."

I wondered if he'd heard only what Baxter's family had heard or if he'd heard the whole story. "Same. It's nice to finally meet you," I replied.

Jerking his thumb at Baxter, he joked, "I'm glad this guy has you to keep him in line," as he gave me an exaggerated wink. It seemed like he knew enough to know I wasn't the enemy.

After we got our drinks and sat down, Joe put a file folder on the table between us. "I don't have all the info the original investigator gathered in here. The official file is stored at the station. These are my personal notes, mainly about people I ran down who were close to the case but not technically involved."

I said, "I think that's what we want, to find people connected to the Baxters and to Marie Collins we may not be aware of."

Baxter said to him, "You know all the players. Who do you think looks guilty?"

Joe shrugged. "Gun to my head, if I had to choose a killer out of the people I spoke to and investigated during Shawn's case, it would be Brock Lovell. But that's my biased opinion based on fifteen-year-old information. A lot can happen in fifteen years, meaning a lot of people could have found a lot of reasons to want Marie Collins dead. I'd start with the more recent altercations she'd had." Smiling at Baxter proudly, he added, "But who am I to tell you how to run an investigation, Mr. Big Shot? I never caught a serial killer, I can tell you that much."

Blushing, Baxter gave his stock answer to this kind of praise, "There was a whole team of us working on those cases, especially Ellie—"

I cut him off and said to Joe, "But when it comes down to it, it's his brilliant mind that always puts all the weird pieces together."

Joe chuckled. "I'm not at all surprised." Then his face grew serious. "I'm sure this case has you thrown for a loop with Tom and Jim being the lead suspects at the moment. I'm sure it's hard to take a step back and look at this objectively."

Baxter stared down at his cup of coffee. "It's been close to impossible." After a hesitation, he added, "Um . . . we just learned the detectives found something belonging to Marie Collins in Tom's house."

Joe harrumphed. "Someone's going to a lot of trouble to make your brother look guilty, huh?"

I was grateful for Joe's unwavering allegiance to Baxter's family. From the look on his face, it was apparent that Baxter appreciated it too.

"Hey," Joe went on, "I know you have help, but if you need me, I'm here."

Baxter nodded.

I hated seeing Baxter so dejected. Any other time I would have put everything else on hold to put his mental health first like he always did with me. But we weren't doing ourselves any favors by not pressing on and using our time wisely.

I asked Joe, "Did you ever speak to anyone named Cody?"

He flipped through his notes. "Not that I can recall. Who's he to Marie Collins?"

"An old boyfriend. Oh, and speaking of old friends, we did manage to put a name to the woman Shawn knew as Rita. Rosaline Suarez. She's in the wind at the moment, but we're looking."

Joe shook his head. "Rosaline Suarez doesn't ring a bell. How'd you find her?"

"Her name was on Marie Collins's prison visitor log. And her last known address was in Bloomington, where Marie Collins held Shawn, so we connected a few dots and made a leap."

He rifled through the file and found a photo and a printed map with a location starred on it. "Good hunch. The cabin where she held him was located just outside the city. This is it, if you're interested."

The modest structure truly was a cabin—it couldn't have been more than several hundred square feet. Surrounded by woods, it was isolated in a rural area between Bloomington and Monroe Lake. The perfect spot to hide out.

"Do you know why she chose that particular area?" I asked.

"I always assumed she had friends there. Once I started digging into her life, I found an old Bloomington address for her from several years prior. Unfortunately, I couldn't tie her to anyone there at the time."

Baxter, who'd grabbed the file and started looking through it, changed the subject. "What about her ex-husband, Javier Powers? It was their child who died at the age of four, which I assumed led to the demise of their marriage. You spoke to him—did he have any unresolved anger toward her?"

Joe thought for a moment. "Not really. I mean, he's no angel. He had a short rap sheet at the time, so it wouldn't hurt to pay him a visit."

Baxter got out his phone. "Speaking of rap sheets, Brock Lovell has a lengthy one." He held out his phone so Joe could see the screen.

Joe whistled. "He's been busy the past fifteen years."

"When he wasn't in prison," Baxter added. His expression turned anxious. "Ellie . . . maybe you'd like to sit the Brock Lovell interview out."

I frowned at him.

Joe nodded. "This guy is a piece of work. Between those battery charges and the disgusting way he spoke about Marie Collins, his view of women is pretty clear in my mind."

Baxter's expression grew dark. "I'm definitely going this alone, then."

My stomach clenched. While I didn't want to tangle with another bad man who had no problem slapping women around, I also didn't want Baxter alone with this guy. Maybe this interview would have to wait until Vic could go along, not that I wanted him to have to be in danger, either.

Joe must have noticed my dilemma, because he offered, "I'd be happy to go with you to interview him, Nick. I haven't had the pleasure of the company of such a lowlife in a long time."

Baxter brightened. "That would be great, Joe. Thanks."

~

BAXTER LEFT the coffeehouse with more spring in his step than he'd had in a while. It was definitely best-case scenario that he interview Brock Lovell with a seasoned professional. Plus to my knowledge Baxter had never gotten to actually work side by side with Joe, which I was sure had been a dream of his since he was a teen. Them leaving me at the coffeehouse alone gave me a chance to drink another much-needed coffee and work on returning emails to students, plan out the last couple of weeks of the semester in case I ended up here for a while longer, and have a lengthy text conversation with Rachel.

An hour later when he picked me up, Baxter was on cloud nine. "I'd never worked with Joe before. It was amazing to watch him with a suspect. He has a knack for tripping people up and making them question themselves. The guy spilled way more than he intended to."

I smiled. "Nice. So you got the information you needed *and* a master-class on interrogation tactics. Can't beat that."

"Best of all, we have a really solid suspect."

My eyebrows shot up. "No alibi?"

"He says he was home alone, asleep."

I frowned. "Wouldn't he have come up with a better one if he was guilty?"

Baxter shook his head. "Joe flustered him. He also let slip that Marie Collins showed up to his work on Saturday night and they had a few words."

"Oh. That's something."

"He works at a gas station here in town. Said she came in alone, evidently to see him. He thought it was one of those revenge body things. He mentioned her being 'a fatty' back in the day."

I took out Joe's file and looked through it until I found a full-length photo of Marie from fifteen years ago. "She was by no means overweight, but she had clearly worked on her body in prison." I felt an honest pang of sympathy for her that she wanted to show herself to the world after all the work she'd put in, but didn't get much of a chance.

"At least she left a sexy corpse."

I gaped at him. "Nick Baxter. That was by far your most horrible gallows joke to date." Ickiness aside, I was happy to see him joking around again.

He smiled and went on, "That puts her in Evansville at ten p.m., so we finally have something to go on her time line."

"Not exactly good news, though. She could have stopped anywhere along the way, and that means infinitely more people to piss off. Personally, I was still holding out hope she bar-hopped her way through Boonville until the fateful incident."

"We're never that lucky."

$\approx$

ACCORDING to the woman who answered Javier Powers's door, he was asleep. She identified herself as his girlfriend, so we went ahead and asked her for his alibi. She said he worked thirds at a local factory and had worked Saturday night. With that information, we could follow up with his supervisor and maybe not have to tangle with him. Baxter and I then headed west to a tiny town called Muddy in far southern Illinois. I was happy he offered to drive, because my black eye was still swollen and felt tired. It was nice to have a break from having to focus my eyes for a while.

On the way, I got an email from Vic detailing his morning's activities. I read the highlights to Baxter. "Looks like Vic did not find a lot of damning evidence on your Uncle Benji. His record's been clean lately and according to his boss, he's been the model employee for the better part of a year."

Baxter grumbled, "He can put on a good face when he needs to."

I looked over at him. "Okay, let's think about this objectively for a moment. I could get behind your uncle creeping around your parents' property thinking he was protecting Shawn from big, bad Marie Collins. I could even get behind him believing she was there in the barn planning to hurt one of the family and taking it upon himself to stop her dead in her tracks. I could get behind him bitching out and not coming forward to confess when Tom got arrested, leaving Tom's fate up to chance. What I absolutely cannot get behind is that he would intentionally take an item Marie Collins was carrying the night she died—because let's face it, she basically had no possessions besides what she had with her—only to plant that item inside Tom's home to make sure his own nephew fried for murder. Change my mind."

He blew out a breath, seeming deflated. "You're right. While I could see Uncle Benji doing it to my dad . . . he'd never do it to Tom in a million years. If the item in question had been found in my parents' house, I would have made a beeline to the station and not left there until Uncle Benji was behind bars."

"Does that mean we can cross him off our list?"

Exhaling again, he conceded, "I mean . . . I guess."

"Good. Now, on to Rosaline Suarez. Funny story . . . that's a stolen identity, and her real name is Rosaline Gonzales. Rosaline Gonzales is currently a guest of Monroe County, charged with, wait for it—"

"Let me guess. Kidnapping?"

I chuckled. "You are correct. I can't imagine how you came to that conclusion. The good news is that she's one less loose end to chase, and the better news is that she's now a captive—pun intended—audience if we want to pick her brain about Marie Collins. I say we save the gas and do it over Zoom."

He nodded. "Agreed. How was Manetti's lunch date with Corinne?"

"That was not covered in the email. However, I'm texting him right now to get the dirty deets," I said as I sent Vic a quick message.

"I meant, how did it go with giving her the names of some of our suspects?"

"Oh, that. I'll ask that, too."

Shaking his head, Baxter let out a soft chuckle. I hoped he could keep up his more positive attitude. We seemed to be making progress, although what was technically happening was that we were narrowing down our pool of persons of interest. Not always a bad thing, but I didn't want to see him spiral again into the discouragement he'd felt this morning.

I put my phone away and perused Joe's file, pointing out a few interesting things I came across. "Aside from Javier Powers's rap sheet, which is paltry compared to Brock Lovell's, I'm not thinking he's much of a contender. It says here that he stated on the record that he hadn't had any contact with Marie Collins since shortly after their child died, which happened nine years before she kidnapped Shawn. I can't imagine he would have initiated contact after that."

Baxter nodded. "I agree. We'll follow up with his supervisor and call it good. What else you got?"

I snickered. "There's a little note in the margin next to Joe's info about Jeffrey Townsend. It says, 'Asshat helicopter dad.' "

He smiled. "That is accurate, but I was asking about information we didn't already know."

"Ha, ha. Oh, we didn't know this—Joe had Margo Watson as a contender for a possible accomplice or at least obstruction charges."

He frowned. "I didn't know that."

"Looks like he took it so far as to give her a lie detector test over what she knew about the kidnapping. She passed, plus Marie Collins signed a separate sworn affidavit denying her sister having anything to do with it, so no charges were brought."

"I wonder if that's why Margo made such a point to try to make amends with my parents afterward. To try to salvage her reputation around here."

"And maybe it's part of the reason she cut ties with her sister—she was pissed about nearly being taken down with her. Or she turned her back on her to save face publicly. To me, she seems a little preoccupied with appearances."

"Do you blame her? Her sister was the most hated person in town for years. In a close-knit community, your status doesn't recover from something like that. She should have moved like Gretchen Hollis did. It would have been easier."

I nodded, continuing to read through Joe's copious notes. "Looks like he even went after one of your mom's church frenemies, Greta Statler. It says she was an older member of the congregation whose disdain for your mom was evident and could be pretty nasty. Her issue was that she thought some of your mom's ideas for church events and fundraisers were garish and too secular, and she did her best to thwart your mother at every turn. Any ideas on that one?"

He chuckled. "You can safely cross Greta Statler off our list. She was about a hundred years old back then. She's long dead now, as are her antiquated ideas of how the world works."

"Sounds like she was a gem."

"You know the old saying about infighting in church congregations, right?"

I shook my head.

"There's nothing a good funeral can't fix."

My jaw dropped. "That's a saying? That's awful."

He shrugged. "I've heard it all my life."

"I believe that one tops your 'sexy corpse' joke for worst thing you've ever said." I reached over and gave him a pat on the leg. "But I'm happy to see you joking around again, so I'll let it slide."

$\sim$

SOUTHERN ILLINOIS WAS AN ODD PLACE. Between the vast acres of farmland were little run-down towns with equal numbers of churches, barbecue joints, and gambling establishments. Even the gas stations had special walled-off areas with multiple electronic gambling machines. Across the border in Indiana, I was used to seeing people throwing their hard-earned money away buying scratch-off lottery tickets in gas stations, but hardcore electronic gaming was a next-level habit reserved for the few and far between casinos.

Muddy, not much more than a wide spot in the road, was exactly like every other little town we'd driven through once we'd crossed the Wabash River. John Kocher owned a dilapidated ranch home on a small wooded lot north of town. A middle-aged man I assumed was John was elbow-deep in the engine of an old truck in his driveway. When we turned into his driveway, he straightened up and looked at us with a wary expression.

His expression only got darker as we approached him and Baxter said, "Hi, Mr. Kocher. This is Ms. Matthews and I'm Detective Nick Baxter. We're here to—"

Suddenly the man's eyes bugged out in fear. "I swear she was eighteen, Officer."

So taken aback by his statement, I blurted out, "Gross." This guy was mid-forties at least and not a catch.

Baxter didn't bat an eye. "It's detective. And I don't care whatever it is you get up to with your spare time. We're here to inform you that a former girlfriend of yours has been killed. Marie—"

"Mary?" he breathed, his expression stricken. "My Mary?"

Baxter nodded. "We're sorry for your loss. We're trying to locate people who knew her to get some background information to help us catch her killer. Did she live here in Muddy?"

John Kocher looked over at the ramshackle house with a mix of nostalgia and pain. "Here in this house with me." Interesting. They were close.

"For how long?" Baxter asked him.

"Pretty near two years."

"Was Mary a nickname you had for her?"

John shook his head. "No . . . no, it was her name."

Baxter frowned. "What did she tell you her last name was?"

"Stevens. Mary Stevens."

"Marie Collins was her real name. Do you know why she might have used a fake name with you?"

Shrugging, John replied, "I always reckoned she changed her name after she left me so I couldn't track her down."

Baxter said, "No, she was Marie Collins before you met and then went back to that name afterward. Was she running or hiding from something or someone when she was here in Muddy?"

"I . . . she never said."

"How did you two meet?" I asked.

John smiled as if remembering a fond memory. "I met her at a bar in

Harrisburg, just down the road." He huffed out a laugh. "One thing led to another, and she come home with me that night. She was down on her luck and needed a place to stay. I gotta admit I fell in love with her the second I laid eyes on her, so I asked her to come live with me."

Marie certainly worked fast. "And you were happy together?"

"Very."

Frowning, I asked, "Then why did she leave? Did you have a disagreement?"

"Uh . . ." He rubbed the back of his neck, suddenly nervous.

Baxter said, "We're not suggesting you had something to do with her death. We're trying to fill in some gaps in her history."

John nodded. "We had a fight over something stupid. She left me."

I said, "After two years of living together, she left without a word and didn't tell you where she was going? Must have been a hell of a fight."

John nodded again. I thought he was starting to act awfully shifty.

I studied him for a moment, then hit him with Vic's assessment of his letter. "We read the letter you wrote to her when she first got put in prison. It was definitely in your words, but the content seemed like something a lawyer might have told you to write. Did someone suggest you write that letter?"

His eyes widened. Got him.

I went on, "Were you worried the authorities would try to implicate you in her crime since you'd been so close not long before she did the deed?"

Voice raised, he said, "I didn't have nothing to do with no kidnapping! Mary did that all on her own. She was . . . a little touched in the head."

I smiled. "Ah. Did the infamous fight end with you calling her crazy?"

Eyes cast down, he nodded.

Chuckling, I said, "Enough said. Did she make any enemies during the time she lived here?"

"I don't think so."

"Did she have friends?"

"A couple. I didn't know them."

"Emily Anders, maybe?"

He nodded. "Sounds familiar."

"Where did she work?"

"She didn't. I provided," he said proudly.

After shooting me an amused glance, Baxter said, "I think that's all we need to know, except . . . did you kill her this weekend?"

John's jaw dropped in horror. "No! I'd never hurt Mary. I loved her."

Baxter squinted at him and blurted out, "Why?"

John shrugged. "Why does anybody love anybody? We fit together real good. It felt right when I was with her." He sighed and rubbed his eyes. "And it feels real bad to know she's gone, even after all this time."

Baxter asked, "Do you have an alibi for between one and three a.m. Sunday morning?"

"I worked third shift that night. I switched with my buddy, Ray. You can ask my boss."

"We'll do that. Is there anything more you want to add, Mr. Kocher?"

John shook his head emphatically.

24

After Baxter got John Kocher's boss's contact info, we left him and headed out to see Emily Anders, a friend of Marie's from the area. Emily lived in Harrisburg, a decent-sized town five minutes south of Muddy. We found her at her work, an animal shelter on the outskirts of town, feeding a group of hungry puppies. There weren't a lot of things I loved more in this world than puppies, and I was going to have a hard time concentrating (and not picking one out to take home) during this interview if we didn't speak to Emily away from all the adorable animals.

Baxter approached her and gave our standard introduction.

Emily Anders stood and walked slowly over to us. "What's going on? Is someone I know hurt?"

We did sometimes get that reaction out of people, especially if they didn't already know our victim was dead. When law enforcement visited an innocent person out of the blue, there was always a decent chance it could be a death notification.

Baxter immediately slipped into his calm, empathetic mode he executed so well. "I didn't mean to frighten you, Ms. Anders. We came here to let you know an old friend of yours has passed. Marie Collins. You may also have known her as Mary Stevens."

I could see from the look on Emily's face she was waffling between relief and sadness. I said, "I'm sorry for your loss. We found your name in the phone and visitor logs at Rockville prison and wanted to ask you a few questions in hopes of figuring out who'd want to take her life."

Emily's eyebrows shot up. "Are you saying Mary . . . Marie was murdered?"

"Yes."

"When? She was supposed to get out of prison Saturday."

"She did. She was killed early Sunday morning."

Emily closed her eyes and opened them slowly. Baxter took her by the arm and guided her to a nearby chair. She leaned over and put her head in her hands.

We let her have a moment, and then Baxter said gently, "When you're ready to talk, can you tell us if you know why Marie Collins used the name Mary Stevens while she lived here?"

Emily sniffled and raised her head. "She was trying to get away from an abusive ex."

I murmured to Baxter, "That tracks."

"Did she mention his name?" he asked.

"Javier."

I said aloud, "That *doesn't* track."

According to Joe's notes, Javier Powers stated that he hadn't had any contact with Marie Collins since shortly after their child died, which was years before she moved to Muddy. Then again, if she'd had to run from Powers and change her name, maybe his word wasn't to be believed.

Baxter asked, "Did he find her here?"

Emily said, "Not to my knowledge. She always said she felt safe here."

"We spoke to John Kocher. He said she left here suddenly because of a fight they had. If she thought she was safe here from her ex, why leave town over a fight? Why not just leave him?"

"Oh, she didn't leave over a fight. I mean, not entirely. She was upset about losing her son. She couldn't bear to stay here anymore without him."

Both of us stared at her. I asked, "Without him? When exactly did she live here?"

"Seventeen years ago."

According to Joe's file, Aaron Powers, the son of Marie Collins and Javier Powers, died twenty-five years ago.

Baxter, who sounded as confused as I felt, said, "Start at the beginning about her son."

Emily explained, "She had a little boy, Danny. She adopted him not long before she moved to Muddy. A couple of years later, there was an issue found in the adoption paperwork that allowed his birth mother to be granted custody again. Mary was sick about it but didn't have the money to fight it in court. She left town to go back home and live with her sister. She said she couldn't stand living here anymore without him."

Baxter shot me a look, which I took as, "Who in their right mind would give that woman a child?" I was wondering that very thing. That, and the fact that adoptions are incredibly difficult, with years of paperwork, waiting, and expense—and that was if the adopting family looked perfect in every way, with long-married spouses, a stable housing situation, and good jobs. From what I'd gathered about Marie Collins, I didn't feel like she could have checked any of those boxes at any point in her life.

He asked Emily, "Did Danny live with her at John Kocher's home?"

She nodded. "Yes."

Baxter turned to me. "Funny he never mentioned a word about a child."

I looked at him uneasily and said to Emily, "Speaking of children, what did you think when you learned Marie Collins had kidnapped a child and was going to prison for it?"

Shaking her head sadly, she replied, "I was disappointed, but not incredibly surprised. She'd lost a child of her own to illness. Then to have her adopted son ripped away so suddenly . . . that boy was her world. She didn't deal with it well at all."

Something was off about this story. I asked, "What was the boy's last name?"

"Stevens. She changed it when she adopted him."

Baxter regarded her quizzically. "To her fake name?"

She shrugged. "I guess. I thought Stevens was her real name until I saw her all over the news when she got arrested, so I never questioned it."

"Did you have any contact with her between the time she left here and when you visited her in prison?"

"Not for lack of trying on my part. Her phone number was 'no longer in service,' and I didn't have another number for her. She wasn't on social media. I couldn't find a way to contact her until I saw that she was going to be incarcerated at Rockville." She sighed. "Look, I know Marie did a terrible thing, but . . . well, she was my friend. She got punished for her crime, so I didn't feel like it was up to me to serve any judgment or punishment of my own. The rest of the world seemed to have that covered. So . . . I was just her friend. I felt like she needed that more than another enemy."

Wow. Emily was a pretty remarkable person to have been able to look past a glaring sin (against a child, no less) and still see the human being behind it. Not a lot of people stood by Marie Collins, including her only family member. Really, the only people who'd had her back besides Emily were other criminals, including her mystery boyfriend, who was likely only kind to her so he could get close enough to kill her.

Speaking of "Jake," I didn't want to let one of Marie Collins's friends get away without asking about him. "Did she ever mention a man named Jake Sampson or tell you about having a boyfriend she was going to connect with once she was released?"

Emily smiled sadly. "I've heard so much about Jake. She was head over heels for him. He treated her like no man had before. I hate that they won't have the chance to—"

I said, "Sorry to cut you off, but you need to know this man is not who he claims to be. He purposely got to know your friend under false pretenses. He stole an identity in order to get into the prison, which could mean he's a felon and wouldn't have been granted access otherwise or that he wanted to hide his real identity. Either one of those reasons makes him troublesome. While we don't know if Marie Collins knew his real identity, we have good reason to believe he could have killed her."

Emily choked out a sob. "No. That would have broken her heart. She was in love."

"Did she ever mention him using a fake name or identity or maybe slip and call him by another name? Do you have any reason to believe she had a clue he wasn't Jake Sampson?"

"No, to my knowledge she thought he was the real deal." She winced. "Granted, I did think at first it was a little odd that he contacted her almost like he was a fan or something. I found it . . . a little gross. I warned her to be careful and to seek out his true intentions. She said she'd gotten really good at reading people in prison and I shouldn't worry. After that, everything she told me about him sounded wonderful."

"Too good to be true?" I asked.

She sighed. "In hindsight, yes."

"Can you give us any specifics about what they talked about? Where they planned to meet after she was released? If they planned to live together or run away somewhere?"

"She said she planned to meet up with him the night of her release to celebrate."

I nodded. "We heard from her sister that she thought Marie had left her home with a man that night. It was customary for her to have her dates wait at the end of her sister's driveway when they picked her up."

Emily frowned. "She always did say her sister was judgmental. Of everything."

"Right. Back to the plans they'd made for that night. Did Marie mention a specific bar she wanted to visit or a person she wanted to see?"

She thought for a moment. "I know there was an ex she talked about . . . she wanted to throw her new man in his face. Brock."

"We spoke to him. He said she came in alone when she visited him at work."

"Oh. Well, other than that, she said there was a bar she used to go to near her sister's house that she liked." She closed her eyes for a moment. "I'm sorry, the name escapes me."

"The Depot?" Baxter asked.

She shook her head. "I don't think so. It's . . . someone's name . . . or a nickname?"

"Scooter's?" he supplied.

"That's the one."

I smiled. "That will help a lot. Tell us more."

Emily scrunched her face in thought. "I . . . I'm sorry. I just don't think there's any other specifics she gave me. She mentioned us getting together sometime and gave me her sister's contact information. I was going to call her later this week—" Her voice broke. "I can't believe she's gone."

I said sincerely, "I'm sorry for the loss of your friend, Emily. I truly am."

Emily nodded. "Please find her killer."

"We will."

Baxter was angrily quiet as we left the shelter and headed toward my car.

After shooting a quick text to Vic to tell him we needed to check out Scooter's bar for our victim's time line, I ventured, "I'm guessing we're going to need to speak to John Kocher again."

"You think?" Baxter snapped, then he immediately said, "I'm sorry. I've got a bad feeling about this whole thing."

Refraining from an eye roll, I said, "I'm not sitting in the car for this reinterview. The guy's not dangerous."

"No, I'm not thinking he's dangerous, either. My bad feeling is about the kid."

"Danny? Oh, yeah. She definitely kidnapped him."

Baxter shook his head. "Makes me wonder how many more there were."

～

WE DROVE in an uncomfortable silence back to John Kocher's house. We found him outside again, this time loading up his truck. When he saw us approach, he jumped, looking around as if deciding whether or not to take off on foot. He ended up standing his ground, his posture stiff and his expression super guilty.

"Going somewhere?" Baxter asked as he got out of the vehicle, his eyes steely and fixed on John Kocher.

"Uh . . . no . . ." John darted a glance at the duffel bag he'd just launched into the bed of his truck. "Um . . . I, uh . . . camping?"

I chuckled and walked over to stand beside Baxter. "John, I'll be honest. I didn't think you were smart enough to pull off not tipping your hand when we spoke earlier. Or have you just had more experience evading law enforcement than I assumed?"

He stared at me, wide-eyed. I loved seeing that look on people—the one where they know we're on to them. At this point, it usually didn't take much to persuade them to spill their guts.

Baxter said, "How about you tell us the truth this time?" When John only blanched in response, Baxter added, "We can talk about it at the station, if you'd rather."

Luckily, John didn't call his bluff. "Nope . . . nope, nope. I'll . . . I'll talk here if it's all the same to you."

"I'd much rather talk here, too. Let's start with why you neglected to mention a word about Danny."

I added, "And we already know the truth, but we'd like to hear it from you." That was one of my favorite lines to use while questioning someone. It made people—at least the rational ones—much more likely to tell you the truth so they didn't get themselves in even more trouble.

John Kocher sighed. "Danny . . . he was a sweet kid. Difficult at times, but I liked him. I, uh . . . didn't say nothing about him because I . . . don't know where he ended up. You see, he run off. Mary, she was sick about it. Looked everywhere for him but couldn't find him. She wouldn't eat; wouldn't sleep—"

Baxter interrupted him. "Wait. When did he run off?"

"Right before she left town."

The picture was becoming clearer by the second. I asked, "Danny ran away and she never found him?"

"Yes, ma'am."

Baxter must have put it together, too. He asked a little too casually, "Was there no search done for him by the authorities? No civilian searches or media campaigns to find him?"

John started to become squirrely again, darting his eyes around and rubbing his hands together. "She, uh . . . she didn't want that."

Baxter said, "She didn't want a police search done for her child. I take that to mean his disappearance wasn't reported. Is that correct?"

John nodded.

Oh yeah, Danny was definitely a kidnap victim. I asked, "How old was Danny at the time?"

"Four when I met him. Six by the time he run away."

My heart ached for that poor little child. It would have been a huge deal for a six-year-old to have had the guts to run away from the only home he'd known for two years, no matter if it had been good or bad. His mind could have barely understood the scope of being kidnapped, especially if Marie Collins had been kind to him, which I'd assumed she had been based on how she'd handled Shawn. But he'd still made the choice to leave and do it so well that two adults with everything to lose couldn't track him down. That was, unless we were missing a piece of a bigger picture.

Evidently Baxter had put all that together, too, and more. "Did she kill him, Mr. Kocher? Is that why she wouldn't go to the authorities?"

John's jaw dropped, and his knees buckled. His back hit the side of his truck, where he had to prop himself up to stay standing. Shaking his head forcefully, he choked out, "No. Never. She would *never*."

If this guy descended into a panic attack of some sort, we weren't going to get anything else out of him. I said, "Let's back up. You said she left just after Danny . . . disappeared. How long are we talking?"

John replied uneasily, "She left me right quick after he run away. Couldn't have been more than a couple of days."

Baxter and I shared a glance.

I said, "This woman physically lost a child—he ran away from home— and she only stuck around a couple of *days* to look for him?" *What, did she just cut her losses?*

John nodded.

I turned to Baxter, deciding to give John a bit of a break from the questioning and make him think we were believing every word of his version of this story. "Does that seem strange to you? Don't parents spend decades searching for their missing children, staying in the same house in the off chance they'll return on their own?"

Baxter evidently didn't pick up on what I was doing, because he said, "Unless they killed their kid, in which case they wouldn't need to wait around."

John Kocher let out a sob. We were going to lose him if we didn't rein it in.

I said, "John, let's quit talking about murder and say Danny did run away. You lived here with them. You said Marie didn't work, so she would have had all the time in the world to devote to him. Was their relationship not good? Was that why he ran off?"

He wiped a hand down his face and composed himself. "Danny was a sweet kid most of the time. He was pretty clingy to Mary. I don't think the two of them was ever out of each other's sight except for when they was sleeping."

"Did he not go to school?"

"She didn't believe in none of that. She homeschooled him." First rule of kidnapping—hide the kid from the world.

"Did he have any friends? Any neighbor kids he played with?"

"Not especially. Mary played with him all the time. He didn't need no friends." Sounded like what she'd done to Shawn—she'd become his world. Another good kidnapping tactic.

I asked uneasily, "Did either of them ever leave the house?"

"They went to the grocery store every once in a while." He shook his head. "She kept him home because he could be a difficult child in public. Mary loved him, but sometimes it didn't seem to be enough. He'd get in a mood and holler things like, 'You're not my real mother,' that would hurt poor Mary to the core."

Baxter had finally caught on to what I was doing. He prompted John, "Because he was adopted, right?"

John's eyebrows shot up. "No, he was her blood." Marie Collins hadn't been truthful with anyone, ever.

I stared at John. "You never once thought it was odd that Danny would say she wasn't his real mom?"

Shrugging, he replied, "Kids say mean things to their mamas."

I tried again to get John to analyze this situation. "And you also didn't think it was odd that she wouldn't ask the police for help and only stuck around days to look for her *biological* child who'd gone missing?"

"She, uh . . . she went a little cuckoo."

"A little?" Baxter snapped.

"A lot," John conceded. "She . . . she snapped."

"What happened? I asked. "What exactly did she do when she snapped?"

His face twisted in anguish. "She asked me . . . she asked me if I'd help her . . ." He shook his head. "I shouldn't have done what I done."

I smiled and said softly, "It's okay, John. Go on. I think you need to work through this."

Wiping a hand down his face, he admitted, "She asked me to help her . . . kidnap a kid."

So he had no idea he'd already been helping her kidnap a kid for two years. Poor bastard.

Baxter stiffened next to me. I put a hand on his arm, belatedly realizing the kid in question was most likely Shawn. I couldn't help wondering what the Baxter family's life would have been like if John Kocher had at least tried to talk her out of it or tried harder to find her after she left him. I managed to shake it off. None of that mattered now.

Luckily, John was too caught up in his own pain to notice Baxter's or my reactions. "She wasn't in no shape to take better care of a different boy than his own mama. I told her that. That's the real reason she got mad and left me."

"I'm sorry you had to go through that, John." As gently as I could, I asked, "Could we go back to what you said earlier about wishing you hadn't done something? Do you wish you'd said something different to her to make her stay with you?"

"No, I said what I meant. I didn't want nothing to do with no kidnapping. What I wish I done was . . . when she started her crazy ramblings about it, I should have took her to the doctor instead of telling her she wasn't a fit mama. I hurt her feelings and drove her away. I should have stood by her and helped her get better."

Barely containing his anger, Baxter asked, "Am I to understand it was only a couple of days between when the boy allegedly went missing and when she snapped and decided kidnapping was the logical next step for her?"

John seemed dazed. "It all happened real fast."

"Still, you did nothing to talk her out of it or stop her, besides refusing to help?"

"I tried to find her."

Baxter demanded, "Did you ask the authorities to help you find her, considering you knew she was planning to commit a heinous felony?"

John shrunk back. "I . . . no . . . I guess I should have . . ."

"Hindsight, right?"

My hand was still on Baxter's arm, so I gave it a quick squeeze to get his attention while I murmured, "The police couldn't have done much merely on his word that Marie Collins was *planning* to kidnap a child."

He said tersely to me, "They would have at least questioned her and kept an eye on her."

"After she moved and changed her name?"

Baxter held up his hands. "Fine. I'm done here." He stormed back to my car and left me with a weeping John Kocher.

I said gently, "Do you suppose Danny found his way to safety and told his story to the police? Did no one come out here to question you?"

He hung his head. "The police come out after Mary left, asking if I seen a little boy out here or if I knew anything about a boy being missing. I, uh .. . figured something wasn't right, so I played dumb. Mary'd took all her things and all of Danny's things, so there wasn't nothing left of either of them."

"John, you do realize she kidnapped Danny, right? And that makes you an accessory."

A tear rolled down his cheek. "I didn't have no idea 'til it was all over. Why should I be punished for loving the two of them and giving them a home?"

I sighed. Theoretically, he shouldn't have been punished for those particular actions. But he deserved some kind of punishment for not 'fessing up to the truth.

"Look, we have no jurisdiction in this county. We can't take you in. But I suggest you turn yourself in within the hour, when we go visit the sheriff and turn you in ourselves. Trust me, it will make a difference to do it voluntarily." I started walking away, but when I heard a muffled sob behind me, I turned and added, "You seem like a decent guy, John. I hope you make the right choice."

25

I looked across the table at Baxter, eyeing the pile of smoked brisket he'd left on his plate. "You gonna eat that?"

Baxter had been in a furious daze since we'd left John Kocher's house. It was further exacerbated by the text he got from his mother letting him know that she'd spoken to Tom's lawyer. The piece of evidence the detectives had found in Tom's home was Marie Collins's new phone. That was not a good development.

Baxter replied, "Oh, uh . . . yeah, I guess so," and shoveled a forkful of brisket into his mouth. He didn't seem to be enjoying the barbecue joint I'd suggested, even though it was some of the best I'd had in a long time. I was pretty sure it wasn't the food he was having problems digesting. He set his fork down and pushed his plate away. "Can we quit wasting time and go nail that guy's ass to the wall?"

I stole a bite of brisket from his plate. "Slow your roll. I gave him an hour."

"Why? He doesn't deserve it. If he hadn't—"

He was starting to raise his voice, so I cut him off quietly. "I know. If he'd only said something, maybe Marie Collins wouldn't have gotten away with kidnapping Danny and done it again." My phone buzzed, and it was a Face-

Time call from Vic. Saved by the bell. "It's Vic," I said to Baxter as I held the phone so we could both see the screen. I answered with a "Hey, how was your day?"

Vic's smiling face filled the screen. "Fruitful. I just got done with Tiffany Clarke, and she had a lot to say."

I smiled back at him. "Great. Did you crack this case wide open, Agent?"

"Maybe. Most importantly, she gave us a last name for Cody—Barnhill. And would you believe he has a record?"

"I'd believe it."

"Get to it, Manetti," Baxter griped.

I gave him a reproachful look and said to Vic, "Let me guess—assault?"

"Drugs actually, but good guess. However . . . he was responsible for a one-car accident that put a child in a wheelchair for the rest of her life."

"What does that have to do with Marie Collins?" Baxter asked impatiently.

Vic replied, "The child in question was her niece, Laurel Montgomery."

I frowned. "I don't get it."

Vic's screen turned and Detective Barnes's face filled the screen. She said, "Laurel Montgomery was Margo Watson's daughter."

Baxter and I both stared at her.

I blurted out, "Barnes . . . what are you—" I remembered I had to be nice to her now. I pasted on a smile. "I mean, hi, Corinne."

She replied, "I hope you don't mind me spending the afternoon with your *friend.*"

"Not if it means you're helping our cause. But don't you have an investigation of your own to do?"

She shrugged. "I'm at the 'mountain of paperwork' stage of the investigation. I took a page out of your book and figured it would be more fun to bring it with me and tag along on Vic's road trip."

Baxter nudged me under the table. It sounded like they were pretty well done with evidence-gathering and interviews. That could mean they either had enough to charge Tom and Mr. Baxter or they'd exhausted their ideas. Neither was too good a sign. But it was a good sign that Barnes was using company time, so to speak, to help run down one of our suspects.

Back on-screen, Vic said, "I think you missed something. Marie Collins's loser boyfriend was driving her sister's child around in his car and as a result made her a paraplegic. It had to have been a tough existence for Laurel. Then about five years ago, she took her own life."

I gasped. "She's L."

Baxter gave me a strange look. "What?"

I said to him, "Marie Collins got a heartbreaking goodbye letter from someone calling themselves 'L' about five years ago."

Vic nodded. "Exactly. That letter was a suicide note. It's pretty obvious that Laurel Montgomery blamed Marie Collins at least in part for her condition, maybe for no better reason than bringing Cody Barnhill into her life. What do you want to bet Margo Watson feels the same way—and attributes her child's death to her as well? She neglected to tell me any of that when we spoke Sunday night."

I said, "So you're thinking she could be the killer?"

"That's where it gets tricky. Corinne already verified her alibi. She worked the night shift at Covenant Nursing Home, eleven to eleven." Frowning, he added, "As much as I hate to admit it, my money's still on Fake Jake. We're on the way back now. I'll let you know when we get there, and we can talk about next steps."

"Cool. Can you email me that accident report?"

"Already done."

"Thanks. Our news isn't so earth-shattering. It's just kind of sad. Marie Collins kidnapped another little boy a few years before she took Shawn. He wasn't her first."

Vic shook his head. "That is sad."

I gave him a quick rundown of what we learned as Baxter hailed the server and settled up. The moment I hung up with Vic, he said, "It's been fifty-two minutes. That's long enough."

I held in a chuckle and followed him out the door.

∿

I WAS PLEASED to see John Kocher's truck in the parking lot of the Saline County Sheriff's Department when we got there. I pointed to it. "See? Our boy did the right thing."

Baxter grumbled, "We forced his hand."

"He still could have run, but he didn't. Come on. Aren't you always the one with way more faith in humanity than me?"

He mumbled something I didn't catch as we got out of the car.

Inside, Baxter gave our credentials to the front desk officer and told him why we were here. We waited only a few minutes until an older detective came out and waved us back to follow him into a conference room.

He said, "I'm Detective Tony Mathias. I hear we have you to thank for sending John Kocher our way."

Baxter shook his hand. "Our pleasure. Detective Nick Baxter. This is Ellie Matthews." I shook hands with Detective Mathias.

The detective smiled. "We were having a quiet evening around here until you two rolled into town and blew up a seventeen-year-old cold case. I'm sorry to say we got nowhere back in the day with the Michael Stockwell kidnapping, other than returning the kid to his family, sort of."

"What do you mean, 'sort of'?" I asked.

His smile vanished. "He'd been missing for two years, and the parents had lost hope. Dad turned to drugs, lost his job, and left mom around a year into it, then mom killed herself. The grandparents picked up little Michael, but you could tell the moment they laid eyes on the kid they didn't want him. I don't know, maybe he reminded them of his mother and it was too much for them to bear, but it didn't make it any less heartbreaking to watch."

"Poor kid." I knew what it felt like when the family members who were supposed to take care of you didn't want you around.

"We were hoping it would all turn around for him after what all he'd been through, but . . ." He shook his head sadly.

Baxter asked, "What were the circumstances of how he was found?"

Detective Mathias replied, "A hunter found him in the woods and called it in. The boy was catatonic when we got to him. Best we could tell, he'd spent the night in the woods. Practically had hypothermia. Scared out of his mind. The only thing he'd say was that his name was Michael—nothing else. Not where he'd come from, where he'd been, or who he'd been with. With no other information than a first name, it was hard to figure out where to start. We sent deputies out to all the residences in a five-mile radius, which included a visit with John Kocher. No one reported seeing a boy running around, and no one had heard of a child who'd run away. Once we thought we'd exhausted local possibilities, we figured the kid could have been transported here from anywhere. It took a few days to wade through every missing persons case in the country for the previous five years, but we finally figured out his identity. He'd been abducted two years prior while playing in a park in Evansville, Indiana."

Baxter and I shared a glance. Another local connection. Even though she made it a point to spirit her victims away to rural areas where they wouldn't be noticed, Marie Collins didn't tend to stray far from home when she did the actual kidnapping.

Baxter said, "So since Michael was unable to articulate the location of where he'd been or the names of his captors, there was no way to charge anyone."

"Yes. It was like he'd been dropped out of the sky, for all we knew. The foster family who took him for the week we ran the investigation said they tried everything to get him to talk, but he wouldn't. The social worker had a therapist work with him, but nothing helped. I assume he never breathed a word about it, ever, since we've yet to have any kind of information come our way."

"Did you follow up with the family? Ask them if Michael finally was able to talk about his kidnapping?"

Detective Mathias nodded. "That's where this story gets even sadder. We did check on him from time to time through his local CPS. There was never any abuse that they could determine, but the general vibe in the home wasn't loving or nurturing. By the age of fifteen, the kid had run away from his grandparents. There was no record of him after that, and—"

A knock at the door interrupted him. A man in a suit stuck his head inside and said, "Tony, a word?"

As Detective Mathias excused himself, Baxter slumped in his seat and seemed to wither right in front of me. "Fifteen and living on the streets?

You know what happens to those kids, Ellie." His eyes shone with tears. "That could have been Shawn."

Leaning toward him, I drew him into my arms and held tight. "That could not have been Shawn. Your family didn't give up hope."

"My family only had to be in hell for seven months. We wouldn't have lasted two years."

"You would've."

"My mother wouldn't have."

I pulled back so I could look him in the eye. "Nick, there's no reason to dwell on what might have been. It's not helping our investigation, and it's definitely not helping your state of mind. I'll drive back and you try to sleep. It's been an eventful day. You could use the rest. Okay?"

He nodded. I doubted he could turn his brain off for that long.

Detective Mathias returned to the room. "Sorry about that. I'm afraid I'll have to wrap this up. We're getting ready to book John Kocher."

"Good," Baxter muttered.

Detective Mathias said, "Where was I? Oh, right. Michael Stockwell disappeared at fifteen. We coordinated with the Vanderburgh County Sheriff's Department to keep an eye out for him, and when he turned eighteen, well, he was an adult, so we quit looking for him. Now, when John Kocher came in here tonight and started telling us his story, I had a deputy run Michael's social one more time. I figured we owed it to the kid to try to find him and let him know he finally got a little justice, but there's still no trace of him. He'd be about twenty-three now. I don't know if he's dead, homeless, or what, but he never set up so much as a credit card in his name."

Baxter frowned. "One more thing, which is the real reason we're here— do you know of anyone connected to this case who might want Marie Collins, AKA Mary Stevens, dead?"

The detective let out a mirthless laugh. "Maybe Michael Stockwell. From what I understand, he'd be about the only person aside from John Kocher who even knew her around here."

Baxter's expression clouded over as he gave the detective his card. "If you think of anything else, please reach out."

Detective Mathias accepted the card with a nod. "Will do. You all drive safe."

~

As I drove, Baxter did not in fact rest, not that I'd expected he would. He spent the drive engulfed in his laptop, learning everything he could about Michael Stockwell and his family. At least the swelling had gone down in my eye enough that I could finally focus on the road without straining, and my head didn't feel like someone was continually pounding on it. For once, I turned my brain off and immersed myself in the drive, hoping some downtime would allow my subconscious to work through what we'd learned today. I felt like the easy rural drive helped my anxiety level, but the same couldn't be said for Baxter. I could feel the tension rolling off him.

I finally ventured, "What is your obsession with the missing kid?"

Without taking his eyes off the screen, Baxter said, "He could be our killer. I sent all the info to Manetti to get his take on it."

I said gently, "Given his circumstances, Michael Stockwell is probably dead."

"And if he isn't?"

"Then he's a crackhead. Or a prostitute. Or so mentally ill he doesn't even know who he is anymore. Or all of those. The fact that he couldn't verbalize anything about two whole years of his life, even later on, speaks to a monumental break that occurred to his mental state. Untreated throughout his adolescence, which I assume was the case considering his grandparents were shitty guardians, it would screw him up practically beyond repair."

"Thank you for the astute analysis, Dr. Freud."

"I'm being serious."

"So am I. What if he's Fake Jake? You called him a ghost. Michael Stockwell is nothing if not a ghost."

I shivered, even in the warmth of my heated seat. "When you put it like that, I could be persuaded. But that doesn't negate the fact that he has to have some incredibly debilitating mental issues after bottling up being kidnapped. I mean, Shawn has had professional help and was able to talk out what happened to him, right? And he's still got issues. Rachel, too. This shit doesn't go away. But repressing it? I can't fathom Michael Stockwell being able to function at all."

Baxter shrugged. "Repressed feelings don't have to cripple you. They can turn into rage, which can motivate you. Making him a perfect murder suspect."

"Seventeen years is a long time to wait for revenge. Young people aren't known for their patience. The more I think about it, the more I like Margo Watson."

His eyebrows shot up. "As the killer? I thought she had a solid alibi."

I said, "In a twelve-hour night shift at a likely understaffed nursing home, someone lucid had eyes on her the whole time? Doubtful. I would concede that she may not have swung the axe, but she's involved. She's had a lifetime of having to clean up after her sister, and then after what happened to her daughter . . . I don't know. I feel like she had a score to settle."

"Would you ever consider killing Rachel?"

Clearly he wasn't on the Margo Watson train. I shrugged. "Okay, I'll play, only let's tweak the scenario a little. Say I revert back to my delinquent teenage self. I start drinking again. I start dating complete tools. I mooch off Rachel and embarrass her nonstop. Then, because of the bad company I keep, Nate is permanently hurt, which Rachel has to deal with and ultimately results in him taking his own life. During all that, I keep being a piece of shit, go to prison, get out, and go right back to being a piece of shit when Rachel finally comes around and tries to reconnect with me. I would hope she'd want to kill me."

He frowned. "I see your point. But if Margo Watson was going to kill her sister, why not do it right after the accident?"

"Because the accident wasn't the last straw for her. She still had yet to endure the ostracization over being assumed as a party in Shawn's disappearance, years of the mental and physical stress of being a caregiver to a paraplegic, and the death of her daughter. Saturday would have been her first chance to kill her sister."

"Why not kill her on the way home and dump her body somewhere remote?"

I cast him a dubious glance. "So she'd be the prime suspect by default? Margo Watson's not stupid. Marie Collins's fingerprints are in AFIS, and her DNA is probably in CODIS. IDing her would be a snap, and there's a record of who picked her up from prison." I shook my head. "No. She brought her delinquent sister back home, knowing she'd go out and get hammered and hang with a bunch of randos, any one of whom she could pin a murder on."

"Except she chose my brother."

I shrugged. "Maybe not. Maybe she chose the location because she wanted a Baxter to go down for it and didn't really care which one. She could have been pissed at Shawn for the vandalism or pissed at your mom for not accepting her apologies over the years."

He nodded. "I could see it."

"Or maybe the barn was a random but convenient location and she didn't even know whose property she was on."

"Don't see that one."

"How far is Covenant Nursing Home from there?"

His eyes widened. "Not far at all. About a mile."

"And there you go. One lengthy coffee break would have given her all the time she'd need." I went on, "On to my next point, I think planting the phone at Tom's house was one hundred percent calculated, *but* not until later. Margo waited until someone—it didn't matter who—got arrested, and she made sure the charges stuck."

Baxter thought for a moment. "That phone has been bugging me all evening. The only ways the police would have known where to find it would be if it suddenly got turned on and they could track the signal or if they got a tip. Either way is fishy. Tom was already in jail at the time it was found and Janelle wasn't home. She'd gone to stay with her sister in Newburgh to get help taking care of Olivia. Based on that, the only person who could have turned it on was the person who planted it. And anonymous tips always scream tainted evidence."

There was the brilliant Baxter I knew. "Ooh, that's a good point. Text Barnes and ask her." While he did that, I added, "Other than that little oversight, it's a brilliant plan, actually. If the crime hadn't been pinned on your family, I feel like we'd be standing in awe of Margo Watson's capacity for chaos rather than tearing apart her character right now."

After finishing up the text, he said, "So by your logic, our next order of business is to question Margo Watson."

"Not yet. I think we need to find Cody Barnhill first."

"Why him?"

I'd taken a look at the accident report Vic had sent me while we were waiting for Detective Mathias in Harrisburg, and I'd been mulling it over ever since. "I've got a feeling."

26

Cody Barnhill lived in a run-down apartment building south of downtown Evansville. As we left my car parked on the street, I wasn't confident it would be in one piece when we returned. The apartment was an unfortunately fitting place to live for someone with as many drug charges on his record as Cody Barnhill. We had to push aside some trash in the hallway to stand in front of his door. The stench was not a lot different than most crime scenes, only missing the aromas of blood and decomp.

Baxter pounded on the door to apartment 203 and waited. Across the hall, there must have been a party, or at least an asshole with a loud stereo system. If we wanted to be able to hear our conversation with our interviewee, we'd have to enter his apartment, and I was betting it was even less clean than this hallway.

A man answered the door, but it wasn't Cody Barnhill. He looked us up and down and flexed. "We don't like cops around here."

Baxter said dryly, "I'm sure you don't. We're here to make a death notification to Cody Barnhill about someone he was close to."

"Oh." The guy relaxed and backed off, allowing us to step inside and close the door. Over his shoulder, he yelled, "Cody! Come here."

Cody Barnhill stood from the couch and staggered toward us. The first guy clapped him on the back and stood next to him to steady him. Cody looked at us with bleary eyes. Damn. I hoped he was sober enough to be of use.

"You cops? I didn't do nothing," he slurred.

His friend said, "Um, they're here to tell you someone died, buddy."

Cody's face fell. "Who?"

Baxter replied, "Marie Collins, your former girlfriend, was murdered Sunday morning." He didn't even bother to give our names. This guy wouldn't have remembered anyway.

Cody squinted at him. "Oh." Then he shrugged. "Oh well. I ain't seen her in years."

"She's been in prison, but we thought she might look you up when she got out. Did she try to contact you Saturday?"

He shook his head. "Nah. We're long done."

I asked, "Have you had any contact with her sister, Margo?"

Cody laughed. "That bitch? No. She hated me."

"Because of what happened to Laurel."

He sneered. "Yeah."

I took my opportunity. "What exactly happened that day? Why were you driving your girlfriend's niece around? Was Marie with you? Were you high?"

His friend said, "You don't have to answer her, Cody. They're asking too many questions. Kick them out."

Cody stared at me for a moment. "Marie's really dead?"

I replied, "Yes, very. I saw her with my own eyes."

He nodded slowly. "Then I guess I don't have to keep her secret anymore, right?"

"Right," I agreed. This sounded promising.

"Marie was driving, not me. She was high as a kite." He let out a chuckle. "For once, I wasn't."

Baxter wrinkled his brow. "Then why weren't you driving?"

Cody shrugged. "Margo hated my guts. She didn't want me driving her precious daughter around because she thought I was a loser, so Marie always drove when the girl was with us."

I saw where this was going. "So when Marie crashed the car, you covered for her because you were sober. Her name wasn't even on the accident report. Did she run?"

"Yeah. She would have gone to jail for sure. Plus her sister would have killed her if she knew."

Baxter and I shared a look. He asked, "If Laurel was in the car, she would have known who was driving, right? She could have told her mother."

"Well, she was in a coma for a long time, so she didn't tell nobody nothing. But I think she ended up not being able to remember the accident. At least that's what Marie said."

Marie got lucky. That, or she was able to convince Laurel to cover for her as well. It certainly sounded like Laurel remembered the accident, especially since in her letter she stated, *I still can't find it in my heart to forgive you for what you did.* I had to wonder if Margo knew the truth as well.

Baxter asked Cody, "Where were you Sunday morning between one and three a.m.?"

Cody rolled his eyes upward. I wasn't sure if he was actually thinking or wanted us to think he was thinking. So far he'd seemed to be a docile and truthful addict. "Uhh . . . I dunno."

I asked, "Is it safe to assume you were high?"

He smiled. "Oh, yeah."

I said to Baxter, "I don't think our friend here has the level of precision we're looking for in a suspect."

Baxter nodded. "Agreed." To Cody, he said, "Thanks for your time."

As we left, Baxter said, "I think I get why you think Margo Watson could be guilty. How did you know this guy had covered for Marie Collins?"

"Sister Code. You don't let your degenerate boyfriend drive your sister's kid around by himself if you're not there."

"Ah."

"It clicked for me because her name wasn't on the accident report as a passenger or a witness. Plus, it's become increasingly clear that for some odd reason Marie Collins could talk a man into damn near anything."

"Yeah, I don't get that, either."

∿

WE PULLED up at the Baxter home to find a party going on out back around the firepit. Several of Shawn's friends had come over to cheer him up, I assumed, which unfortunately was being done with the aid of multiple cases of beer and a joint that was being passed around and then clumsily hidden as we got out of the car. I wasn't surprised. Mr. Baxter was indisposed, and Mrs. Baxter couldn't very well put a stop to their drug use and underage drinking while she was passed out on the couch.

When Baxter headed for the house rather than toward the multiple misdemeanors being committed, I said, "Do we do something about this or let it happen?"

He groaned. "I'm too tired to deal with those idiots. Plus the minute we go inside, they'll go back to doing whatever we want them to quit doing. If we tell them to leave, they'll just move the party to another location. It's an exercise in futility."

"Sounds like this isn't your first rodeo with them."

"I have a history of ruining their fun. They call me Officer Buzzkill."

I chuckled. "Ooh. Well, then, could we score some brownie points with the cops by tattling on them?"

"Where do you think that would land Shawn?"

I frowned. "Oh, right. Good point. So we look the other way."

"Basically."

We went inside to find Mrs. Baxter right where I imagined she'd be, exactly the way I'd found her last night, passed out next to a bottle of gin. Damn. I guessed what I said wasn't enough to get through to her, if she even remembered it, which I wasn't convinced she had. I knew it killed Baxter to see her like this, but the poor man had no more cycles left to give. I did what I did last night, taking her bottle and burying it in the trash. Since she was asleep this time, I saved the lecture and came back and laid a blanket over her. I then stood next to Baxter as he looked out the sliding patio doors toward the group of young adults seated around the firepit.

"What do you think about Shawn's friends?" I asked.

He replied, "I thought we'd gone over that. I think they're idiots."

I chuckled. "Yes, you made that clear." I looked at them thoughtfully. "I mean, do you think one of them might have any insight into this mess?"

"I doubt if they have much insight, period."

"Maybe not, but I bet everyone in town wants to gossip with them about what happened, considering they're Shawn's best bros. I want to know what the townsfolk think about who did it."

Smiling, he said, "That's not a very professional investigational approach, Ms. Matthews."

"So fire me."

His face fell. "Too soon."

"You think they'd talk to us?" I asked.

"You, maybe."

"Oh, right. Because of the whole Officer Buzzkill thing."

He nodded.

I felt like since this afternoon he'd been slowly losing hope that we'd figure out who the real killer was. I believed we'd made headway and learned a lot, but at the end of the day all we really did was uncover more of Marie Collins's sins and cross off nearly all the suspects on our list. If Margo Watson could get someone to vouch that they had eyes on her nonstop during the time of death window and we couldn't come up with a motive for Brock Lovell other than the fact that he was a violent asshole, our two most solid leads were toast. To me, Michael Stockwell was a medi-ocre contender at best, but that was if we could find him *and* he wasn't out of his mind. Fake Jake still seemed like the most likely suspect, but you couldn't pin a murder on someone you couldn't locate. Granted, Michael Stockwell and Fake Jake could have been one and the same, but that didn't make him any easier to find. It was starting to feel like we needed a new angle, and hometown gossip wasn't looking half bad to me.

"I'll be back," I said, sliding the door open and stepping out into the crisp evening air.

I approached the boys' circle and got some stares. "Hi, guys. I'm Ellie. Nick's friend from work."

I got a scattering of disinterested "hey" responses.

After a pretty lengthy silence, I began to think they were going to completely ignore me, so I sat down on the edge of one of the chairs around the firepit and said, "Is there anything else to do for fun around here besides sit around and drink?"

One of them shrugged. "Not really." Then a look of realization seemed to hit him. "Oh, shit. You found the body."

I feared Shawn would be sensitive to this, but I had to do something to gain a little cred with these guys and get them talking. "I did. It was gross, and there was so much blood."

The same kid, the one with the short mullet, said, "I heard the axe was lodged in her head."

Where in the world had he heard that? Although I hadn't followed the news coverage, I couldn't imagine the cops had leaked that particular detail. And then I remembered Mrs. Baxter had seen the body and wasn't one to keep her mouth shut.

I went with it. "That is also true. I've seen a lot of murdered people, and this one was pretty far up there on the gruesomeness scale."

One of the others, the one with the long mullet, said, "She had it coming. I hope it hurt."

Short Mullet chimed in, "Yeah, that bitch didn't deserve to be breathing fresh air for what she did to Shawn."

The bulked-up guy who looked like a total gym rat said, "Scotty trying to come up with a new catchphrase challenge—impossible. You've said that like a thousand times, bro."

"Eat me, asshole," Scotty fired back.

I said, "So, speaking of what she did to Shawn . . . we found out today that he wasn't her first kidnap victim."

It went quiet around the firepit.

Shawn, who'd yet to say anything, stared at me in horror. "She . . . she kidnapped someone else besides me?"

I nodded. "A boy from Evansville. His name was Michael Stockwell. It happened about four years before she took you."

"How in the hell did you find that out?" he breathed.

"We talked to a lot of people today."

"Did you talk to him?"

"No, he's . . ." I shrugged. "We don't know where to find him. He was reunited with his family but then ran away from home at fifteen. There's no record of him after that. If he's still around, he's not using his real name."

Gym Rat said, "Whoa, wait. How did she not get arrested for that kidnapping if the kid got back with his family?"

I explained, "The boy managed to run away from her, and then I guess she panicked and left town before anyone could catch her. She was using a fake name during the time she had him and was pretty efficient at not leaving a trail for anyone to follow."

Long Mullet shook his head. "Damn, she was diabolical."

The one with the trucker hat held up his bottle of beer. "To Shawn, for surviving. And to him never having to worry about that psycho again. Cheers, buddy."

After lifting their drinks to Shawn, they all took long swigs. I felt remarkably unmoved to want to join in even though I hadn't been to a meeting in days. With a front-row seat to Mrs. Baxter's spiral amplifying my desire to never come close to that again, I hadn't felt like I'd needed one to keep me on track. I promised myself that once this mess was behind us, I was going to do something to try to help her.

But back to my plan, which had so far been one-sided on the gossip. "So what's the consensus around town about this murder? I know no one's crying over her demise, but surely people are talking, especially to you guys since you're close to Shawn. Is anyone buying Tom and Jim Baxter being guilty?"

Long Mullet said, "People are pretty split on it. Some think they did it. Everybody has a theory."

Now we were getting somewhere. I said, "Let's hear some of these other theories. Who's everyone accusing?"

"Benji McDonald. He's kind of a psycho, too."

Gym Rat reached over and slapped Long Mullet on the back of the head. "Chase, you dick. Don't say shit like that. He's still Shawn's uncle."

Trucker Hat said, "Yeah, I've heard it about Benji McDonald, too. Sorry, Shawn."

Scotty said, "My mom thinks it's her sister, Margo. She's kind of a bitch."

Chase nodded. "My mom works with her and says she's a bitch, too. She thinks she did it."

I turned my attention to the two of them. "Any specific reason why they think Margo would bring her sister out here—or lure her out here—to kill her? There are plenty of other places she could have done it."

Chase shrugged. "To get back at Shawn's mom. They had beef."

"Because Margo kept trying to apologize for her sister and Mrs. Baxter wasn't having it? That's not much beef."

Chase shook his head. "No, it was because Margo and Benji were hooking up and Mrs. Baxter wasn't having it."

My eyebrows shot up. "Whoa. When was this?"

Shawn said quietly, "Right before Aunt Lucy divorced him."

Ooh. I'd yet to hear this little nugget. I wondered if Baxter knew. "Is this common knowledge?"

Shawn shook his head. "Mom told me one night when she was drunk. It wasn't that long ago. I told the guys."

I had a bad feeling about this. Vic and I had pretty much ruled out Uncle Benji on the basis of his recent better behavior and the fact that we didn't think he'd ever have planted evidence on Tom. But if there was someone else in the picture pulling the strings—and making moves behind Uncle Benji's back—then I was beginning to think we'd been too hasty in our quest to narrow down our suspects.

I asked Shawn, "Is your uncle Benji right-handed or left?"

"Both, actually. There's a word for it . . ."

Oh shit.

27

I raced back to the house and into Baxter's room. "I may have made a huge error in judgment."

Baxter looked up from his laptop. "About what?"

"For starters, is Uncle Benji ambidextrous?"

"Yes." Realization dawned on him, but then he shook his head. "Oh, but he bats and plays sports right. He can just write with both hands. That's why it didn't occur to me." He paused again, and then said uneasily, "I suppose he has the capacity to swing left if he wanted to, though."

I cringed. "Well, it gets worse. Did you know Uncle Benji and Margo Watson were doing it?"

Jaw dropping, his response was only a horrified stare.

I gave him an apologetic smile. "Yeah. I don't know how long it's lasted, but it started just before your aunt divorced him."

He finally found his voice. "Who told you this? Shawn?"

I nodded. "Evidently your mom spilled the beans to him."

"Mom knew . . . maybe that's why she hated Margo Watson so much."

"That's what I'm thinking. According to Chase and Scotty's moms, Margo Watson is our killer."

"You learned their names already?"

"Only those two. I didn't catch names for Gym Rat and Trucker Hat."

Baxter let out a slight chuckle. "Gym Rat would be Tanner, and Trucker Hat is Jackson."

"Whatever. So Chase and Jackson said they've heard people going around saying Uncle Benji is to blame. If Margo Watson is half the manipulator her sister was, she could have coerced your uncle into going after his nemesis. I mean, she could have driven their drunk asses out here and locked them in the barn so they'd cage match it out. Either way, she wins. Her shitty sister either dies or goes down for murder. Benji is collateral damage."

"If she had in fact set up such a cage match, don't you think she would have provided each of them a weapon?"

I shrugged. "Maybe she preferred them beating the hell out of each other. Maybe she didn't even want them to die—it could have been about watching them struggle and suffer."

His expression grew dark. "We need to talk to Margo Watson."

"I know you're invested in this. But if any of this has any merit, she won't say a word with you in the room. I think it needs to be Vic and me, with you listening in."

"I hate being on the outside of this case," he griped.

I reached out and took his hand. "I know you do. But I feel like we're finally getting close. We can't afford to screw this up."

He nodded in agreement, and I got out my phone to call Vic. When he answered, I asked, "How far out are you?"

Vic replied, "Just rolling into town. What's up?"

"You and I need to go question Margo Watson. Like now."

Condescension dripping from her voice, Barnes said, "Ellie, Margo Watson has been incredibly open and helpful throughout our investigation. Plus, she has a solid alibi. She was officially ruled out as a suspect almost immediately."

I bit back a growl and put it on speaker so Baxter could hear. "Says the detective who has two wrong suspects incarcerated right now. Besides, this is my investigation, not yours, so I can question anyone I want."

Baxter put his hand on my arm and mouthed, "Be nice."

Barnes let out a huff. "You should be thankful I'm giving your so-called investigation any merit at all."

"No, *you* should be thankful, because without my 'so-called investigation,' you'd never know that Margo Watson has been sleeping with Benji McDonald, one of her sister's biggest haters. You wouldn't think those two had anything in common. Except . . . it turns out Marie Collins was the one who put Margo's daughter Laurel in a wheelchair. Who's got motive now? I think those two are a match made in the hell of Marie Collins's making."

That shut her up.

Vic said, "Damn. That changes things. Marie Collins wasn't listed on the accident report at all."

I explained, "She worked her magic on Cody Barnhill and fled the scene because she was driving high. He admitted to taking the blame because he was sober at the time of the accident."

Barnes sounded almost apologetic as she said, "About Benji McDonald, we did consider him briefly as a suspect, so we began tracking his movements that night. The bartender at The Depot said he got a phone call and left around twelve-thirty a.m."

"Then what?"

"Then . . . we found a better suspect, so we abandoned the Benji McDonald angle."

I snapped, "Great detective work. Let's give the guy with a lengthy assault record, a history of unstable behavior, motive coming out his ears, and no alibi a pass."

Baxter gave me a dubious glance and whispered, "You did that, too."

I ignored his remark as Barnes said, "Well, there was the fact that his prints weren't on the murder weapon. What would be more important to you—a hunch or actual evidence?"

If the cases Baxter and I investigated together had taught me anything, it was that gut instinct and thinking outside the box were just as important as the evidence I gathered and processed. "Right now, my hunch is that I should get off this call before I say something I can't take back. Vic, see you at Margo's." I hung up.

～

BAXTER and I parked behind Vic's vehicle on the road near Margo Watson's mailbox. It was true that you couldn't see her house from here, and vice versa. Barnes was unfortunately still in Vic's vehicle, and she frowned at me from the passenger side as we approached. Vic got out, and Baxter took his place.

Vic said to Baxter, "I'll call Corinne and put it on speaker so you two can listen in. Am I to assume we're not tipping our hand that we think Margo Watson could be guilty of murder or at least conspiracy?"

Baxter nodded, his expression kind of defeated. "I think what we need most is to figure out if she's conspiring with . . . Benji."

On the way over, he'd gotten increasingly quiet and fidgety. It had to be such a double-edged sword for him to know that to free his brother and father, he quite possibly had to deliver his uncle as a trade. I shook off my feelings about it. I had to be on my game for this interview.

I said to Vic, "I think we need to open up by hitting her with the news of the Michael Stockwell kidnapping. If she knows about it, maybe she has some insight she might share to keep our focus off her. If she doesn't, it'll hopefully rattle her."

"Sounds like a plan. You ready?" Vic asked me.

I nodded, falling into step with him as we headed up the steep driveway. To calm my nerves, I tried to take my mind far off the subject at hand. "How was your date?"

He shot a glance at me. As any good friend would, he figured out I needed to get out of my head for a minute and replied, "Good . . . I think."

"What's with the hesitation?"

"She was hard to read."

"It wasn't hard for me to read that she thinks you're hot. At this stage of the game, that's really all you need."

He winked at me. "Lots of women think I'm hot."

I rolled my eyes. "She's literally the female version of you."

"Not really. She seems kind of uptight. And she doesn't get along with you at all."

"Exactly. She's the old you."

"Ah." He thought for a moment. "I guess I can see it."

Snickering, I said, "Have an argument with her and you'll see it."

He frowned.

I shrugged. "So you're not a perfect match. She's gorgeous. You're on vacation. Hit it and quit it."

"That's not my style."

"I know. But I also know exactly how many days it's been since you got any. No one should have to suffer for that long."

Giving me a knowing glance, he said, "I can say the same about you. Because unless you've suddenly gotten a lot better at keeping a lid on your afterglow, I'd wager you and the good detective have been keeping things PG."

I barked out a laugh. "You mean you don't think we're getting it on in his childhood bed with his disapproving mother down the hall while we have to keep pretending there's nothing between us? You're correct. It's decidedly PG in my world. Someone might as well be getting some action."

"You and Barnes aren't exactly besties, yet you're pushing me toward her with both hands. Are you angling for me to screw some information out of her or what?"

"No. I may be a lot of things, but I'm not a pimp. And no, we're not besties, but . . . I think we could be if we weren't on opposite sides of this thing. Besides, if Baxter dated her, she can't be all bad, right?"

He smirked at me. "He chose you. I'm not sure I trust his judgment."

I elbowed him. "Dick."

We were fast approaching Margo Watson's front door, so Vic took out his phone and called Barnes. After a quick check that they could hear us, Vic knocked on the door.

We only had to wait a couple of moments before Margo Watson answered the door with a smile. "Back again, Agent? I didn't hear you pull up." She flicked her eyes toward her driveway and then gave me a questioning glance.

Vic smiled. "Yes, Ms. Watson. We parked on the road and walked up. We needed to stretch our legs after a long drive this evening." He put on a more serious expression and continued, "We learned something upsetting about your sister we'd like to discuss with you. We don't want this particular information becoming public knowledge before you have a chance to process it. May we come inside?"

Her face fell. "Oh, yes. Please come in."

As we entered the home, Vic said, "This is Ms. Matthews. She's working with me and the police on this case."

Margo Watson turned and stared at me. "I know that name. You're that Baxter boy's detective partner."

I knew she'd have some sort of opinion about whether or not she'd want to talk to me based on who I was. I tried a little preemptive damage control before she got the notion to kick me out of her home. "Nick Baxter and I do work together up in Hamilton County. I came to town to help him with a legal issue and found myself in a much bigger situation. I want to offer my condolences on the passing of your sister."

She frowned. "Passing? I heard you found her. Of anyone, you should know that 'passing' doesn't quite seem to describe what happened to Marie."

I nodded. "I didn't mean to downplay the situation, Ms. Watson. Your sister's death was tragic, and I'm only interested in making sure the correct person is punished for the crime, no matter who it is."

"Even if their name's Baxter?"

"Even if their name's Baxter."

She seemed to settle down a bit, so Vic took the opportunity to say, "You may want to sit down to hear what we came to tell you, Ms. Watson."

She nodded and sank into a side chair. She motioned for us to sit on the couch, facing her, so we did.

Vic began, "We went to Rockville Prison to find out who your sister had been in contact with during her incarceration. We tracked down several people, and our search led us to a town called Muddy, Illinois. Do you remember your sister living there for a while?"

Margo's eyes went a tad wide as Vic named the town of Muddy. I felt like she knew something. She didn't give it away, though. She sighed. "No, but that's not unusual. Marie moved around a lot and didn't always tell me where she was living. I usually had a phone number for her, but not always. We'd go for years without speaking, mainly because . . ." She paused to huff out a breath. "Mainly because it was never a priority to her to keep in touch with me. That was, unless she needed money, and then she'd come and visit me and pretend she hadn't ghosted me for months on end."

Maybe I could play the empathy card here. Like Margo, I watched out for my sister, taking her into my home when she was seventeen and pregnant. Unlike Margo, I'd never regretted my decision or begrudged my sister even for a moment. But then again, my sweet Rachel had never given me the slightest bit of trouble, aside from dating the occasional loser, which up until lately I was guilty of as well. I could see where it would be difficult if your sister wasn't a good person to be able to walk the line between helping and enabling. And that wasn't even considering the emotional toll Marie's actions had taken on Margo.

I gave Margo my best sympathetic smile. "I get it. My sister and her little boy live with me. Some days, I feel like all I do is give and all she does is take. It's not a good feeling."

Margo nodded. "It's really not. So many times I've told myself 'this is the last time I bail her out,' but I can't seem to ever stick with it. I guess now . . ." She trailed off.

I didn't want her to clam up, so I said, "You know, even if she didn't tell you or show you, I'm sure she appreciated what you did for her. Even if it felt like you were being used, you were still giving her the help she needed."

"Needed. It wasn't always deserved."

"We all have times we don't deserve the love we're shown. Even if you judged her or were angry with her, you still had it in your heart to make her life better. That's what makes a great sister." Except that a great sister would never kill her sister or have her killed. I hoped this woman didn't pick up on the truckload of smoke I was blowing up her ass.

If she did, she didn't let on. "Thank you for saying that. It hasn't been easy being Marie Collins's sister."

"I imagine it hasn't been. And that's why we wanted to bring you this news before it gets out. This isn't going to be easy for you to hear, but . . . Shawn Baxter wasn't the first child your sister kidnapped."

The split second she took to compose herself before breaking into an expression of utter shock was all I needed to see to know this was not news to her. She was good, but she wasn't that good.

She gasped, "What? There was another?"

"Yes. Michael Stockwell, a boy from Evansville. We don't know much about the actual kidnapping, but she took him to Muddy, Illinois, and held him there for two years. We spoke to the man they lived with at the time. He had no idea the boy wasn't her son."

"How could she . . . ?" Margo put her head in her hands.

I had to say, her acting was top-notch. She was convincing. So much so, I imagined it wasn't hard for her to talk Uncle Benji into confronting her sister. However, the one thing that continued to bother me about Uncle Benji committing the act of killing Marie Collins was his demeanor when I met him. All the pieces fit, but my feeling was one I couldn't shake.

Vic had picked up on where I was trying to take the conversation and had gone quiet, but once we got onto a different subject, he jumped back in. "We understand if you need a moment."

Margo nodded, head still in her hands.

Vic gave her a couple of minutes. When she raised her tear-streaked face, he asked, "I hate to bring this up, since I'm sure it's a sore subject, but did your sister covet your daughter, Laurel?"

Holy shit, he went there. I had to work to keep a straight face.

28

Margo stared at Vic, her jaw going slack. "Covet . . . Laurel? No . . . I . . . I don't think so."

He asked, "Was she a good aunt? Did she take Laurel places and do things with her?"

She was starting to look uncomfortable. Perfect. "She . . . well, before she lost Aaron, she was great. Our kids were a year apart, and we were all inseparable. Say what you want to about Marie, but she was a wonderful mom."

He pressed, "After Aaron died, she had some difficulty working through her loss, correct?"

She nodded. "She never got over his death."

"Which is why she kept kidnapping four-year-old boys."

"I imagine so."

Vic kept digging. "Back to Laurel. Did you ever have a reason to believe your sister might try to take your daughter from you?"

She blinked. "No, she wouldn't have."

Nodding slowly, he said, "Okay." After a purposeful pause, he asked, "Then why, on the day of the accident, were they halfway to Indianapolis? It was shortly before she kidnapped Michael Stockwell. It stands to reason that could have been her first attempt."

Again, I had to restrain myself from reacting. I'd read the accident report, but I'd paid little attention to the location listed. I wasn't familiar with town names in this end of the state, and I didn't think to map the location.

Margo seemed to have to restrain herself as well. She clasped her hands on her lap and smiled tightly. "Marie wasn't in the vehicle."

Vic played dumb. "So her boyfriend was driving your eight-year-old daughter around alone, miles from home?"

"Yes," she replied.

"Were you aware of this?"

She cleared her throat. "Yes."

He settled back into his seat, comfortable and in his element as he began to argue in earnest. "And you had no problem with a known drug abuser driving your eight-year-old daughter around alone, miles from home?"

"He wouldn't have been my first choice."

"Where were they going?"

"To Indianapolis for a short vacation."

He raised an eyebrow. "Just the two of them?"

She frowned. "They were meeting Marie there."

"Hmm."

He was veering toward bad cop territory, so I jumped in with a gentle tone. "Why do you still feel the need to cover for her now that she's dead? You don't have to keep up the charade. Cody came clean about Marie being high and crashing the car. You can, too."

She whipped her head toward me. "What?"

I got the feeling she was more worried than angry, which meant I was right and she knew about the accident and had helped cover up the truth. "I get it. My sister and I always cover for each other, no questions asked. But this is different. If I were the person responsible for hurting my nephew like that, my sister would straight-up kill me." I feigned a gasp as Margo's eyes got fiery. I'd said what I meant, but she didn't need to know that. "Oh, Ms. Watson, I'm so sorry. Poor word choice. I didn't mean to insinuate that you—"

Vic was able to step back into the good cop role and smooth things over.

"I can assure you that Ms. Matthews meant nothing by that turn of phrase, Ms. Watson. We believe we have a solid lead on who really killed your sister, and the detectives on the case have been looking into his background and interviewing people around town. In fact, Detective Barnes is sending out deputies to pick up our suspect for questioning this evening."

Margo had been able to rein in her emotions so far, but now she lost it. "What? They have two suspects in jail already. Why are they wasting time chasing your half-baked theories?"

I said calmly, "Honestly, it was because of the evidence they found at Tom Baxter's home. It was fishy how it fell into their laps like it did, and because of that, it'll be inadmissible in court. The circumstances made the evidence seem planted, which actually hurt the case against Tom instead of helping it. The killer thought he was being smart, but it was a stupid move."

She closed her eyes, I imagined in an attempt not to blow a gasket in front of us after learning she'd screwed up *and* getting called stupid. "I'm . . . not feeling well. This has been a lot to process. If you don't mind, I need to go lie down." She stood.

Vic stood also. "Completely understandable, Ms. Watson. Do you need help getting settled?"

Damn it. We didn't get around to bringing up Uncle Benji, and it didn't look like we were going to get the chance tonight.

"No," Margo said as she left the room and stormed down the hallway, not even bothering to see us to the door.

Once we were outside, I said, "We definitely rattled her. I'd love to stay and peep in her windows to find out what she's going to do next."

Vic chuckled. "I'd bet money she's packing a bag, and that's why I'm going to stay behind and tail her."

"Smart. I think she's going to call Benji and give him a heads-up."

He shrugged. "Maybe."

I looked up at him. "What, are you not on board with the Margo-Benji angle?"

"If I'm honest . . . I'm still Team Fake Jake."

"Is that why you didn't bring up her hooking up with Benji and didn't name-drop him as our suspect? Because you don't think he's our guy?"

"Yeah, same reason you were vague about the phone found at Tom's house. You weren't sure of the details, so you let her fill them in. I'm not convinced Benji McDonald is the killer, but I *am* convinced Margo Watson knows who the killer is. Marie Collins wasn't the only sister who left a trail of broken-hearted losers in her wake. I'm confident Margo Watson could come up with any number of delinquents to do her dirty work. If she doesn't lead me straight to one of them tonight, I'll start running them down tomorrow morning."

My jaw dropped. "And when were you planning on sharing the fact that you have a whole new pool of suspects—any of whom, I assume, could be Fake Jake—with the class?"

"Hey, you were the one who ditched me to hang out with your boyfriend all day. I did some actual investigative work with *my* time."

I scoffed. "You want to go, Manetti? We haven't had a good fight in a long time."

Laughing, he said, "Damn, woman. Take a joke. I emailed you all of my information for you to peruse at your leisure."

I smiled. "Okay, fine. Too many suspects is better than not enough, I suppose. And speaking of suspects, is it true that Barnes is having deputies pick someone up tonight?"

"She likes Benji McDonald for it with Margo Watson being a low-key accomplice, so she's having him picked up. I disagree with all of that, but hey, at least she's leaning toward the dark side with us."

"Yes, you seem to have put some sort of spell on her. Her head's almost out of her ass."

Grinning, he said, "Thanks, I think."

～

VIC STAYED BEHIND to keep an eye on Margo's movements, so Baxter and I had to drive Barnes to the station. She grilled me the whole way there about our interview with Margo Watson. She'd even taken notes on what points she wanted clarified. It wasn't quite as exhausting as being on the opposite side of an interrogation table from her, but it was close. For the sake of not getting into yet another argument with her, I didn't voice my opinion about Margo Watson running the murder show and Benji or some other sad schmuck being nothing more than her puppet. To her credit, she didn't push her theory on me, either.

Once Barnes was out of our hair, Baxter and I headed back to his parents' house to rest for a while, figuring there was a decent chance the case could break wide open in the next few hours if Barnes's interrogation of Uncle Benji went her way. Mrs. Baxter had gone to bed, and Shawn's party was winding down, with two of his buddies sticking around to help put out the fire and clean up.

I was in the middle of reading Vic's email about Margo Watson's myriad exes when Baxter said, "I think I should break the news to Shawn about Uncle Benji being a serious person of interest before he hears it from someone else."

I looked up from my phone. "You think it could wait until we hear if Barnes gets anything out of him? Vic's list of Margo's minions is a treasure trove of possibilities."

He frowned. "You're still wishy-washy on Benji?"

"So is Vic. I firmly believe Margo Watson is the mastermind. With that being true, her enforcer wouldn't have to have a motive to kill other than to please her. It opens up infinite possibilities." I scanned the rest of the email and counted the number of minions Vic had compiled. "Well, four possibilities. But that's way more than we have now."

Baxter got up off the couch and headed toward the door. He paused when he got there, looking back at me. "I haven't been myself for a while. But you've stuck with me through it all. I haven't said enough how thankful I am for what you've done and what you continue to do. You're my rock, Ellie. When we get back home, we're not going back to how things were. We're not going to sneak around. I'm finding a way to be with you, no matter what it takes. I promise." As he disappeared out the door, he said, "I love you," leaving me shell-shocked.

I sat there replaying his sweet words in my head, allowing myself to enjoy a glimmer of happiness in one of the hardest weeks of my life. I had been so focused on this case that I hadn't given a thought to the hurdles we'd have to overcome once we got home. But knowing Baxter loved me and would be with me every step of the way made me confident I could get through anything.

My phone rang, breaking me out of my reverie.

When I answered it, Amanda said, "I finally got the info on that print."

I smiled. "That's great. What was up with it?"

"The only information listed for the print was an index number, which I'd never run across before in a case. I had to jump through a bunch of hoops and wait for permission to get the name released. The print ended up belonging to a missing child named Michael Stockwell."

I sucked in a gasp. Michael Stockwell had been out here. The only reason for Michael Stockwell to have been here was to kill Marie Collins.

"Ellie?" Amanda said, her tone worried. "You okay?"

"I think you just solved our case, Amanda. Shawn wasn't Marie Collins's first victim. She kidnapped Michael Stockwell a few years before she took Shawn. This poor Stockwell kid was really messed up because of it."

"Holy crap. I didn't realize I'd be delivering that big of news." I could hear the excitement in her voice.

"Amanda, I can't thank you enough."

She said warmly, "I'm happy to help. Anything to get you and Nick back here again. It's not the same without you. I'll let you go, because I'm sure you want to share the news. Keep me updated, okay?"

"I will. Thanks again."

I headed out to the barn to tell Baxter what Amanda had found and to stop him from tarnishing Shawn's view of their uncle. On the way, I gave Vic a quick call. Before he could say hello, I blurted out, "You are never going to believe this. Are you sitting down?"

He replied, "Technically I am, but more importantly, I'm tailing Margo Watson on her way into town. Make it snappy."

"You know the ill-gotten vape pod I found?"

"The crime scene evidence you stole."

"Whatever. Guess whose fingerprint is on it."

Vic didn't even pause to think. "One of Margo's exes? I was right, wasn't I?"

I chuckled. "No, think crazier."

"Okay, Margo herself."

"Crazier."

Now there was a long pause. Then he breathed, "No . . ."

"*Yes*. Michael Stockwell. He's alive, and he's the killer."

"Good luck proving that with your tainted evidence."

I huffed and slowed my pace. "Oh hell. I didn't think about that. I'm on my way now to tell Baxter the news. I was thinking he'd be thrilled, but now I realize he's not going to take it well at all."

"Ah, don't worry. Evidence isn't everything."

"Huh. When I met you, I never would have believed I'd ever hear those words come out of your mouth."

"The new me is a super cool guy."

I laughed. "He was until you said that. I'll let you get back to it. Be safe."

"You too," he replied.

I hung up and put my phone in my pocket. When I reached the barn doors, I came upon a scene that stopped me dead in my tracks. I sucked in a horrified gasp.

"Ellie, run!" Baxter yelled.

29

"Don't run, Ellie, come join the party. My first bullet goes in your boyfriend if you don't," Shawn's friend Jackson said smoothly, standing in the middle of the barn with a nine-mil pointed at a distraught Baxter. Shawn was a few feet away, barely conscious and tied to a chair.

Not wanting to press the guy to find out what he was capable of, I began walking his way with my hands raised as I replied cautiously, "Sure, I'll join the party. No need to shoot anyone."

He smiled. "You're a little nicer than these two. Maybe you'll make it out of this alive."

I shivered.

Baxter choked out, "Jackson, she has nothing to do with anything. Let her go."

It dawned on me that Baxter had no idea who this guy really was. I said, "Um, Baxter, meet Michael Stockwell."

Jackson/Michael and Baxter both gaped at me.

Jackson/Michael said, "I didn't expect you to figure that out. I mean, I'm impressed, but at the same time kind of pissed you stole my thunder. I was waiting until later for my big reveal."

Shrugging, I said, "Sorry. What did you do to Shawn?"

Gun (notably held with his left hand) still trained on Baxter, he waved his free hand. The fact that he was a lefty wasn't lost on me, even in my agitated state. "He's fine. I put some Xanax in his beer to make him easier to deal with."

I stared at Shawn's slack body, knowing he'd had way more than the recommended dosage. "How much, exactly?"

"Enough."

Still in a daze, Baxter said to Jackson/Michael, "You were here all along. Right under our noses."

Now that the initial shock of our situation had worn off, my mind began playing out every worst-case scenario possible. To keep my thoughts from spinning out, I started babbling. "So, do you prefer we call you Jackson or Michael? Mike, maybe? You don't look like a Mike."

"Jackson's good. I never liked the name Michael."

I nodded. "Ah. I guess that's why you ditched it at the tender age of fifteen."

He chuckled. "Someone's done some stalking."

"Uh, yeah—you. I'm not saying I condone your actions, but I'm at least impressed with your patience for the long game. Speaking of that, did you used to have long hair and a beard?"

Jackson stroked his clean-shaven face. "I did, and they served their purpose. You really have done some extensive stalking. Oh, I almost forgot. I'll take your phone, please."

Damn. If only I'd stayed on the call with Vic for another ten seconds, someone would have known we were out here. As it was, we were going to have to buy ourselves some time to figure out how to get Jackson's gun away from him without getting any of us shot. I preferred this not be a repeat of the last time I tangled with a killer, only days ago. Even though Sterling and I had made it out alive, it hadn't been without injury.

I got my phone out and handed it to Jackson, who pocketed it. "If you don't mind me asking, why didn't you leave town after you killed Marie Collins? You're a ghost. We would never have found you."

He chuckled. "Where's the fun in that?"

"I imagine getting away with murder is a lot more fun than prison."

"It is, and getting away with more murders will be even more fun."

Fighting to keep my composure, I replied, "I don't know. Surely at some point your conscience would keep you from having too much fun with it."

Jackson grinned. "It hasn't yet."

Baxter finally seemed to wrap his mind around the situation and turned to me. "How did you figure out he's Michael Stockwell?"

I explained, "Amanda called. It was his print on the vape pod."

"What vape pod?" Jackson asked.

I said, "The one you dropped near the driveway, presumably when you brought Marie Collins out here to kill her."

He seemed impressed. "I had no clue I'd dropped anything. Good detective work."

Baxter glared at me and ground out, "Tell me you're joking."

I was surprised by his reaction, because I'd thought we worked out our issues about my evidence. I replied evenly, "No. It took a while for her to find a name to go with the print. His identity was listed in the system under an index number since it was from a missing child case."

Baxter took a few steps toward me so he towered over me. "So you're saying if you'd spoken up on Sunday afternoon instead of hiding and stealing evidence that we would have known about Michael Stockwell days ago?"

Jackson snickered. "Ooh, boyfriend sounds mad."

I'd fought with Baxter plenty of times, but this exchange was off. His eyes were scared, not angry. I was pretty sure he was picking a fake fight with me to distract Jackson and buy us some time.

I raised my voice and went with it. "Don't put this on me, Baxter. You know as well as I do the investigators did not do a thorough job. Even if they'd taken the vape pod into evidence, they wouldn't have given it priority. It would still be sitting in a box, untouched, for who knows how long."

"You don't know that."

"Uh, yeah I do. I work in evidence, remember?"

Stupid rebuttal, but I was distracted by a flash of headlights outside. My stomach clenched. Were we saved, or would this person stumble blindly into Jackson's little trap like I had? The headlights went out, and after a moment, Margo Watson appeared. I nearly let out a yelp of relief. If Margo was here, Vic wasn't far behind. I noticed Baxter's posture relax a bit as well.

Jackson drawled, "Oh, hello, Margo. Now it's a party."

Her eyes ping-ponged from me to Baxter and Shawn and then to Jackson and his gun. "What the hell are you doing, Jackson?" she cried. "They're cops."

Jackson replied calmly, "Just tying up all the loose ends."

She stalked toward him. "There were no loose ends until you insisted we put a nail in Tom Baxter's coffin. It was a red flag for the police when the phone suddenly started putting out a signal from inside his house."

He shrugged. "Oh. My bad. Anyway, it doesn't matter now, because I've decided to go back to my original plan and let my pal Shawn take the fall."

Margo glared at him. "That's a shit plan. I thought we already went over this."

Baxter and I shared a glance.

Gun still trained on Baxter, Jackson replied, "My plan was always solid. *You* decided it was shit because you have a soft spot for your sister's victims."

"Because you've all been through enough, Jackson. It was bad enough you talked this poor child into trashing my house and nearly got him arrested. Let him be."

I didn't quite follow her logic. I interjected, "So you don't want Shawn taking blame for your sister's murder because he's 'been through enough,' but you figure it won't do any damage to his psyche to have two of his family members go down for murder?"

Margo stared daggers at me, but Jackson took my side. "She's not wrong, Margo. I think all you cared about was sticking it to Mama Baxter for ordering you to stay away from her brother and bitch-slapping you in the Walmart parking lot."

Margo's expression turned absolutely murderous, so I figured I'd push her a little farther. "From what I hear about Benji, it sounds like she did you a favor."

She snapped at me, "Do you ever shut up?" Then she addressed Jackson, "Let that boy go. He did nothing to anyone to deserve any of this."

"Of course you'd take his side. Everyone loves Shawn and his heart-warming story about how the whole town looked for him for months and how his perfect family never gave up hope of finding him." Jackson took a fistful of Shawn's hair and wrenched his head back. Shawn was so out of it he didn't even make a sound. Jackson pressed the muzzle of the gun against his forehead. "Always the Golden Boy, aren't you? Everyone always looks out for Shawn. No one *ever* looked out for me."

Baxter bellowed, "Maybe no one looked out for you because you're a little bitch."

Jackson let Shawn go and started to come at him, but I held out my hands and said, "Settle down, boys. Yes, Shawn always got a pass because he'd had a traumatic experience. But it's not like his life went back to normal after his rescue. There's no 'back to normal' for a kidnap victim. He's screwed up as bad as you are, Jackson. You both need help."

Gesturing wildly with his gun, Jackson spat, "That's bullshit. *His* mom didn't kill herself. *His* dad didn't disappear. *He* didn't have to live with my crazy grandparents or on the street!"

I said as calmly as I could, "Your life situation was worse. No one's contesting that. But you can't claim your *trauma* is worse, because you have no way of knowing what goes on inside Shawn's head. We've all had bad experiences, but it's how we process and deal with them that makes the difference in whether or not we ever recover. Don't hate Shawn because you perceive that he had it easier than you."

Jackson had finally let the gun fall to his side. "I don't need a psychology lesson."

"No, what you need is psychiatric care."

His expression darkened. "Thanks to everyone in my life abandoning me and refusing to love me."

Margo scoffed. "Excuse me? I was there for you, and I loved you. I helped you get away from your grandparents. I took you in and treated you like my own child."

He rolled his eyes. "Don't try to play the surrogate mother card, Margo. I was practically an adult by the time you did anything to actually help me. Besides, you were a shitty mom. No wonder Laurel killed herself."

Oh damn.

She stared at him, pale and shaking. "You ungrateful little bastard. We're done. We killed Marie, and that's all I ever wanted. I won't let you kill

Shawn, too. I wouldn't wish losing a child even on that drunk bitch Elaine Baxter. This is over."

"It's over when I say it's over."

Infuriated, Margo began barreling toward him. Jackson raised his gun and fired one shot into her torso. Margo dropped onto the ground right on the spot where I'd found her sister.

Disoriented by the shock of what I'd just witnessed and the pain in my ears from the shot, I cried, "What did you do? Why . . . ?"

Jackson showed no remorse. "You heard her. She was going to stop me, so I stopped her first."

Baxter made a move toward Margo, but Jackson shoved the muzzle of his gun against Shawn's head again and said, "Don't help her. You do, and your baby bro gets one, too."

His face ashen, Baxter backed off.

Hoping I could rattle Jackson enough to pull him away from Shawn, I said, "Like I said before, had you just exacted your revenge and got the hell out of town, none of us would be in this predicament."

Jackson shrugged. "I'm not in a predicament."

"The hell you're not. You're making your mess bigger, not smaller."

"I'm making *Shawn's* mess bigger."

Turning to Baxter, I said, "As dastardly plans go, this one kind of sucks, don't you think?" I turned back to Jackson, who was finally starting to look a little pissed. "We've put a stop to our fair share of dastardly plans. If you want, we'll critique yours and tell you why it won't work."

Jackson sneered. "It'll work."

Baxter must have realized what I was trying to do, because he managed to shake off what he was feeling and bark out a laugh. "It won't if you're the genius who planted the phone."

"Shut up, Officer Buzzkill."

I said, "So you're planning to pin all your crimes on Shawn . . ."

I trailed off as my attention was drawn to Margo, who was struggling to put pressure on her wound and not looking so good. If we got her some medical attention soon, she could live to tell about this. And speaking of people coming to the rescue, where was Vic? If he'd tailed her here, he'd be a minute or two behind her, which meant by now he had to be somewhere on the property. Assuming he'd heard the shot, he'd be contemplating barging in here, but I desperately hoped he would wait for backup. He had no gun and worse, no jurisdiction. Anything he did to physically stop Jackson he'd have to answer for as a civilian. However, that fact wouldn't deter him from doing whatever was necessary to keep Shawn, Baxter, and especially me from being harmed. Maybe he was listening and monitoring the situation from outside. If so, I was going to give him as much information as I could about what was going on in here.

I shook off my worries and went on in as loud a tone as I dared, "Let's break this down. You're going to stage this so we're supposed to believe Shawn just now shot Margo Watson in the gut. What's his motivation?"

Baxter supplied, "He blames her for taking her sister in after she got out of jail. He already established that when he vandalized her home. Or, rather, when Michael here made sure he got wound up enough to do it." Baxter must have had the same thought about Vic or picked up on what I was doing.

I held back a smile and nodded. "Right." I looked at Shawn. "Only Shawn's not in good enough shape to do much damage to anyone tonight. It's not going to be believable if the cops see him passed out like he is among the carnage."

Jackson said, "He won't be passed out. He'll be dead. I already have his suicide note written."

Baxter's breath hitched.

I managed to keep my composure enough to say, "You know they'll autopsy his body after an apparent suicide, right? And when they do, all that Xanax you gave him will show up on his tox screen and maybe even in his stomach depending on the timing. Manufacture all the evidence you want, but no one's going to believe he had the capacity to shoot anyone tonight."

Jackson was unfazed. He smiled and slapped Shawn's cheek. Shawn roused a little. "I know. That's why I switched over to dosing him with Adderall in his last couple beers. He should be waking up any minute now."

My jaw dropped. "You speedballed him? That could kill him."

He gave me a strange look as he tapped the end of his gun on Shawn's forehead. "Have I been unclear about my plan?"

Baxter managed to keep his cool to point out, "No, but the moment I stepped in here, you had to pivot on the fly. I think you're a meticulous planner and being forced to deviate makes you prone to mistakes. Like the phone."

"I've got the situation under control," Jackson griped, his temper not quite under control.

Baxter went on, "I get that you lured Margo out here to kill her so she couldn't have a change of heart and turn on you later. She was clearly a loose cannon and you knew that going in. You had Shawn vandalize her property so there'd be an issue between the two of them you could use later if needed."

Having calmed down again, Jackson said, "You got me. So what?"

While the two of them had been busy arguing, I took an opportunity to glance around the barn, looking for cracks between the wood wall planks that might have been big enough for Vic to see and hear through. I spied one decent-sized crack that seemed to be a good candidate. Most of the other cracks had light shining through them from the dusk-to-dawn light mounted on a tall pole outside. I noticed that the crack in question was sometimes lit from the outside and then would suddenly go dark, as if someone had moved and blocked the light. I hoped that someone was Vic. Hell, at this point, I'd be happy to see Barnes come to our rescue.

Baxter continued, "So what's your plan for us, Jackson? You can't shoot us and blame it on Shawn, because that would make zero sense. No one would believe Shawn would kill me. We're tight. And he has no motive to kill Ellie."

Jackson shot me an apologetic look as he replied, "He doesn't actually like Ellie all that much, though. He told me she treated you real bad, and even if you've forgiven her, he hasn't. So I figure he's got decent enough motive to shoot her. But then big brother gets pissed and tries to take his gun away, a struggle ensues, the gun goes off, and big brother takes a bullet. Shawny-boy is anguished over accidentally killing his big bro and turns the gun on himself." His face lit up with a wicked grin. "I have to say, it's morphed into an even better plan."

Shawn raised his head and moaned.

Jackson looked down at him, repositioned the gun, and gave him another slap on the cheek. "Hey, buddy. Wakey, wakey. We've got stuff to do."

While Jackson had been waxing poetic about his amazing plan and beating up poor Shawn, I noticed the shadow behind the crack start moving toward the door. And then I noticed a second shadow moving behind it. Hot damn! Vic had backup, and hopefully that backup had a gun, or several. I figured the best thing I could do was to give whoever was there a clear shot at Jackson and get his attention turned away from the door.

I let out a fearful whimper and started wringing my hands. "Uh . . . Jackson, you're seriously starting to freak me out." I feigned some panting and started pacing back and forth, tweaking my path each time to press further and further toward the back of the barn. I caught his eye and stared him down, trying to come off as distraught as my acting chops could manage and still be believable. "I don't want to die. Please. Is there anything I can do to get you to change your mind?"

He smiled at me sincerely. What a sociopath. He said kindly, "I'm sorry, Ellie, but you know too much now. There's really no other way."

I started panting again. "There has to be. I'll . . . I'll help you stage the scene. I can make it perfect. Seriously, you need my expertise if this batshit little tableau is going to work out the way you want it to." When he frowned, I added, "I'm one of the best criminalists in the state."

"Hmm . . . and how would I know you wouldn't turn on me afterward?"

I shrugged. "Knock me out. When I come to, make sure you're gone. I mean, I know your real name and some of your aliases, but I'm sure you have a new identity with no strings attached to this area that you're planning to use after doing this job. You can disappear again and I'll never be able to find you."

Jackson nodded. "Fair point. I like you, and I could use the help."

Did he seriously believe I'd turn on Baxter and Shawn that fast? I guessed he was crazier than I imagined.

Smiling, I said, "Let's get to work. First, untie Shawn. He's waking up, and once he realizes he's bound, he's going to start struggling. Anywhere the rope touches his skin, it'll chafe and bruise, and that will be super obvious at autopsy and raise all kinds of suspicion."

He took a step away from Shawn and pointed his gun at Baxter again. He ordered me, "You do it. I need to keep Officer Buzzkill in line."

As I worked to free Shawn's hands, feet, and torso, Baxter griped, "Quit pointing that gun at me with your shaky-ass hand, Jackson. You're going to accidentally discharge it in my direction."

Out of the corner of my eye, I saw Jackson purposely waggle the gun at Baxter and had to suppress a wave of panic. Baxter wasn't wrong—I'd noticed Jackson getting increasingly shaky and sweaty as the minutes ticked by. I wasn't sure if it was the stress of the situation or if Shawn hadn't been the only one ingesting stupid amounts of Adderall this evening.

I put one arm around Shawn's shoulders and used my other hand to give Shawn's hands a squeeze. "You awake, Shawn? Can you squeeze my hand?" I got back a gentle squeeze. "You need to sit up on your own now, okay?"

His eyes fluttered open and he looked around, dumbfounded. "What's going on? Nick?"

Baxter's jaw clenched. "Everything's okay, Shawn. Just stay calm and quiet and try not to move."

I stood. "Okay, that's done. Jackson, next, no one is going to believe Shawn shot Margo if he's got zero gunshot residue on his hands and his fingerprints aren't in the proper place on your gun to have pulled the trigger. Wipe it down with your shirt and hand it to him. We'll have him shoot it into the hay over there in the corner so they won't find the bullet."

Jackson very nearly followed my orders, but as he was reaching to hand the gun to Shawn, he pulled back and pointed it at me this time. "Nice try. I'm not that stupid."

I felt a wave of panic, staring down yet another psycho with a gun, but my disappointment in my near miss swept in and overrode it. I'd almost had him. Just as I was starting to reformulate my plan, I spied Barnes's silhouette at the door, gun in hand and ready to take him down. I tried to catch Baxter's eye to let him know we were saved, but he was fixated on Jackson. Surely he'd figured it out and would stay out of the way.

Relief coursing through me, I couldn't resist taking a dig at Jackson. "To be fair, you were about two seconds away from being that stupid."

"Shut up!" he screeched.

It took everything I had to ignore the wildly shaking gun pointed at me in order to give Barnes a few more seconds to close in on her mark. "Damn, you really have got all kinds of issues, don't you? Marie screwed you up real good."

Finally I'd hit the right button, because Jackson let out a guttural scream, upended poor Shawn out of his chair, and came barreling at me. I dropped to the ground. As I did, I saw Baxter tackling Jackson from behind at the same time two shots rang out.

30

Barnes and Vic came charging toward us.

"Ellie!" Vic shouted. "Are you okay?"

I could barely get out a "yes," as I scrambled toward Baxter, who was lying on his side next to Jackson. Neither of them were moving.

I cried, "No! Nick . . ." as I saw two bloodstains blooming on his shirt, one on the right side of his chest and one several inches away on his back. I clamped one hand over each hole and pressed down to slow the bleeding. When he grunted in pain, hope bubbled up inside me. "Hey, Nick, you're going to be okay. I got you."

Vic rushed to attend to Margo, but his attention was on me. "Ellie, you're doing great keeping pressure on his wounds. We've got an ambulance only a couple of minutes out."

I nodded, tears starting to spill over as I watched the color drain from Baxter's face and his breathing get shallow. The position of his wounds around his right lung was troubling.

Barnes kicked the gun away from Jackson. Her face a mask of horror, she reached down and checked him for a pulse. "He's . . . gone." She raised her head and fixated on Baxter. "Nick, I'm so sorry. I didn't think you were going to—" Choking on a sob, she got out her phone and walked away from us to make a call, screaming at someone to get three ambulances up here.

Once she was done, she hurried to tend to Shawn, who was starting to try to sit up.

Baxter wheezed out a scary-sounding breath. I also heard what sounded like a hiss.

I said, "Nick, what's wrong?"

He croaked, "Hard to . . . breathe . . ."

My heart felt like it was going to rip in two. I said, "Just stay calm. I'm right here."

Vic snapped, "Corinne, take over for me. Ellie, we need to roll him over so the wound is facing the ground."

"What?" I asked blankly as Vic came my way and started gently rolling Baxter to his other side. Baxter let out a groan of pain.

Vic explained calmly, "I'm pretty sure the bullet passed through his lung. This position will make it easier for him to breathe and lessen his pain."

I nodded, thankful he was here and knew what to do. I repositioned my hands around Baxter's torso to keep pressure on the wounds and murmured, "Easy breaths, Nick. Help is on the way." He grasped my arm and held on, which broke my heart all over again. I had to fight to hold back a sob.

When I thought I was going to lose it from helplessly watching the love of my life fight for air, two EMTs rushed into the barn with a gurney.

Vic started barking orders. "Take this man first. He has a through and through to the right lung. Difficulty breathing. It's been about four minutes since he was shot. We've got the female gunshot victim's blood loss slowed and she's conscious. Other male gunshot victim has no pulse."

One EMT took over for me putting pressure on Baxter's wounds, and Vic led me aside as they went to work on him. I didn't want to break down where Baxter might hear me, so I focused my attention on holding everything in for a little longer. I about lost it when I heard Shawn's voice croak, "Nick? What happened? What's going on?"

Vic and I rushed over to him and caught him just as he tried to stand and instead collapsed.

Vic said to him, "Shawn, your brother is injured, but he's got help. We need to get you some medical attention, too. Just try to stay calm, okay?"

"Nick!" he cried, unable to take his eyes off the EMTs hoisting his brother's slack body onto the gurney and preparing him for transport.

I broke away from them. "I'm going with him."

Vic said, "Go do what you need to do. I'll handle everything here."

When I passed Barnes, who was on her knees holding pressure on Margo's wound, she looked up at me. Tears streaked her cheeks. She said, "Ellie, I'm so sorry. I had a clear shot, and Nick moved just as I pulled the trigger. I would never have—" She stopped short and shook her head, anguish evident on her face.

I said, "I know it was an accident, Corinne. Don't blame yourself. I'm thankful you came to our rescue."

                                         ∾

THE AMBULANCE RIDE to the hospital, even at full speed, felt like it lasted a lifetime. I rode up front to stay out of the way but at the same time agonized over leaving Baxter's side. Equally as bad, I couldn't seem to rip my eyes off the sickening amount of his blood that stained my hands all the way past my wrists.

The rest of the night descended into a blur. Vic arrived with Mrs. Baxter, who was understandably beside herself. Detective Martin showed up and took me aside to question me while Baxter was being prepped for surgery. He then did the same thing to Vic while an Internal Affairs officer questioned me about every detail surrounding Barnes's actions at the scene. I remembered this well from the first case Baxter and I worked together where he'd had to shoot someone who was about to shoot me. Just as he had, Barnes would be suspended and investigated before she'd be cleared to return to duty. And then she'd have to deal with the emotional aftereffects of taking a life, not to mention the guilt she was already feeling for accidentally harming a friend.

We finally got word that Baxter was in recovery and allowed one visitor. Since Mrs. Baxter had been keeping Shawn company in his observation room while Nick was in surgery, I got to be the first one to see him when he woke up.

Baxter's eyes were closed as I approached his bedside, but when I murmured, "Hey," he opened them slowly.

He smiled, and I thought my heart would burst. "Hey." He winced. "Ouch. Everything hurts."

I gently took his hand. "That's what you get for being the hero."

"Yeah, but it's lame I got hit by friendly fire."

"Not when you put yourself in danger to save me and your brother. Thank you."

His face clouded over. "How is Shawn?"

"He's going to be fine. They're keeping him tonight to watch him, but he's good. Your mom's with him. And in other news, I heard from Detective Martin that your dad and Tom are being processed out as we speak."

He closed his eyes and relaxed back into his pillow. "Best news I've heard all week. Made it all worth it."

My heart again swelled. I didn't want another moment to go by without telling him how I felt. "Nick, I love you, too."

He opened his eyes. "Okay, *that's* the best news I've heard all week."

~

THE FOLLOWING DAY, once I'd given the Baxter family some private time to reunite and quietly celebrate their return to normalcy, I was able to have some alone time with Baxter. Evidently he'd had a lot of time to think of all kinds of questions to ask me about the case, starting with the most difficult one.

"Why in the hell didn't you run when I told you to run?" he demanded as I walked into his room.

"Good morning to you, too, Mr. Grumpypants." I leaned down and gave him a kiss, then sat next to him on the edge of his bed and offered the cup of coffee I brought for him. "Maybe some decent coffee will help your mood."

He frowned and took the cup. "Answer the question."

I smiled. "You're cute when you play bad cop."

"Ellie . . ."

"Fine. I didn't run because, first, I don't take orders from you. And second, a mentally ill murderer told me he'd shoot you if I did. There was only the one option for me."

He set the coffee on his tray table and took my hands. "Next time, please just run."

I laughed. "Let's hope there's no next time."

"Considering this is the second time in three days you've been in a frighteningly similar scenario, I'm resigned to the fact that there's a good chance there'll be a next time."

"Maybe not. We're both kinda fired right now, remember?"

"I'm sure yesterday's events will more than erase any black marks against either of us."

Shrugging, I said, "True. We were pretty badass at exonerating ourselves and your family. And in record time without our usual tools."

"We got lucky. Speaking of lucky, I hear Margo Watson is alive and mostly well."

"She is. I had brunch with Vic and Corinne, and they filled me in on her side of the story."

His eyebrows shot up. " 'Corinne'? I figured you'd be more likely to try to punch her in the face than have brunch with her."

I laughed. "I don't blame her for shooting you. Plus . . . I like her. She's being super nice to me now. I think she's trying to get my blessing for her and Vic to get together."

"Does that mean she no longer thinks you two are an item?"

"I told her the truth. We're like besties now."

He shook his head. "Back to more adult conversation, did you find out how Margo Watson knew about Michael Stockwell?"

"Oh, yeah. So once Marie Collins got sentenced for kidnapping Shawn, she confessed to Margo about her other kidnapping. Margo was understandably appalled. But evidently not appalled enough to go to the cops with what she knew.

"Still protecting her sister after finding out she was a monster?"

I smiled. "The sister bond is like the brother bond. It's hard to break."

"I get it."

"So like she had with Shawn and your parents, Margo reached out to

Michael Stockwell and his grandparents. Unlike your family, Michael and his family accepted her apologies and they even became friends."

"Friends? That's hard to believe."

"It's not when you know that Margo's friendship came with a monetary gift."

Nodding, he said, "Ah, there it is."

"Margo was Marie's power of attorney, so she was in charge of her finances. She sold the cabin where Marie kept Shawn, but instead of using the money to retain a lawyer, she let Marie take her chances with the public defender. She threw a little of her ill-gotten gains to Michael Stockwell's grandparents to use to spoil Michael, but soon realized they weren't cutting him in on his own blood money. She also realized they were abusing him, so when he was ready, she helped him disappear. She was there any time he needed money or a place to crash. He visited enough that he and Laurel became good friends. He took her death really hard."

Baxter frowned. "They both had a boatload of reasons to want to get back at Marie Collins. It wouldn't have been enough to rat her out for the rest of her sins. They wanted to have a hand in dishing out the punishment."

"It would seem so. What I want to know is how long ago Michael took on his Jackson persona and how he managed to befriend Shawn."

"He leeched onto their group through Tanner a few months back. Now that I think about it, I met him and thought he seemed off, but I chalked it up to the fact that Shawn's friends are usually punks." He shook his head. "At the time, Shawn was becoming more and more depressed and apprehensive with Marie Collins's release date approaching, so . . . I decided it wasn't the time to question his choice of friends."

I squeezed his hands. "Don't beat yourself up. Jackson was good at getting close to people and making them like him. Hell, I thought he was borderline charming at times when he was holding us at gunpoint."

Baxter stared at me. "What? Why?"

I shrugged. "I don't know. There was something compelling about him in a Ted Bundy kind of way."

A grin pulled at the corner of his mouth. "You find me more charming, though, right?"

"I suppose I should say yes since you took a bullet for me."

"Would it make a difference to know I didn't intend to take a bullet for you?"

I laughed. "No, because I know you'd take one for me if necessary."

He made a face. "I don't know. After taking one, I'm not so sure I'm interested in taking another one."

Giving him a fake glare, I said, "Oh, I see how it is. Maybe I'll go back to being partners with Sterling. He took a concussion for me."

"Don't make me laugh," Baxter said, chuckling. He winced and clutched his side. "Ow. Seriously, don't make me laugh."

My phone rang, a FaceTime call from Jayne Walsh. I said uneasily, "This might make you stop laughing. It's Jayne." I answered, "Hey, Jayne. What's up?"

She said, "I figured I should check in with you. It's not every day I get notified you've been held at gunpoint." She gave me a pointed look and added wryly, "But it is sometimes twice in one week. Knock it off. You're making me prematurely gray."

I smiled. "I'll try."

"I take it you're with Detective Baxter." There was only a hint of reproach to her words.

I moved the phone so she could see him as well.

Baxter said, "Hi, Sheriff."

"I'm happy to see you're not looking too much worse for wear, Detective."

Nodding, he said, "I'm hanging in here."

"Good. The local sheriff brought me up to speed on your investigation as well as your heroism. I hated to have to come down on you like I did, but I knew it wouldn't take you two long to clear yourselves and your family, especially with Agent Manetti's help."

Knowing Baxter wouldn't give her any pushback for being fired so unceremoniously, I said, "We weren't thrilled about being let go, but we understood. We already had a hell of a fire lit under us to solve the case, and you canning us was like adding gasoline. So thanks, I guess."

"Watch it, smartass," she muttered at me. To Baxter, she said, "Detective Baxter, in light of your name being completely cleared for any suspected wrongdoing, your job is officially reinstated effective immediately . . . although now I suppose you'll be on medical leave."

"Thank you, and yes, I'll be out for a while," he replied. I knew he was bummed about the prospect of being on medical leave for the next several months, but the relief about his career was evident on his face.

She looked at me. "And Ellie . . . I guess I have to hire you back now, too."

I chuckled. "I don't know about that . . . Who would I be partnered with while Baxter's out? Sterling? We all know how that turned out last time."

"Maybe you can be a lab jockey for a while."

"Maybe." I glanced at Baxter. The job wouldn't be the same without him.

We said our goodbyes and hung up with Jayne.

Baxter took my hand again. "You didn't sound too excited to get your job back."

I squeezed his hand. "It's funny how your priorities shift after a traumatic event."

"Don't tell me you don't want to work because of me."

"It won't be fun if you're not there."

"That's not a good reason to quit your job."

"It's only my extra job. Besides, I'd rather use any free time I have to help you recover." I leaned toward him and gave him a kiss.

I heard someone clear their throat from the doorway and quickly sat back up. Of course it was Mrs. Baxter who'd walked in on us. I pasted on a smile. "Good morning, Mrs. Baxter."

She actually smiled back. "Good morning, Ellie." It was the first time I'd heard no slur to her voice. "May I speak with you outside?"

My heart thudded. I couldn't imagine a private conversation with her going well, but I dutifully got up and followed her to the hallway.

She said, "I . . . want to thank you for everything you did for my family. Nicholas said if it hadn't been for you, no one would have known the identity of the killer."

I smiled. "It was a group effort."

"He also said you kept Jackson occupied while he was holding my boys —" Her voice broke, but she quickly composed herself and continued,

"That you bought enough time for the police to arrive and stop him. Nicholas said you're strong in dangerous situations and that getting criminals to trust you and talk to you is something you're very good at. He said you're better at it than he is, and better than most policemen he knows."

I blushed. "He said that?"

"Nicholas adores you."

"I love him, too. I'm sorry we had to keep that from you, but—"

She held up a hand. "He already explained everything, and I won't breathe a word of it to anyone. More importantly, I owe you an apology. I'm sorry I was so cold and rude to you."

"I understand. You thought I'd broken your son's heart."

"You did do that."

I sighed. "Fair point."

She assured me, "It's already forgiven. Now I hope you can forgive me, because I need your help."

"Absolutely. Anything."

She blew out a heavy sigh. "Will you . . . would you be able to . . ." She sighed again. "I want to quit drinking. Forever."

I took her hands. "Good for you. What can I do to help?"

"I think you've been sneakily helping me already."

I chuckled. "Sorry I kept throwing out your gin. I mean, I'm not sorry, but I feel like I owe you a few bucks."

Smiling at me, she said, "Help me get to the right kind of meeting and we'll call it even."

"Sounds like a plan."

SINS OF THE FATHER
Book #6 of the Ellie Matthews Novels

When the sins of the past come knocking on her door, Ellie Matthews must confront her darkest fears.

The relative tranquility of Ellie Matthews's life is shattered when her estranged stepfather Marcus resurfaces, pleading for help against an unknown danger. Ellie's peaceful sanctuary is quickly tainted by an ongoing murder investigation. The victim: Marcus's ex-wife, Katie.

When investigators set out to question Marcus, he is nowhere to be found. In a jarring twist, Marcus dies in an apparent drug overdose. When Ellie and Detective Baxter search Marcus's residence after his demise, they find unsettling evidence linking him to a series of murders, including the death of Ellie's own mother. Despite the mounting evidence against Marcus, the case isn't sitting right with Ellie. Was Marcus a cold-blooded killer, or was he being set up for the perfect crime?

When the FBI is pulled in to help with the case, Ellie is brought onto the task force to uncover Marcus's dubious past. It is only after she receives a threat of violence that Ellie realizes that her own family may be the next target. But with every secret exposed, Ellie finds herself further ensnared in a mystery that not only threatens her life, but has her doubting everything she's ever believed about her past.

ACKNOWLEDGMENTS

Thanks to the Severn River team, with special thanks to Julia Hastings and Chloe Moffett for all of their help, guidance, and support. Thank you to my early readers as well. And a big thank you to my family for cheering me along to get this novel done on time!

ABOUT THE AUTHOR

Caroline Fardig is the *USA Today* bestselling author of over a dozen mystery novels. She worked as a schoolteacher, church organist, insurance agent, banking trust specialist, funeral parlor associate, stay-at-home mom, and coffeehouse owner before she realized that she wanted to be a writer when she grew up. When she's not writing, she likes to travel, lift weights, play pickleball, and join in on vocals, piano, or guitar with any band who'll have her. She's also the host of a lively podcast for Gen Xers called *Wrong Side of 40*. Born and raised in a small town in Indiana, Fardig still lives in that same town with an understanding husband, two sweet kids, and three exhaustingly energetic dogs.

Sign up for Caroline Fardig's reader list at
severnriverbooks.com/authors/caroline-fardig

Printed in the United States
by Baker & Taylor Publisher Services